DETOUR TO LOVE

CEDARWOOD SPRING CLEAN ROMANCE SERIES
BOOK ONE

ERICA SAMS

Detour to Love
The Cedarwood Spring Clean Romance Series

Published by Hudson House Publishing
Pennington, NJ 08534

ISBN: 979-8-9922671-0-5
FICTION / Romance / Clean & Wholesome

Cover design by N. Brown Literary Services, copyright owned by Hudson House Publishing.

CHAPTER 1

E xit 13? *Really??* Noooo, this was the *last* thing she needed.

Anna Diaz pushed her head back against the leather headrest of her white BMW, pressing her hands against the steering wheel in frustration.

A state trooper clad in dripping rain gear directed the crawling line of cars merging onto the exit ramp off the flooded Pennsylvania interstate. As she pulled near him, she rolled down the window and immediately got pelted with fat, fierce raindrops. But it was worth it to try.

"Sir?! Excuse me, sir!" The officer squinted at her as she pushed her voice to the level of a yodel, trying to twist her own squint into some version of a smile. He cupped his ears and mouthed, "What?"

She motioned wildly past him. "Can't I just go ahead here? I just have a few more exits to go."

But the officer grimaced impatiently and kept waving her to the ramp. "Trees are down on the road just ahead, and it's starting to flood, miss. Keep going."

As she reluctantly inched onto the exit, following the bleary taillights in front of her, she groaned to herself. Out loud. Just to really make the point.

She knew this exit. It had been awhile—years actually. But she still remembered every telephone pole and road marker, and every charming grove of charming trees. She just hadn't realized she'd ever need to see them again. Enough with the charm.

This was the exit that headed away from civilization, as she thought of it, back into the Pennsylvania Dutch countryside, down wooded roads leading to Cedarwood Spring. Her hometown. Where she hadn't been for more than a decade. For good reason.

And now she was headed right into it, in the midst of a huge storm? This was *so* not the idea.

What *was* the idea was the posh Poconos spa where she'd made the reservation for herself—"Reservation for one, please … yes, one … yes, I'm sure." But that exit agonizingly still lay miles ahead.

She flipped on her favorite Philly traffic radio station— which, she realized ruefully, she probably should have done earlier. The meteorologist's voice came in over the scratchy AM airwaves: " … the unexpected turn this storm took, flooding has caused road closures all the way through the county, on the turnpike and the interstate. Backroads are unpredictable. Please avoid being on the road unless it's an emergency."

Anna snorted to herself. In her book, this definitely constituted an emergency. So even with Googlemaps, there was no way to know how many downed lines and trees she'd run up against on alternate roads, not to mention even more flooding. The only thing worse than this mess would be this mess in a gasless car.

Shoot. Anna sighed, eyeing her muted phone on the seat beside her. The cool of the AC combined with the aggressive humidity outside made her feel both chilled and clammy in her silk tee—her fave top that always worked totally fine in New

York in any circumstances but somehow now seemed like an unwanted guest. With slender manicured fingers, she wiped dark, damp curls from her temples and moisture from under her nose.

She could still smell the morning's croissant on her finger-tips, and this time she said "shoot" out loud. If only she'd stayed in the cozy coffee shop in her Brooklyn 'hood and listened to her annoying manager who had predicted the storm would be worse than she thought—not because he ever had any insight into anything vaguely scientific but because Rubin had a penchant for predicting the worst.

For once she'd ignored him, and for once, he'd been right. It's just that she'd wanted so badly to get to the resort, she thought, lightly tapping her fist on the steering wheel. Work had been so stressful, and the calm luxury of the resort had been dangling in front of her like a carrot for a Central Park horse. And she'd known, positively *known*, that she could handle getting through some punky storm, just like she was able to get through all the other storms in her life.

I guess sometimes life has to stop you in your tracks to get you to notice where you are, she thought. Hey, that's good. I'll have to write that down.

It was late afternoon, though you couldn't tell it from the strange gray light coming through the leaden clouds. Fat drops of rain plunked across the windshield, and the red brake lights of the car right in front of her peppered the blur.

Enough of this, Anna thought, with another emphatic thump on the steering wheel.

At the end of the ramp, she put on her blinkers and pulled slowly out of the line of cars and onto the shoulder, wincing as lightning cracked the sky. Picking up her phone, she was grateful to see it still had plenty of juice—and several missed calls from said manager. And no messages. She hated it when he did that.

She tapped into the phone. "Hi, Rubin."

His high-voltage voice made her hold the phone slightly away from her ear—the normal pose for phone calls with Rubin.

His voice cut through the whirr of the windshield wipers. "Are you at the resort yet? I've been calling and calling."

As if she didn't know. "Hey, Rubin, can you remind me again why a pastry chef needs a manager?"

"Oh, not this again!" She could hear his verbal eye roll. "You're a true pâtissière." He always delivered that word with such a flourish. "You're young, you're talented, you're a glamorous Latina woman, you're a great interview on NY1. You need me."

Anna's eyes rested distractedly in the blurry middle distance. "For what?" She knew she was being provocative, but there wasn't much else to do in the clammy car.

He took the bait, his voice spiking. "To handle the reality TV show that's being handed to you on a silver platter. Pun intended. The legal stuff, financial, PR, coordinating with the director, setting up your social media …"

Her stomach clenched a little tighter in what was becoming a common and depressing reaction to the idea of the show. He was right—it was amazing. So why couldn't she shake this little grip of negativity at the mention of it, even in the backwoods in the rain?

Fatigue. Right, that's it. Fatigue. She'd been burning the candle at both ends for too long. A little rest at a posh resort would make everything bright again. Or that was what Rubin was always saying.

"Hello-o-o-o-o?"

She snapped back to attention, guiltily aware she'd indulged in yanking his chain. "Sorry, Rubin. Yes, I absolutely need you."

"Well, don't let me twist your arm or anything."

Anna sighed, noticing the thick drops thunking on the windshield. "I am sorry. It's not you, it's me. I mean, the help I need right now is how to get to the darn resort."

"What are you talking about?"

"I'm kind of rerouted. The interstate's closed. The wind's really bad and apparently trees are down on the road. There might be flooding. The trooper said I couldn't get through."

"Well, then, turn around, for heaven's sake, and come back!! I told you you should never have gone out with this storm coming! Don't you remember this morning when I …"

As he droned on, Anna's eyes drifted again. What she wouldn't give to be cuddled up back in her Brooklyn apartment, its blurry view of the rainy Manhattan skyline lost in the steam from her favorite mug—made, of course, by an artisan also in Brooklyn who was just starting to go national. Rainy days were always great for holing up and scanning her favorite baking blogs for new adventures in pastry recipes. The most recent one she'd stumbled upon was a young French woman who made sure to source all her blackberry extracts locally. Great publicity both for her and for the local farmers. Come to think of it, nice idea for—

A distant boom of thunder reminded Anna that she was in neither Brooklyn nor France. Wind whipped the blurry treetops lining the local road ahead and cars sloshed by slowly.

"Yes, you did tell me. And no, I can't turn around, Rubin. Not that I wouldn't love to. But the roads are a mess. I'm not sure it's even possible to go back the opposite way on the interstate."

"So where are you exactly? You're, like, in the middle of nowhere?" Rubin was an inveterate city dweller. To him, Hoboken, New Jersey, was nowhere.

"Not exactly nowhere," Anna hedged. "Exit 13, actually."

"I have no idea what that means."

"It means …" Sigh. "It means I'm going home."

～

Jake Petersen scanned up and down Cedarwood Spring's main drag, squinting through the rain to the closed-up shops and stores. The hardware store and the farm-supply store had all their merchandise safely inside. Collectibles antiques and Between the Lines bookstore had their awnings rolled up. The Bread-and-Butter Bistro and PT Events—Pete and Tina were doing such a great job with their new design enterprise—had their lights out and windows shut tight. The early-summer banners that always adorned the lampposts up and down Main Street on Memorial Day weekend, supposedly to welcome all the tourists, were flipping wildly in the wind above empty sidewalks.

The timing of this storm was really lousy. Such an important week ahead for his inn just outside town, which of course meant important for his whole life. Too much hung in the balance. All his friends whose lives were poured into these little shops—shops Jake had given heart and soul to helping—had done so well. They'd really gotten traction.

Now his inn just needed to finally join the trend. Jake felt a nervous twitch in his stomach that didn't have anything to do with the weather.

Assured for the moment that everyone seemed to have battened down the hatches, Jake leaned back against the front door of the Filling Station café, pushing backward with muscular legs to heave it open. This place was another one of the success stories in Cedarwood Spring, taking the motif of an old-fashioned filling station and converting it into a cozy pastry café. Was even written up in the Philly papers.

His thick, wavy gray-blond hair stuck in rain-darkened wisps along the sides of his face, his broad jaw framed with two days' reddish-blond growth. But he couldn't care less. Helping his grandmom prep the inn to weather the storm had been on the top of his mind. And in all his "tons" of spare time, he wanted to make sure his friends in town had enough supplies in case they lost power.

Jake's arms were heavy with a sizable stack of wood—enough to hold the café for several hours of light and heat if necessary. "Hey, Haven," he called. "Where d'ya want it?"

A short, fair woman in her mid-twenties emerged from the kitchen, wiping her hands on an apron with frazzled distraction. "Oh, thanks so much, Jake, you're the best god-brother a gal ever had. There, by the wood stove." Haven Martin pointed to the stove at the end of the room set with urban-farm style cozy chairs and tables. "How are things at the inn? How's Iris?"

Jake knelt by the stove, holding the wood against his chest and lifting it off piece by piece. "Grandma's OK, just nervous. It's almost dark out, and a storm like this can really screw things up." He paused, glancing meaningfully at her. "And right now we can't afford any setbacks."

"Exactly!" Haven's eyes widened at the looming deadline. "Let's keep our fingers crossed. The wedding is less than a week away. Everything has to be perfect."

"Yep, everybody's gonna be there. It could make all the difference for us."

Haven eyed him gingerly. "Any update on the line of credit?"

Keeping his eyes on the wood, which he arranged more carefully than was necessary, Jake shook his head. "Just got word from the bank. That was the second extension of our line of credit, and they've already pushed back the due date once. They're great over there, but they've done all they can, and they can't give us any more breaks on the loan. Time to make it work."

Jake paused to shove back the anxiety of the week ahead—made all the uglier by this damn storm. Then remembering that Haven had to be pretty anxious too, he gave his old pal a weak smile. "And the wedding *cake* will be fantastic."

Haven grimaced and looking appealingly at him. "Yeah, everything's on the line for me too. Doing wedding cakes is what I've always dreamed of. Even when my family thought I was

7

silly. And then finally I get a chance and ..." She gestured toward the skies, helplessly eyeing the display case and antique green-glass cake stands scattered across the counter, now holding only a few stray muffins and strawberry tarts from earlier in the day. Haven attempted a weak smile. "I mean, if I make great muffins, can a wedding cake be far behind?"

Jake forced a normal-sounding chuckle. "No doubt, kiddo." Though to be honest, he was probably as nervous as she was about the cake. The whole point to him was using local talent, for sure, and Haven deserved a break as much as anyone. She'd done great at birthday cakes and stuff. But a huge wedding cake wasn't part of her wheelhouse yet.

Still, when she'd breathlessly offered to do it for free so she could begin branching out her business into wedding cakes, his good-guy side that always helped his pals up and down Main Street had overreached his business-school-trained side, and he'd said yes. Which had only added to the feeling that this make-or-break event was teetering on nothing more than popsicle sticks and glue. He forced a breath into his lungs.

Just then a sharp ring from her cell phone in the kitchen made them both jump—at exactly the same moment that the headlights of a car swung into a parking spot right in front of the café.

"Who can be coming to a café with this storm?" Haven asked, irritated. The phone rang again, and she shook her hands at the air. "Jake, I gotta get that. Can you take care of whoever is dumb enough to be muffin-shopping at this hour?"

"Sure." Jake finished laying the last of the wood, as Haven darted back into the kitchen.

As he got back up, brushing off his creased jeans, the bright meme of shattering glass cut through the low boom of thunder, and he stepped quickly to the window. Peering through the blurry rain beyond the window, Jake could just make out a white compact car—standing out all the more because the brilliant white was spattered with mud. A large tree branch lay against the front headlight on the passenger side. Geez, he hoped no one was hurt. It didn't look that way. But best to go out and see.

He pulled up the collar of his oiled, canvas raincoat and reached for the old, stained leather Stetson-style hat that had been his grandfather's during his growing-up years. It always somehow made him feel most connected to all the things he'd staked his life on—in more ways than one. He squinted out the window once more, running his fingers nervously over his beard stubble, and heard another crack of thunder. At a time like this, he needed the hat. He pressed it onto his head and tugged it low on his face for protection

Jake strode back through the café toward the front door, side-stepping the tables and chairs. Just as he got to the door and reached to pull the handle toward him, it burst open, and someone in a dark, hooded rain poncho barreled through it and right into his chest, knocking him backward against one of the tables.

Instinctively, he grasped the edge of it, his wet work boots making squeaking sounds as they skidded on the bare wooden floor. A nearby chair fell back against its neighbor.

The hooded poncho—or rather its contents—slammed the door closed as if to slam shut the whole storm, then, wheeling back toward him, gave a yip.

"Oh my gosh, you scared me!" The poncho apparently had no problem speaking. A woman's voice. And something about it fleetingly tinkled a tiny, distant bell in Jake's memory.

The poncho shook itself, and slender, manicured fingers reached up to push back the hood, revealing first a woman's full, dark swath of curly damp hair, and then a face—a stop-the-presses-beautiful face.

And ... a stop-the-presses ... *familiar* face.

As Jake stared at that face, his breath spiked and his blue eyes shot wide. His words, however, took their time.

"Uh, wow," he began, slowly processing how quickly this moment had gone from something so unknown—a strange car he'd never seen before—to something that … he *had* seen before.

This face, he knew this face. No wonder the voice had rung a bell. Even as his mind was playing catch-up with his eyes, something deep and old moved inside of him, something from long ago. But something that was also alive right now.

Time froze for a moment.

The woman—no longer a poncho—didn't seem to freeze. She shook her hair, smoothing the curly wisps back toward a now almost-defunct ponytail and wiping her damp face with the backs of her fingers. The warm steam of her breath combined with the damp in the room. He could sense more than smell faint perfume.

Her wide brown eyes betrayed a mix of indignation and—to the extent that he could get his wits about him—a touch of fear?

Damn! Jake's wits quickly returning, he realized that with the low hat and coat-collar, he must look like the proverbial dark nameless stranger. He reached up and pulled the hat off, raking his hair back from his face with his fingers in his age-old habit.

The woman stopped, frowning into his now-visible face. Jake noticed a series of quick emotions flickered through her large, dark—beautiful—eyes, her lips damp and slightly open as she took a sharp intake of breath.

Finally, his own emotions coalesced into recognition, and he managed to reclaim his words.

"Annie?" he asked incredulously, in an almost hallowed whisper, his mouth slowly opening to a half-smile. "Annie Diaz?"

The woman apparently struggled to gather herself, visibly taking a deep breath. She paused for a moment, looking down, then flashed those eyes shyly back up at him.

Suddenly, she seemed like a little girl. "Hi … Jake."

Fifteen minutes later, Anna found herself in the cab of a truck, a large, newish silver pickup with a tarp covering the contents of the back, and she didn't feel one bit more in control of herself now than she had back in the café. Not one bit.

What had become her normal confident flair in her city life progressively shrank smaller and smaller as they drove deeper into the dark, limb-littered road in the rain.

The sky was shades of gray as they drove in near silence to Jake's place on the outskirts of the small town, a drive that echoed with the countless times she'd taken that same route before, hoping to glimpse him at the end of it. Anna leaned against the passenger-side door, reaching down to reassure herself that her handbag and suitcase were still at her feet. And that all of this was real.

I'm in a truck with Jake Petersen in a storm, she repeated incredulously to herself, since each piece of it felt equally hard to believe.

A truck. Not an Uber, not a cab, definitely not her white BMW. Which, she thought ruefully, was now sporting a bashed-in headlight and sitting where she and Jake had left it, back at the café.

In a storm. When she was supposed to be enjoying the springy green of the Poconos on Memorial Day weekend.

And … with Jake Petersen. That was the hardest thing to believe.

Some ideal memory she'd always carried tucked away in her mind like a photo in a locket was suddenly flesh and blood—big-time, she thought, glancing over at his damp, intent, profile and the muscular forearms under the rolled-up cuffs of what seemed to be an old corduroy work shirt. He'd always been the Golden Boy who fit in so easily, while she looked on from the edges.

Yet now he simply seemed … real. Gone was the locket. She

11

fixed her eyes straight ahead. She was feeling a little too real herself.

In the wink of an eye—or a storm—she was perilously close to going from being Anna, the confident, successful professional woman driving her BMW to a spa resort, to Annie, the shy, tongue-tied teen who'd lived for the moments when Jake would stop by her papi's farm-equipment supply store on the main street of Cedarwood Spring. They'd take a walk around town, chatting and licking ice cream, while Papi smiled knowingly. Then Jake would drive back off to a world that seemed so close and yet so far away.

The memory made her feel even more vulnerable. Especially since her dad had passed a few years ago—and had never been treated all that well in Cedarwood Spring anyway. But this was no time to walk into that memory bank.

Get it together, girl, she told herself, and shuddered as images from the past quickly evaporated.

"You cold?" Jake asked, glancing over at her before turning quickly back to the hazardous road. He hadn't said much. Only that they needed to get back to the inn before the storm got much worse, and they could put her up for the night. He'd introduced her to Haven, whom she thought she vaguely remembered, though Haven had been several years behind them in school.

But Haven had remembered her—or more to the point, knew what she was doing now and seemed to be super excited about it. Which had felt surprising, if not downright alarming, to Anna. How could anyone in Cedarwood Spring be excited about what she was doing when it hadn't occurred to her to wonder about anyone in Cedarwood Spring?

"No, I'm OK," Anna said quickly. She reached up to smooth her hair again, then realized there was no point. Curls gonna do what they do. "Jake, thanks again for helping me with the car and for giving me a room at your inn. I remember it." She shifted at the old images, which had a bit of patina in her mind's eye;

there just wasn't time to process all this, at least not until later. "This is all so totally unexpected. I don't know what I would have done—about the car, or about a place to stay. You've clearly got plenty of other things going on." She glanced meaningfully out the window.

"I'm glad I was there," he said, with startling firmness, his voice low. "You wouldn't have been able to drive that car anywhere, and it would have been a bad idea. Trees are down in all kinds of places, the roads are a mess. And there was nowhere else to stay around here anyway. The Cedarwood Spring Hotel at the end of Main Street is totally booked up for the holiday weekend."

Anna gave a dry snort. "Some holiday."

"Yeah, not much chance to meander down country roads in the middle of all this." He cast a sidelong glance her way. "Nice car, by the way."

"Thanks," she said, and for a second, it occurred to her that maybe he thought it was *too* nice. She'd always been simple and plain when she lived here—that was the person he'd known. Heck, that was when she began her lifelong habit of consignment clothes—not because it was hip, as it was now, but because she and her mom had to.

But then she reminded herself of what she had known of Jake: His family were long-timers in Cedarwood Spring, descended from the town's founders. Whereas her folks had moved there from Texas after her papi had immigrated from Mexico and met her mom. He'd started out in farm work and rose quickly to managing the Cedarwood Spring farm-supply store, dedicated to taking their family life into a future he couldn't really see. But his name, his skin, his accent had all marked him out. He hadn't spoken Spanish at home, so she never did either. But she'd known it was part of him.

She'd known, and the whole town had known, or at least that's how it had felt to her back then. Especially when she was helping Papi out at the store. She'd hear the family who owned the store make comments stereotyping where he'd come from, the food he ate, his pronunciation. He worked so hard, and they'd taken it for granted. No wonder she'd cock her emotional fists when she was at the store to help out.

Not that Jake had ever treated either of them that way. In fact, that's what had been so special about him; he seemed to treat everybody like it was a level playing field. But feeling like an outsider had just been her default back then. She wouldn't have known any other way to think.

Well, not now. That was Annie. *This* is Anna, she thought defiantly. Inch by inch, she was regaining confidence, if only through the sheer force of will. She squared her shoulders.

"Yeah, I love that car. It's beautiful, drives super smooth, and it's really safe. Besides ..." She tossed him a flirtatious glance. "I look good in white." When feeling awkward, resort to banter.

Jake gave a weary chuckle, his face crinkling around his smile. "Yes, you do."

Anna felt a shot of pleasure and grabbed the gumption to steal a glance at his profile.

It was the same Jake, but different. Golden Boy handsome, of course. But something softer around the eyes and mouth, and maybe a few strands of early gray at the temples of his sun-and-honey hair? It was hard to see in the semidark of the story afternoon. Ah, but there was the same little scar on the side of his right eye. How was it that she even remembered it was from an impromptu football game his senior year of high school?

A damp musky smell rose from sweat and rain—not sweat from heat so much as clammy perspiration—and she found it oddly comforting, with a note of familiarity. Could body chemistry stay the same for years? Pheromones, was it?

She was looking at him too long. Quick, something else to say.

Anna cleared her throat. "So bring me up to date on your family's place. Since we're on our way there."

Jake's smile faded. "Cedarwood Spring Inn. A few years ago, we officially named it that for the stand of cedars out back. I'm not sure how much you've followed what's gone on around here the past few years?" His voice sounded vaguely reproachful.

"Not much. After Papi passed, my mom moved back down to Texas to live with her sister. I wasn't in touch with anyone else in Cedarwood Spring after that."

"Well, the town's done great," he said, and she definitely heard pride in his voice—in fact, was it almost defensive? "In the last twenty years or so, it's really become known as a getaway out here in Pennsylvania Dutch territory—or near enough. We've still only got the one hotel in town, but it's doing really well. Lots of people are doing Airbnbs. And lots of other spots have opened up—restaurants, galleries, antiques, cafés. Some really smart, young entrepreneurs. Like the Filling Station. Haven is doing a really cool job with that. I've really tried to encourage her."

"It looked great, the little bit I saw of it," Anna agreed. "Neat concept. And I know about this stuff. Haven is doing all the baking?" Suddenly it occurred to her: Even if Haven seemed to know something about what had gone on in her life, did *Jake*? Best to play it cool and see what came up.

"Most of it. She's got a couple of college kids working for her. She's going to do the baking for—" Jake broke off.

Anna eyed him. He wasn't answering her. That much was coming up. "I'd asked you about your family's place."

He shrugged, keeping his eyes intent on the road. "Well, we've tried to grow with the town. It's been in our family a long time—since my great-great-granddad. But then you know that."

Anna nodded, remembering the lore. "You're named after him, right?"

Jake looked over at her, faintly impressed. "Right. How'd you remember?"

Anna suppressed the need to say, *You have no idea how much I remember about you. Including your football scar.* But this wasn't a moment to walk on the wild side. Better to go with a safer line: "How are your folks?"

Jake looked back at the road, making sure to dodge fallen limbs. "They've both passed. Was years ago, first Mom, she got sick. Then Dad soon after that. They'd been real partners for so long, I don't think he knew how to function without her."

Anna felt a flash of guilty embarrassment. OK now it was painfully clear how much she *hadn't* kept up with things. "I'm so sorry," she murmured. "I never knew them well, but they always seemed ... well, right together."

"They were. Now it's just me and my grandmom. Do you remember Iris?"

"I do," Anna said thoughtfully. She had always liked the tall, graceful, post-hippie woman whom she'd often see out and about on Main Street and who came into her papi's store to buy seeds for her herb garden. She'd talk to Anna—Annie, then—about things like exactly what herbs would go best with what dishes and when the best time was to plant strawberries based on how early or late spring was.

Anna squinted, retrieving an old memory. "She used to talk to me about recipes. I remember how she liked making pastry dough, and how she told me how to keep a pie crust from being tough. Turned out to be a valuable lesson. I cashed in on it." She held up a finger emphatically. "I'll have to thank her."

Jake gave a small grin, his tension visibly broken. "Yeah, that's Iris. She's not able to do as much these days. The whole thing is ..."

"What?"

"Well, a lot has happened. We took some pretty bad hits." He paused, and Anna felt her curiosity rise, but he continued before she could query him. "I want to bring the inn back up to being great, you know—being what Granddad, and Iris, and Mom and Dad always imagined for it. And why Jacob had built it in the first place. As a place for people to gather and … well, just love how special the place is, I guess. I want people to see it—only *better* than anybody imagined," he ended, with an air of aggression.

Anna's heart flipped a little. Wow, that was honest—and a little bit scary in its fierceness. The ease this Golden Boy always seemed to have before was rougher now. Her curiosity to know more rose.

"It's such a beautiful place," she said, watching him. She remembered the old stone house perched on a low hill over-looking the town, with front-yard gardens of climbing wisteria and hydrangeas. Of course, she'd only ever seen the front yard in passing, and not much more of what she—and everybody in town—knew was quite a large property. It had to be, based on the quantity of supplies Jake's dad had bought at Papi's store.

And now she was going there with Jake. In a truck. In a storm. It all felt a bit surreal.

"The place always seemed like it would be a great destination," she added, trying to keep on track.

"That's exactly the idea," Jake said emphatically, thumping the wheel. "I've been working hard for so long, and we're almost there. I've got a good team of people helping me. Haven is one of them, but I'm using a lot of these new local businesses in town too. We're trying to launch the barn and the inn as a place for hosting big events. And this week, we've got this great chance. The Abbott wedding." He glanced quickly at her. "You remember them?"

Once again, a specter darkened the edge of her memories, and this time it was harder to push it back down. Did he remember all the prickly moments that were resurfacing in her own memory?

"Of course," she said, trying to keep her voice light and praying Jake didn't remember her defensiveness back then. "Powerful family, had their fingers in all kinds of business. They owned the farm-supply store where Papi worked."

Her inner mantra: *Anna, not Annie; Anna, not Annie.*

If Jake noticed her emotional tempest, he was gracious enough not to comment. "That's right. Well, their youngest is getting married, and there'll be lots of people, lots of publicity, lots of connections I can make. A chance to show what we can do—what we always wanted to do. It's just …" Jake shifted the truck into low gear. "But enough about all that. Here we are."

The truck rounded the curve of the winding paved driveway, and through the gray-green sheets of rain, Anna saw the old stone house rise into view. Even in a storm and the mind-spinning disorientation of the day, her mind cleared for a second: "Oh, Jake, it's still so beautiful."

The old inn had always held magic for her, and no less so now. Her heart bumped at the sight of its three tall stories—the top one, gabled beneath a slanting roof—rising against the stormy sky. Stout chimney tops stacked at either end of the roof, with a third in the middle; she wasn't sure whether the white mist she saw was smoke or just the effects of wind-swept rain. Dark cedars, for which she knew the town had been named, framed the old inn on either side, and vines clung stubbornly to the stonework in the shifting wind.

Even in the waning light, Anna could make out where the gravel drive circled up to the edge of the small, highly tended front yard, typical for the farmhouses of that era and aesthetic; Jake and his family had always kept it up, and she flashed on unloading mulch with her papi from their truck. She knew that the drive then led through the woods around the inn, down the hill that was behind it, and down to a barn in the back. But she and Papi had never ventured that far with deliveries; in fact, she didn't remember the barn even being functional, come to think of it.

As Jake pulled up to the front of the house, Anna saw more clearly the raised garden beds lying in neat rows on either side of the curving brick walk that led to the large front door, with old-fashioned copper lanterns gleaming from both sides, undaunted by the weather. A welcoming glow burned inside the smaller multipaned windows that spanned the first and second floors, though the gabled windows on the top floor were dark. She'd always tried to imagine what was inside those windows.

Jake's voice softly called her back to the present. To Anna, not Annie.

"I called Iris from the café. She's expecting you. She's excited," he said, pulling the truck up close to the brick walkway. He paused, and she couldn't quite tell if his face was intent or playful or both. "And I should tell you—it's not just the two of us living here."

Anna looked down, forcing herself to appear nonchalant, though why that would need forcing, she had no idea. "Oh, who else?"

Jake looked at her teasingly—for the first time that night and yet also deeply familiar from the distant past. "Putz. The one-eyed cat. He'll love you."

Anna grinned in relief.

Jake turned off the motor and turned his face fully toward hers for the first time since they'd dashed through the rain and climbed into the truck. Things might have been happening fast, but his smile was slow and warm.

"Welcome home."

Oddly, it felt to Anna as if the journey had only begun.

CHAPTER 2

"Annie, it's so lovely to see you," Iris Petersen said, easing carefully into one of the cream-and-blue striped wingback chairs that sat on either side of the matching sofa.

The air inside the wide, gracious front room of the 150-year-old house was cooler and drier than the odd humidity of the stormy afternoon outside.

"The fire's nice," Anna said, nodding toward the central fireplace—also wide from the days when it had to warm an entire family—which glowed with a small fire that flickered and danced from the downdrafts the winds pushed down the chimney.

Iris nodded, smiling. "Feels a bit strange at the beginning of summer, but I thought I would help dry you two wet strays out. And this one too." She nodded toward the large orange cat with ears that looked like they'd tussled with another cat or two, sleeping soundly on the rug in front of the fire.

Anna smiled, realizing she hadn't used those muscles much today. "So that's Putz."

"He's what we call the X factor around here. Never know where he'll pop up or what he'll get into."

Anna relaxed into the couch, tucking her legs underneath her, feeling a bit like a stray cat herself. She gratefully picked up the cup of green tea Iris had made for her as she gazed around, hoping her amazement at being in this house—actually inside it —wasn't too obvious.

Her sleek black-leather sneakers sat damp by the front door where she'd left them. On the other side of the room, glass-paned French doors to the adjoining dining room stood open, and a touch of the smell of wood-smoke mixed with the scent from the lavender diffuser on the coffee table and something delicious —Anna couldn't tell quite what—coming from the kitchen.

She'd grown up seeing it from outside, always eagerly watching Jake Petersen stride out, gangly and smiling warmly, to shake her hand—and her papi's. That had meant a lot; a Mexican immigrant and his daughter delivering supplies often went unseen. But Jake saw them. And she always, always saw Jake.

And out of the corner of her eye, she saw him now. Standing in the doorway to the kitchen, framed by the light from behind. Leaning against the door jamb, holding his mug, watching and listening.

Anna snapped out of the hazy past, suddenly feeling more on-air than for any live interview she'd done for NY1. She quickly refocused on the woman before her, who was just as kind as Anna remembered, if more frail. Iris had always reminded her of some enviable combination of Pennsylvania Dutch and '60s flower child. She still had her loose ponytail, now totally white, at the nape of her neck and charming small round Lennon-style spectacles.

"Iris, thank you so much again for taking me in. I really don't know what I would have done if I didn't happen to ..." She glanced sheepishly at Jake.

"I'm so glad Jake found you," Iris said quickly.

Warming to the fire and the company, Anna couldn't resist a little honesty. "Actually, Iris, I found him—almost ran right into him when I was trying to get out of the rain." She looked hesitantly at Jake, who simply gave a small smile.

"Well, I think you have good aim," Iris continued. "And you got settled into your room OK? Everything is looking its best this weekend. We have a big event later this week, and we've spent months getting ready for it." She glanced worriedly out the window.

"Jake told me—a wedding here, in this beautiful place. It will be perfect," Anna said, reassuringly. "Believe me, it's sort of my business." She took a breath to continue, suggestions for how well the inn could be used popping unbidden into her head. But glancing uncertainly toward Jake, she took a different turn. "Iris, I really wish you'd let me pay for the room. Surely you have other people who are needing it. And I was all set to pay for the resort, after all."

Iris shook her head firmly, floating light wisps of white hair. "We're not renting out rooms yet—just open for events in the big barn down the hill, with some use of the kitchen and dining spaces up here."

"Grandma keeps that guestroom made up like she's waiting for someone she knows is coming," Jake spoke affectionately from where he stood.

Iris smiled at him just as affectionately. "Well, I was right, wasn't I? You never know what traveler may need a bed. That's always been the idea here." She turned back to Anna. "See, it feels predestined that you were here."

Goosebumps bristled invisibly along Anna's arms, as she kept her voice calm. "Well, clearly I was in the right place at the right time." Wow, that was weird; hadn't everything about the day been wrong?

"I hope so." Iris settled her hands in her lap. "Well, speaking of your business, bring us up to date. I'd heard you were living in the city."

Anna cupped the tea in her palms. "That's right, I live in New York now—in Brooklyn."

"And what are you doing up there, Annie? I remember you always said you wanted to become the greatest baker in the world. I used to talk about recipes with you! So how did that go?"

"It went great." It was Jake who answered quietly but with disconcerting clarity. "And, Grandma … she's not Annie anymore. She's Anna."

Both women turned abruptly to look at him—Iris, in delight, and Anna, in surprise and a bit of annoyed embarrassment, the goosebumps completely gone.

So maybe he *did* know something about what she'd been up to. Though it would have been nice to find out about it some other way. She arched an eyebrow at him—a gesture all the more striking when she remembered it had been one of her standard ways of teasing him some twenty years ago. Only this time she didn't mean to tease—she meant to push back.

Iris turned to her, smiling and clearly assuming she had simply filled Jake in in the car. "Really? That's lovely. And you made your dream come true?"

Once more Anna felt a bit caught in headlights. Jake's presence seemed to be having that effect on her, even with all her media training. Where was Rubin when she actually needed him?

"Yes," she said, ignoring Jake—or rather, ignoring her awareness of him. "Well, I'm not the best in the world, that's for sure. But things seem to be going pretty well for me in the city."

"Where are you working?" Iris asked.

"I was heading up the pastry team at a couple of restaurants in Soho that are well known for their pastry menus. You know, all kinds of breads and specialty desserts. But it was getting tiring spreading myself out that way, and …" She glanced inquiringly at Erstwhile Golden Boy, as if to say, *Do you want to answer this one, buddy?*

Evidently he did.

"Grandma, Anna's famous—she's all over NY1, the local TV channel up there, and she's about to be part of a TV show."

Anna's eyes widened. *Geez, he did know.*

Iris clapped her hands together. "Why, that's wonderful. Congratulations, I'm so proud of you, Annie ... I mean, Anna."

Anna spun her attention back to Iris. "Yeah, the name worked better professionally." *And I was trying to leave behind the version of me that used to do exactly what I'm doing now: getting all self-conscious in front of someone like Jake. Or make that just in front of Jake, since there had never been anyone else sharing his particular, um, energy in my life.*

"Well, we all have to make changes and concessions for work," Iris said gently. "We sure have done that around here. You've clearly got a good head for building your career. Good for you. But it sounds like an awful lot of stress."

"Exactly," Anna said. "It is a lot."

"So this new show is going to help?" Iris sounded a little incredulous.

"That's the point. See, I've had this idea for a place that only has drinks, breads, and pastries. But they're geared to match perfectly with each other and the time of day. The idea is that it's open morning, noon, and night with pastry options and gourmet drinks tailored to the time of day." Anna shifted, clearly warmed, as she always was, by the idea of the café. "So, for instance, coffee, tea, cocoa in the morning. But with really great coffees, teas, cocoa beans ground right there on a warm stone."

"Oo-ooh, that sounds good," Iris encouraged her.

"Top-shelf sherries or gourmet teas in late afternoon. French cognac and locally sourced coffees in the evening. All paired up with exactly the right sweet or savory bread or pastry."

"How lovely!" Iris exclaimed, looking over at Jake.

"Thank you! But the problem was that neither of the restaurants I worked for were geared to do that. So my manager started up this idea to find a new place—"

"Another restaurant?" Iris asked.

Anna tilted her head. "Not quite. Probably something more intimate, like a bistro or a café. But what could help us get started is this, um, show." She looked warily toward Jake. "See, we were having trouble finding a place to get my idea going— getting the funding, getting it set up with all the logistical and legal stuff. And my manager, Rubin, knew a TV producer who was looking around for a new concept. They went out one night for drinks, and the next morning, all I knew is that they'd hammered out this idea to get my café funded and publicized by making it into a reality TV show …" There went the stomach clench again. Deep breath. " … and I got a call from Rubin saying it was the answer to everything."

"And you are the star?" Iris asked.

Anna glanced into her tea. "That's the idea."

"So that's how it came together?" Jake asked from the doorway.

"Yes, or at least how we hope it's coming together."

"I'm trying to imagine this," Iris said. "Do you mean like the baking shows on TV?"

"Sort of. It's a reality TV thing. So we'll have staff and customers and all, but also, well, cameras and 'soft script' and …" She sighed. " … stuff I still have to learn a lot about. It's not like other TV baking shows where the bakery is already established, like *Cake Boss* or *Ace of Cakes*. Those use bakeries that are already well established. Been in the families a long time. That's just it; I don't really have that, some place belonging to my family forever." Anna averted her gaze to the fire. "So we're using the show to establish the place I belong—wherever that ends up being."

Iris watched her thoughtfully. "Sounds … exciting?"

Anna's eyes stayed on the fire, and she knew she should be smiling but didn't feel like it. "It does sound that way."

"What's the name of the café?"

Anna giggled shyly, looking back at her. "It's 'Love Bite'! Can you believe it?" She was never quite able to get used to saying the name and sort of abashed to say it to Iris.

"My, sounds snappy." Iris wiggled her brow.

"Well, my manager came up with it that night after a few too many margaritas."

"Sounds like your manager has a lot of … drive," Iris said, turning to Jake. "Jake, maybe you should think of adding something like that into the plan for the inn. Anna, we're developing the place as an event venue with the barn as the main space. But that would be for big one-time things, like wedding receptions, birthdays, things like that. Up here at the inn itself, we haven't figured out a way to make these rooms a place for local people to come on a more regular basis."

"I think we have enough in the pipeline, Grandma," Jake said, with a bit of bite, it seemed to Anna. "I'm not sure I could take on something like a café. Right now, we need to get this wedding scene to work. Like, really well."

"You're right, it's not easy," Anna said, looking alertly back and forth between them as if she were glimpsing what was an ongoing debate. "It's safe to say, I'm learning a lot. I've ended up doing a lot with the director, who's this really cool woman, super experienced. It's soon. The pilot, the first show that's going to decide whether the Eats Network wants to do a whole series, is coming up on June 21."

Jake's voice softened. "Ah, the summer solstice."

"Right," Anna said. "The director, Sierra, wanted to kick it all off on the first day of summer, the longest day of the year. There's sort of a romance to it." She smiled at Iris.

"It's also the shortest night," he added.

Anna's smile disappeared. Why was he insisting on these little asides? They were quite distracting. Where was the easy-going teenage football prince she'd known so well? In the mix of the storm and the cozy fire, she was having trouble integrating the two.

"Right," she said again, turning emphatically to Iris.

"And," Jake continued, "did you know that in Sweden and some of the old Dutch countries, it was believed that if girls picked seven wildflowers and lay them under their pillows on the solstice, their future husbands will appear to them in a dream?"

Anna wrinkled her nose at him. What was he, friggin' Wikipedia?

"Jake likes the family's old cultural lore," Iris cut in fondly. "Apparently, there are lots of Swedish babies born nine months after the solstice. And I believe I heard that in Greece," she looked inquiringly at Jake, who shrugged, "unmarried women put something special to them in a pot and leave it under a fig tree. It's said that the next day, they say rhymes that help them predict their romantic future."

That words "unmarried" and "romantic future" seemed to leap annoyingly out of a conversation that was supposed to be about work, and Anna felt a little kick in the gut. As full as her work life was, this other "romance"-type category in her life was pitifully empty. Not that she'd worked so hard to fill it. There was just too much going on for romance. Or was it like Sierra had once said—that the busyness kept the loneliness at bay.

This was getting into a weird space.

Thankfully, Iris got the conversation back on track. "So Anna, with all that going on, is it work that brought you up this way?"

Ah, solid ground.

"The pressure got to be too much for the new show and all. I was having trouble sleeping … I don't know, I needed to get away and get centered before we got into the filming. Clear my head, get a reset. My manager even said I needed to get some rest and it had better be good."

Iris smiled. "In other words, you're under pressure to relax?"

"Yeah. I was headed up to Silverwood Resort, in the Poconos, but the storm sort of …" She glanced at Jake. "… had other ideas."

A shutter banged hard somewhere toward the back of the house. Jake started and turned to set down his tea. "Speaking of which. Excuse me, ladies—I need to go see what's about to fall apart this time." Looking from Iris to Anna, he nodded and headed up the stairs.

Iris watched his feet disappear, then turned back to Anna.

"Well, you're at the right place to relax," she said. "In fact, how long do you think it will take to fix your car? Was it bad?"

Was it? Anna shook her head. "I have no idea. A headlight was bashed in."

"Well, I hope you'll consider this your getaway instead. It might not be what you planned, but it's special around here and we don't get many overnight guests." She took a sip of tea. "That's what this inn is meant to be in the first place. Did you know it's what my husband's grandfather built it for?"

Anna shook her head. "Tell me."

Iris looked toward the fire, as Putz jumped up beside her, and she absently rubbed his head. "Jacob Petersen was from a strict religious family. There was a lot about it he valued. I remember my husband saying he started talking about it only toward the end of his life."

"I know Jake was named for him. What did he look like?"

"Handsome, a lot like Jake," said Iris, glancing knowingly at Anna. "I never met him of course, but my late husband said he had the same hair, same eyes as Jake, and we've got a photo of him when he was in his seventies. I'll show it to you sometime. No football scar though." She laughed. "I'm told Jacob's character was like Jake's. Stubborn, he could be a bit gruff. But he gave his heart to what he believed in. And Jacob believed in this land. He loved its beauty, especially this time of year, when the fields become so green."

She rubbed Putz thoughtfully, her gaze in the middle distance: "But what he didn't like about his upbringing was how it left out too many other people. So Jacob left home, staked out his claim here—starting right where the grove of cedars are, around the sides of the house. And there's a small pond out by the barn. It's how Cedarwood Spring got its name," she added proudly.

"I've only ever seen the front of the house." Anna stayed away from too many details of the past. She preferred the present.

"Jacob built a small shack where he could live while he worked on this house. Stone by stone, using the material of the land. The stones were from the nearby quarries. In those days, you can bet it took a lot of hauling to get them here. He met Jake's great-great-grandmother from one of the local families. Together they finished the house and made it a place for different families to come together. For meals, for weddings, for mourning when someone passed." A shadow crossed over her face.

"I heard about Jake's parents. I'm sorry, Iris."

Iris gave a small smile. "Thanks. They tried to keep that dream alive. But it's hard maintaining such a big old inn. Let alone taking it into the future. They got pretty far. And Jake's determined to take it all the way."

"Like Jacob?"

"Like Jacob. And like you," she said, smiling proudly at Anna. "You've been pretty determined and successful yourself."

In the flash of that smile, Anna realized she wasn't sure anyone had shown pride in her lately. Her mom, for sure, but it was different when you're Skyping with Texas. And she had plenty of people smiling at her in New York, but sometimes it felt like they mainly just wanted things from her. Of course, she had close friends whom she knew she could trust, like Sierra. But she was always so busy. At least that was one good thing about the show—they'd get more time to hang out. And there was her friend Colleen, though now that she was engaged, her time seemed sucked into wedding planning.

And Anna was always pushing herself to grab the next rung of the ladder, never feeling like enough. The simple affirmation of someone like Iris being proud of her made her realize she was hungry for it.

Iris seemed to read her thoughts, or at least her vibe. "You must be tired."

"True, it's been a long day. And a pretty unexpected one." That was a massive understatement.

"Tell you what. Go lie down for a bit. I'll have Jake call you when dinner's ready. It's not Silverwood Resort. But it should be plenty good."

"That sounds as wonderful as any resort," Anna said. And she meant it.

Heading up the two flights of stairs to her room on the third floor, she heard Iris bustle into the kitchen, and another waft of good smells reached her. She got to the top hallway, headed to her room down at the end, and pulled the door closed behind her.

There she paused, looking gratefully around her suite, its gray and white punctuated with clusters of flowers and small pots of aloe and camphor. Plants meant to help you sleep, she thought. Someone, probably Iris, had a good eye.

The ceiling angled down one side, sloping toward what she knew was the back of the house, and a fire popped in a small fireplace on the far wall. The heat felt good in the cool damp of the night. Against the double-sized dormer window, a four-poster bed with simple white canopy was set so that she could tell that morning light would flood in on her, a plain white quilt contrasting with the dark stained wood. A small wooden table was set with a Brown Betty pot of tea, a delicate blue teacup, and rounded cookies. From the smell, her expert nose told her they were both ginger and fresh.

Through the bathroom door, the claw-foot tub, sparkling and new, sat beneath a stained-glass window that also overlooked the back. A soft white robe lay over a small Dutch-looking dark-wooden chair, and lavender soap, lotion, and body wash—all bearing handwritten labels sporting a logo saying "Seed & Grass, made in Cedarwood Spring"—were out on the counter. Anna reached to unwrap them.

Wow, this was better than any resort.

The ageless peacefulness of the old space under the eaves was shattered by the unwelcome ringtone of her phone. She sighed, reaching for it. Rubin, natch.

"How are you, dear, I've been worried. There are reports all over the news about falling trees and floods and pretty much the end of time!"

"Thanks, Rubin, it was crazy, but I'm totally fine now. Everything's actually worked out really well." Anna paused. How to describe what had happened—or for that matter was happening?

"Where are you staying?"

"Let's just say I ran into an old friend, and they're putting me up for the night. Or two."

"An old friend? He or she?" Rubin always patrolled her personal life, or total lack thereof. But then again, he didn't have one either.

"He. Just … an old friend." She hoped she'd made it through that lie. "He and his grandmom have an old inn here, and they had a spot for me. It's really nice."

"Are you still going to go to Silverwood? Or get yourself back here?"

Looking at herself in the dark-metal-framed oval mirror over the white, raised bathroom sink, Anna saw a tired face with disheveled curls of hair going up, down, and sideways. The skin around her eyes looked grayish. She held her hand lightly to her chest, feeling how her heartbeat was rocketing simply from the conversation—and she knew in her gut that she really needed to power down.

Besides, she was really liking this room.

"Actually, neither one. I think I'm OK staying here for now. They've invited me to stay on, and anyway, the roads will take a while to clean up and I have no idea yet how long it will take to fix the car. I might as well take my break here." The relief she felt in saying that told her it was the right thing to do. The relief was also speckled with a bit of excitement.

"But the whole idea was for you to get away and get rested for the pilot."

"I can get rest here." She glanced appreciatively at the tub.

"OK, have it your way. Stay put. And keep checking the traffic app for news on the roads."

"Will do."

After texting Sierra, Colleen, and a couple more friends to make sure they were up-to-date, Anna tapped the phone onto silent and pulled off her clothes, laying them carefully over an old oak rocking chair. Thank goodness she had enough clean vacation clothes with her.

She lit the fresh, grass-scented candle beside the tub, remembering sitting in traffic that morning in the Lincoln Tunnel, waiting amid exhaust and honking horns to get out of Manhattan. She silently shook her head and mouthed the word "Wow."

She'd had no idea where the day would bring her, thrown—gently or wildly, she wasn't sure—back into Jake Petersen's world. Which used to be her world too. Kinda, sorta.

It definitely wasn't her world now. Her world was back in New York where she'd been visible and heard and valued for her Latina heritage. And where that visibility had led to the next big step. Her idea for her café of her very own: the concept, the recipe pairings, right down to the atmosphere she wanted to create in it. And the show that could make it happen.

Anna's stomach tightened.

She had to make the show work if she wanted to get her café off the ground. And Rubin had made clear that for the show to work, she needed to be refreshed, reset, and ready to go. But more than that, Anna knew, she didn't just need the show to work out; she needed to really *want* the show. And surely, this break back in Cedarwood Spring was the way. After all, wouldn't an unexpected immersion back into the very place she'd tried to leave all those years ago make getting back to the show seem ... *irresistible*?

Right, that had to be it!

If she had to be here, which the storm and her car seemed to have determined, then that was the deal she'd make with herself.

This *will* be the break I need from the city, she thought. The chance to rest, stay out of the kitchen, and let this whole detour make me all the more ready to get *out* of Cedarwood Spring and back to the city.

Anna ran the hot water and poured in the bubble bath. She let herself sink into that knowledge as she sank into the warmth, lavender bubbles beginning to build in the spray.

The top floor was really looking nice, Jake thought as he reached the guest floor he and his father had extended and remodeled from the old attic. The clean, white walls contrasted nicely with the brown of the beams and posts. And it smelled good too. Fresh.

Or was that Anna?

His heart gave an annoying bang. He didn't know whether to stride authoritatively toward her door as the builder and owner of this place—or just yell "supper's ready" and turn tail.

What was he anyway, thirty-seven years old—or seventeen? Seventeen sounded about right.

This was all so strange and disorienting. He felt both too young and too old at the same time. Such a big moment for the inn with the big Abbott wedding in just days and so much at stake, and now a storm that could hurt the property and delay the deliveries that were all due for Tuesday, the day after Memorial Day, so they'd have a couple of days to get everything in place.

And then out of the blue—or rather, the rain—this girl from the past literally landed right into his present. He fleetingly remembered the sensation of the damp scent and past-life voice that had emanated from the poncho back in Haven's bakery. Kind of a nice memory.

Sure, he'd always cared for Annie Diaz when they were pals back in high school. Why wouldn't he? She was warm and smart and pretty—with the same smiling eyes as he was finding so captivating now. Every time he was around her—he remembered this so clearly—she would listen and laugh and tease and discuss so easily that it didn't feel like he had to work for it at all. It had always felt like a mini vacation from his usual set of friends, who seemed to take more work.

Of course, he'd run with a different crowd than she did, a crowd that had all the right people. After all, he's been brought up aware of his legacy as part of the town's founding family, a legacy he'd tried to outrun. Somehow, he'd felt pressure to chase after status even though, in retrospect, he knew he wouldn't have known what it looked like if he caught it. Of course, subsequently getting married to and then divorced from one of that crowd had brought that process to a screeching halt, and he'd downshifted to working on the inn and reshaping his friendships in town, stepping up for those who needed help, while keeping himself to himself.

While Annie—Anna, he corrected himself—hadn't really had a crowd back then. She always seemed fine doing her own thing. In fact, he'd envied it, especially when his own clique hadn't treated her—or her father—very well. He winced at the thought and wondered if she remembered it the same way he did. And as each step unfolded memories he hadn't unpacked in a while, he suddenly remembered that the most wince-worthy memory had actually involved the Abbott's—as in, the same family with the make-or-break wedding that week.

And here she was, sliding into his home base.

A beautiful, sophisticated Anna, whose wide dark eyes seemed to sparkle as much as her silver bracelets did, and in whose gaze he felt special—once again. And here he was, over-worked, overworried, on the border of failure, and beginning to go gray in the temples. Not to mention he suddenly felt embar-rassingly single; he didn't usually worry about the fact that he hadn't dated in an eternity—it just wasn't a priority. But suddenly he felt inadequate in that department too. He bet Anna had a rich, handsome boyfriend back in the city. His left ring finger felt painfully naked.

Jake shook himself.

Going for the thirty-seven-year-old option, he strode purposefully toward her door.

"Anna?" he said softly. He rapped lightly and heard her tread on the wooden floor. In a few seconds, the door opened and damp, light perfume greeted him. Yep, that fresh smell was her. It was the first time he'd really stood close to her when they were alone and not dodging tree branches in the car. He had to admit, he kind of liked it.

Her hair was brushed and loose around her head, and she'd put on a bit of makeup, set off by her simple, white open-collar shirt. Jake could have gazed a bit longer. He knew he should step away, and he was working on it—really, he was.

Focus, man.

"Hey, um, Iris has dinner ready. If you feel ready to eat?" He managed to turn and start back down the stairs, gesturing to her to follow.

"That would be great, thanks. She's been amazing." Anna pulled the door closed behind her. "You both have."

Anna followed Jake silently back down the stairs, watching his broad frame move easily in the space he knew so well, silhouetted against the light coming from below. It felt both freakishly familiar and totally unprecedented. As did all the memories that were beginning to climb out of the hole where she'd left them. Maybe this was the new normal.

As they turned to head through the French doors into the dining room, she stopped with a sharp intake of breath, gazing around. "Wow, this is beautiful."

Like the living room, white ceilings and walls were framed with restored wooden beams matching the rich dark wood of the mantel that was over another, smaller fireplace. A simple, elegant wrought-iron chandelier—its plain arcs of dark metal contrasting with the gentle white light at the end of each graceful arm—hung over a wooden table covered in a plain damask cloth. A sideboard held a rack of stacked dishes and what looked like a fresh pound cake, a small vase of blue flowers adding a pop of color at its center.

Iris was just placing two plain-white china plates on the table, which was set with pewter and silver, cloth napkins, and candles—amid serving plates holding a roast chicken and vegetables, and steaming fresh popovers.

Jake gave Iris a playful side hug. "You set one great table, Grandma."

Iris smiled. "I hope you like it. Anna, have a seat. Just make sure Putz doesn't get on the table. He's a big chicken fan and has a crazy radar for the one moment you're not looking." She affectionately toed the fuzzy orange tail protruding from beneath the tablecloth.

"I'll defend it with my life," Anna said, sliding into a chair. Noticing there was only one other place set, she looked up questioningly at Iris.

"Oh, I always eat early," the older woman said. "I like it that way. I leave Jake's helping waiting for him—only this time, for once, he doesn't have to eat alone, thanks to you. I'll head to bed soon, but Jake knows how to close up shop. Sleep well, Anna. We'll keep our fingers crossed about the storm." Iris disappeared into the kitchen.

As Jake called out a good night to her, Anna suddenly felt not just alone with Jake—but *decidedly* alone with Jake. There was no car ride, no catching up with Iris. Just Jake and … her. And the cat circling her feet in hopes that she was a messy eater.

She turned back to him in time to catch his small smile. "Wine?" He picked up the bottle of red from the sideboard.

Was he kidding? "Definitely," she said, watching while he poured.

He set the bottle beside them and sat down, lifting his glass to her. "To … storms."

She held up her glass. "To storms."

As if in answer, another clap of thunder shook the air.

Anna laughed nervously and glanced at him before picking up her fork. She paused, feeling the weight of the pewter in her hand. Looking back up at him, she noticed his light hair was no longer in damp spikes along his face, but combed back, gleaming a bit from the candlelight. He'd changed out of the damp work clothes, and a clean, long-sleeved gray T-shirt lay loose across wide shoulders. Whoa, his masculinity was aging like … fine wine.

Time to take the lead.

"Jake?"

"What?"

"Got a question for you." She met his eyes.

"Hmm?" He took a bite.

"How did you know … about me? I mean, what I was doing, the show, all that?" Her gaze was gentle but unwavering, as insistent as his voice had been back in the living room. "How did you know I was going by Anna?"

Looking like a kid who was caught doing something he wasn't supposed to, Jake became very interested in his food, pushing it emphatically around on his place. "I happened to be at my computer after we got in and just kind of, uh, looked you up."

"You mean you googled me? Should I be flattered?"

"Sure, I google most old friends from time to time," he said nonchalantly. "Just part of the drill around here. After all, it's been a while."

"True." She took a bite, feeling more comfortable. No reason not to have fun with this. "So what else did you find out about me?"

He shifted in his chair. "Not much. That you're a really good cake chef."

Anna raised her eyebrows. "A *cake chef*."

He looked at her then back down at the food. "Well, you know. All the stuff you talked to Iris about."

This wasn't adding up. How did he know about her? Anna frowned teasingly, looking at him askance. "You found this out in the time it took me to get settled into my room? While you were getting cleaned up and checking on the storm? Come on, dude, that doesn't make sense."

He took a breath, averting her gaze, though she could tell he was suppressing a smile. "Well, I might have … seen you a bit on Instagram from time to time," he added.

"You mean you followed me?" Anna resisted the rising heat she felt in her face. After a certain point, she'd given up trying to notice who followed her and who didn't. This was no time to show him he could still make her blush.

The idea that he would have followed her had simply never occurred to her. All these years, she'd kept Jake nestled in her memory like an inspiring painting or a special old photo—something that existed more in her mind than in reality. Maybe because the memory was so good that she didn't want to find out the reality wasn't. Maybe because it had never occurred to her that the real Jake would have been thinking about her, let alone following her.

But he apparently had.

"Sure," Jake said, sounding casual, if also a bit forced. "Didn't you follow people you knew in high school? Places here in Cedarwood Spring?"

She shook her head. "No, honestly, I haven't. My life is in New York, and it's really demanding. I have enough people to deal with right there. Besides, I wasn't all that close to kids here." She paused, looking down. "Other than you." Should she add that the way she'd found out her then-longtime boyfriend was seeing someone else was a Facebook tag that she happened to click on?

Let's see, I'm eating dinner with a handsome interesting man I haven't seen in years, crackling fire, nice wine …

Nah. No need to go there.

"I got more and more people either following or tagging me or expecting me to follow or tag them," she continued, trying to sound blasé. "I got too anxious about keeping everybody else happy. Then I got a therapist and learned about boundaries." She laughed, keeping her gaze on her food. "I officially decided to spend only a little bit of time every day on social media, only with close friends. Otherwise, it makes me crazy. And besides, all that stuff is what I have a manager for."

Jake lifted his eyebrows. "To get crazy for you?"

That was so spot-on that Anna all but coughed up the bite

she'd just taken. Her hand flew to her mouth. "Yes, exactly. Only I don't seem to be delegating it very well."

"He … she … is intense?"

"He. Rubin Maxx. And he was born to be intense." She sighed. "But he's a good soul. He's the one who brought me up to Sierra—she's the director of the show. Then she got in touch, and we clicked on the idea. Really cool woman, super smart."

"Clearly she's smart," he said. Jake's eyes lingered on hers, and Anna felt it.

"I'm excited," she hurried on. "Only that stuff gets crazy around shooting a pilot episode—I'm told, since I've never done it before. There's lots at stake. This could make or break everything for me. Sierra's been involving me so much that all kinds of doors could open from here. If it goes well, I get to take part in directing a future season of the show."

"And you'd like that?"

"Of course, who wouldn't?" Though as soon as she said the words, Anna caught herself. They kept sounding a little too automatic, and she was trying to get past that.

Jake shrugged. "I guess someone who didn't really love directing."

Forks tapped lightly against china. She looked at the fire. Jake waited; he doesn't seem afraid of silence, she noted. A good sign—means he's made some peace with himself.

Anna decided to step into the silence. "I'm not sure if I'd like it. I … it's just that, when you asked me that just now, I said whatever seemed the right thing to say. I keep hoping it'll start rolling off my tongue—taking the lead in a reality show. Helping to direct. But I can't make it feel all that natural. At least … not yet."

"I didn't know you could make feelings do anything." Jake peered into his wine glass.

"Touché. You can't. Hundreds of dollars in therapy later, I do know that. I guess I'm hoping they'll catch up on their own. After all, that's why I was getting away."

"To make the show feel better?"

He did have an annoying way of calmly nailing exactly what was bothering her. "Well, not the show," she hedged. "Just getting rest, stepping away from it all so that it would feel good to get back to it." As she heard her own words, they sounded lame.

"So, what *do* you like?"

There he went again. But it was fair enough; she'd pressed him for answers.

"Just the chance to make a whole … place, you know? A vibe, a concept. Not just part of a big restaurant, however glamorous and successful it is. I want to do my own thing. Plan the whole thing, oversee it all, not just the desserts. I feel like I've got so many ideas. And at the two places I've been working, they just slot me into a narrow role. I need a place … of my own."

Jake nodded. "The whole thing, like concept, decor, budget, menu?"

"Exactly. All of it. Soup to nuts." She paused to swallow a bite of popover, which she pointed at with her fork. "This is amazing, by the way."

"Thanks. Iris."

"I figured. She's got so much talent, Jake, and you have such a gorgeous place here. You've been so great taking me in. I'm sure this will give me the break I need. We'll just see how long the car takes." She glanced around appreciatively and let herself take a deep breath. "Isn't there something I can do to help out while I'm here? I have a lot of experience from these places I was working in Soho, as well as tons of others where I go with friends. How it works behind the scenes, new layouts. You know, totally new ways they are integrating the cooking area with the serving space. I could take a look down at the barn for you—"

Jake stiffened and pressed his fork harder into a piece of chicken. Anna glanced at him, curious. "Are you OK?"

He nodded, avoiding her eyes. "Yeah, thanks, just tired. I think hauling stuff around all day before the storm took more out of me than I thought."

"Oh, I'm sure." What had just happened? The air between them cooled. How to show her good intentions, and that she wasn't taking this for granted?

"Of course, and here you took me in and everything. But maybe as a way to help out while I'm here," she pressed, "I could at least give you some pointers—"

"We're good, thanks," Jake broke in, uncharacteristically abrupt, then softened his tone. "I mean, thanks anyway, Anna. Really. I know you're super at everything that you … do. But I've got local people working on it, and they're really good. It's part of the whole concept of Cedarwood Spring Inn." He gave a small but pointed smile. "Locally sourced."

As Anna watched his face in the candlelight, an old pain that she'd forgotten from years ago suddenly waved from a distance. Here she was in Cedarwood Spring—in fact, at the heart of its identity, Jacob Petersen's old inn.

And just like when she was a kid, just like her father before her, she was still on the outside. Wow, she'd completely suppressed that feeling. Which was probably a good thing.

She knew she shouldn't feel that way. She'd dropped in from nowhere, and Jake owed her nothing. She was probably only misreading him anyway: old ghosts and all that.

Her face must have reflected the fleeting discomfort, for Jake leaned toward her, his eyes less distant. "Really, thanks, Anna. You're doing amazing work. I do know that." A smile warmed his face back up. "After all, I've followed you."

Anna felt her face warm again. "It's good to get caught back up with you and Iris. I guess I need to catch up on my followers." She took another breath, her soft dark curls backlit by the rosy light of the fire, and glanced toward the dark window. "Maybe this storm gave me the nudge I needed."

"Agreed." Jake refreshed the wine in their glasses and held his up. "To storms."

She touched his glass with hers. "Storms."

And for a second, it felt like it wasn't just a storm that was passing, but one that might lie ahead.

The storm did rage that night. There were plenty of sound effects from banging limbs and falling branches. But thankfully the power stayed on, and Anna felt sheltered in the homey, elegant room tucked safely under the eaves. In the cool of the room, she slept, warm under the quilt.

At one crack of lightning that popped light through the room, she surfaced, remembered where she was, and pulled up to look through the dormer window over her head. Through the rain she could just make out the silhouette of the ring of cedars, then more distant, the roofline of a large building—the barn, she assumed—and wide fields beyond, where the wild sky was slightly less dark-purple than the horizon. She was eager to see it in the light.

She had forgotten the beauty of this area, even when the weather was fierce.

Anna slid back down into bed. This day had ended light-years from where it had begun. She'd thought she would be snoozing in a resort bedroom with attendants scurrying by outside. How could it be that she was in Cedarwood Spring, in Jake Petersen's house, in a bedroom she'd never seen before that still felt like home?

Yet even for its comfort, fragments of memories had begun to creep out of the woodwork like little goblins. Not that she didn't know them well, she just hadn't seen them in a while. And it didn't help that within an hour of getting detoured back to Cedarwood Spring, the memory of the Abbotts and all they represented in her memory, loomed up from the past.

But that was then, this is now, right? Mentally, she tried to shoo the old images back into their cracks and crevices. After all, she wouldn't be here long, and she certainly wouldn't have to see anyone other than Jake and Iris and a couple of people in town. Then she'd go back to where she belonged, ready to take on the world—right?

A small nightlight shaped like an old-fashioned candle in a holder glowed on the antique wooden desk beside her. Anna ran her hand lightly along the pewter shape where you'd hold it with your forefinger. Then the thought came back to her from the evening: Jake had followed her work.

And he hadn't just followed her work. He'd followed … her.

The next morning, the storm seemed like a dream, erased by the fresh morning light of a regular day. As Anna pulled on snug jeans and a drapey ivory tee, she wondered if the rest of the property was as untouched as her room. She might only have been there one night, but she felt as reconnected to Jake and Iris, and could see their stake in all of this, as if she were picking right back up where she'd left off in high school. Glancing out the window, she could see the barn down the hill, damp mist rising from the ground. She hoped it was as unaffected by the storm as it looked.

As she came into the kitchen, the smell of coffee hit her nose like a gift.

"Good morning, dear," Iris said, pouring boiling water into a French press of ground coffee. "Pull up a stool." She pointed to several that surrounded the work island in the middle of the well-equipped kitchen. Cozy lamps nestled along the counter alternated with brighter light over the range. Over a deep farmhouse-style sink, a wide window opened onto damp green and blue sky.

At the center of the island were OJ, a pot of tea, strawberries, and what looked—and smelled—like fresh cinnamon-sugar muffins.

"Good morning, Iris, thanks so much," Anna said enthusiastically. "These look fantastic. Mmm." Settling onto a stool, she slid a muffin over to her plate. "How's the property? Where's Jake?"

"He's out checking around, but you can bet he'll be in soon. He knows these were coming out of the oven. So far I haven't seen any problems in the house or the gardens other than lots of twigs and branches that we'll need to clean up."

"That's a relief."

"Sure is. He just needs to make sure the wiring and everything in the barn is still OK. It's at the bottom of the hill, you know, and it would flood in the past. When we renovated it, we raised the floor and put drains along the exterior and did all kinds of weather-proofing. So, how'd you sleep? Storm keep you up?"

"Not really I woke a couple of times, but it was fine. That room feels good, like it hugs you. And this kitchen is wonderful," Anna added, looking at the double oven, warming trays, and top-of-the-line mixer. "I know kitchens, and you've done a fabulous job with this one."

Iris looked wistfully around. "Jake and his dad worked hard on it to bring it up to being a professional-grade kitchen. We couldn't become a destination for events without it—or without a pretty hefty line of credit from the bank." She shook her head. "There was just no way around it, but it drove Jake crazy to have to put up the family property as collateral. There didn't seem to be much option. Now we have it all done. We just need the people."

As if on cue, the door to the sparkling white coatroom off the back of the kitchen heaved open, and Jake stepped in followed by a waft of cool, fresh air. His jacket and jeans were smudged here and there with dirt.

He peered from the coatroom into the kitchen. "Morning, ladies, let me pull off these boots," he said, ducking back around the corner to hang up his jacket. As he came into the bright kitchen, his plaid-flannel shirt easily across his shoulders, Anna noticed how powerful he seemed by day—clearly used to physical labor.

He went to the sink and washed his hands. "Those muffins for me?" He winked at Iris.

She laughed, patting his back as she walked over to her stool. "They've been waiting all morning for you, but you'll have to share them with Anna. How does everything look out there?"

"Could be worse," Jake answered, pouring coffee and pulling up a stool across from Anna. The three of them leaned on their elbows, nibbling on muffins.

"There's more work to do than I'd like. A lot to clean up before we can do all the setup but at least the new drains worked." He glanced meaningfully at Iris. "No flooding, and the runoff seems to be going down toward the stream, the way the new landscaping was supposed to channel it. The barn interior looks good. Stuff like the tables and chairs and decorations are all scheduled to arrive in a couple days. This is Sunday, the wedding is Friday. I'll write up a list of what we need help with, and I'll get with the people in town. We'll get it together, Grandma."

Anna felt a small pang at the mention of townsfolk, but before it could get far, Jake put her at ease. "So, Anna. You ready for a trip into Cedarwood Spring? It wasn't exactly at its best yesterday. Time for you to catch up with the town. And anyway, we need to move your car over to the garage."

"Oh, right, the car." Anna grimaced. She had totally lost her sense of time. Which, she realized, felt unexpectedly good. In fact, she wasn't sure how quickly she wanted to find it again.

"Seb's not in today—he's a pretty serious churchgoing guy," Jake continued. "And tomorrow's Memorial Day. We need to park it over at his place so that it's ready when he is."

This car-fixing thing was moving annoyingly fast, and she was just letting herself settle into the idea of a few leisure days in one place. Didn't cars usually take forever?

"I already called him," Jake was saying, "and he'll start in on it first thing Tuesday morning. But I want to go ahead and get your car off the street."

Anna nodded, feeling the day beginning to move under her feet. "Absolutely. Sure. Let me just finish my coffee." And get myself ready to reenter Cedarwood Spring.

CHAPTER 3

Outside, the world was calm and damp. The raindrops left
on the early-summer leaves refracted the bright morning
sunlight, and the air felt brand-new. Jake and Anna walked down
the flagstone path to where his silver truck was parked on the
blacktop driveway.

Jake glanced at her sideways. She seemed thoughtful, peace-
ful. It was as if the storm had passed and taken her worries
with it.

Her thick, dark hair was up in a ponytail, a wide white headband framing her hairline. It reminded him of the ponytail she'd
always worn years ago, only the headband gave it a new sophistication. Annie/Anna, he thought. She was looking down at the
flagstones as she walked, hands thoughtfully in the pockets of
her off-white sweater, her jeans svelte and snug. The storm had
brought her in and had given her some ease, it seemed.

Part of him knew that the last thing he needed right now was
this woman from the past who—through no fault of her own—
reminded him of everything he'd failed at in life.

And then another part of him was just so damn glad to
see her.

Anna paused, looking intently toward the trees that arched over the driveway leading down the hill to the road. "This is so beautiful," she said in something close to a whisper. "I'd forgotten."

Jake smiled a proud satisfaction and slid the saw he was carrying into the back of the truck under the tarp. Clicking the fob to unlock the truck, he came around to her side and opened her door for her. "Well, now that you remember, maybe you can come back and see us from time to time. People would be glad to see you, you know," he ventured tentatively, then suddenly felt too obvious. He quickly closed her door, got to his side, and climbed in.

"Do you really think so," she was saying flatly as he clicked the ignition. She looked back toward the driveway. It sounded more like a statement than a question. "I usually go out to the Hamptons with friends when I get the rare weekend off."

Jake took a dance step backward inside as he headed down the driveway, keeping an eye out for fallen branches. "Right, right, you have a pretty big life up there."

"True," she agreed and seemed to refocus on Jake. "So tell me more about this wedding. It's in, what, five days?"

He nodded. "Friday. It's the Abbott family, their youngest is getting married. Younger than us. James, he's marrying Sarah Smart. You remember either of them?"

Anna kept her face forward. "I remember James's father."

The vague memory that had surfaced last night as he'd been going up to her room came barreling back into life-size view. He rubbed his jaw, slightly grizzled with yesterday's stubble. "I'd forgotten about all that till … till now. There was something that happened around the garden project out at the community college. Right?"

Anna nodded as they reached the end of the driveway and turned onto the road. "I never knew all the details. Papi never talked much about it. But I know it hurt him." She turned to

Jake. "Do you remember what happened? I've always wondered."

Jake wavered. Was it really the right thing to go there? OK, well, better to name it. She already had.

He took a breath. "I don't remember the details all that well either. It was the new set of gardens at the community college. A big deal. They were designing it with all indigenous plantings to attract birds and pollination, I think. I remember talking to your dad about it at the store that whole year. He was so excited."

"Yeah, indigenous plantings were always his real passion. He was always researching it. He was ahead of his time."

Jake nodded. "And he totally knew the species around here, and he put in a ton of extra work after hours on the college gardens, you know, volunteering. I think he even paid for some of the plants himself."

"I remember him going out there in the evenings and on weekends. I think we were juniors that year."

"Yeah, we were. And then ... at the ceremony inaugurating the gardens, Mr. Abbott thanked everyone who worked on it by name, had their names on a plaque ..."

"Except ... Papi."

Jake paused. "Yes. Except Jorge." It felt powerful to say her father's name. As if touching what he knew was probably tender for her. He wanted to ask her what she remembered, what she had thought of the Abbotts back then, and that whole set ... and of him. But he didn't dare. This was all too new.

They drove in silence for a moment before Anna turned toward him. "Thanks, Jake." Her voice was soft.

"For what?"

"For remembering." She turned back to the road. "For not pretending it didn't matter. For not pretending he wasn't there." They rode a little farther, and she cleared her throat. "So. They're the make-or-break wedding for the inn. Ironic."

It was Jake's turn to feel fear. "Yeah, it just worked out that way. They're big into supporting the local economy, and we're happy to be part of it. We need it to go great, every detail. I'd like to say it doesn't matter, but it does."

"I understand. I really do. It'll be fantastic." Anna's voice returned to normal, and hearing her familiar, old support felt deliciously both past and present to Jake. "So the ceremony is at the barn?"

"No, the wedding is down the road at Old Trinity Church," he answered. "You know, one of the oldest churches in town?"

Anna nodded, remembering services at the graceful old stone church. "I always liked the way it smelled in there," she said thoughtfully.

Jake grinned. "I know what you mean. The ceremony will be there, so we don't have to worry about that. But it's the reception that's at the inn, all over the property. The gardens, the kitchen. But mainly in the barn. Food and music, the whole thing. Pete and Tina—you'll see their new outfit on Main Street, called PT Design—have been planning it, and they've hired all kinds of local artisans to help. They're good at it, at making people feel like everything is magic. Something special, but also relaxed."

"Nice. Tell me more. I'm always interested in the details of this kind of thing. There's always something new to learn."

He glanced at her, hoping he wouldn't come across as the newbie he was on this level of the business—a level on which she was clearly expert. "Well, for one thing, they're using long, narrow tables for the dinner seating, instead of round ones, so people are closer to each other and it feels more casual. Easier to get up and move around. You don't feel so stuck."

"They're totally right." She nodded approvingly. "I hate being stuck at a round table."

"And they got a really good band that plays pop stuff but also the old standards. You know, for real dancing?" For a second, Jake's mind snapped a picture of what Anna would be like to dance with. He bet she'd look great.

"Of course, it's the best. I've been to some amazing formal dinner-dances in New York."

He stared at the road, the image of her dancing becoming the image of her dancing with someone else. Not as interesting.

Thank goodness Anna seemed to miss his little mental excursion. "Who's doing food?" she asked.

"Haven is coordinating. She has caterers doing most of the dinner food—Albert Carlino?"

Anna shook her head.

"He was after your time. Really smart guy who's doing great getting his business going here. It's called Purveyor. You'll see them on Main Street too. He uses local food as much as he can, has a good relationship with the farmers and dairy businesses around here. And Haven does too—she's doing the dessert pastries, some of them her own creation."

"And now for the most important part." Anna did a playful drumroll with her fingers on the dashboard. "Who's doing the cake?"

Jake gave her a nervous glance. "That's the thing. Haven wants to try that too. It's just that it's the first one she's done— professionally. I felt like I needed to give it to her—she asked and all. But now she's really feeling the pressure." And so am I, Jake added silently.

Anna nodded. "Understandably. A wedding cake is tough. It's complicated to make, and then everybody's eyes are on the results. And their cameras."

Jake felt his anxiety spike and tightened his mouth.

Evidently Anna saw it. "Everyone's eyes are on you too?"

Might as well give her the whole scoop, she'd find out anyway. "The whole town, and lots of big family contacts in Philly, Bethlehem, Harrisburg. People who will talk about it, tell other people. But mainly," he took a deep breath, "one guy who's coming is a reviewer for Taggarts. You know, the place that publishes venue reviews?"

"Of course I know Taggarts! Every place I ever worked that hosted big New York insider events had a top Taggarts review. It's a huge deal." She looked at him sympathetically. "Now I get what you're looking at."

He nodded. "For Iris and me, it means being able to hire a regular staff at the inn. Put it on the map. It's what my parents and I really worked for. They put so much money into it. And then—"

"Then what? You mentioned before that something happened, but you didn't say what."

Jake kept his eyes on the road. It felt odd, almost like the old days. Talking freely to Anna—Annie—without fearing he wouldn't measure up. Here he was, doing it again, only now, there was so much more to tell, and not all of it good. Adding a divorce to his list of accomplishments had hardly been the stuff of high school chatter. Since she hadn't kept track of Cedarwood Spring, he could only hope she hadn't kept track of that either.

He gave her a quick sideways glance. Her eyes were open and earnest, just as he always remembered them.

What the heck. He probably wouldn't see her again after her car got fixed and she disappeared back into her dinner-dance, Hamptons life.

Besides, Jake was surprised to see that something in him wanted to talk to her about it all. Almost *needed* to talk to her about it. He was always worried about being so chin-up for all the people he hung out with in town, especially after the divorce, and with everything they were going through at the inn. He hadn't realized … it had been a long time since he'd had someone to talk to, really talk to. The way they'd always been before.

"Dad and Mom and I always wanted to bring the inn up to what it was always built for—a place where people could come from anywhere, everywhere, and have a great reception or party or whatever. Of course, we came to understand it's called 'event planning' and 'venue' and 'destination.' A whole industry."

"Sure is."

Jake nodded. "You get it. The inn was so old, and lots of problems come with old homes. It hadn't really been brought up to speed even in the twentieth century. My granddad wasn't as good as Iris at taking care of these things. And when you don't take care of problems with the property, it doesn't just stay the same. It gets worse."

"Like ... plumbing, the roof, stuff like that?"

"Exactly. In our case, the foundation got more expensive to repair, there was mold in a couple of the walls of the barn, things like that. And of course, the whole interior needed a complete redesign if we wanted to be competitive. Fixtures, walls, molding, lighting, sinks, faucets. It finally got to the point that we knew that if we wanted to do it at all, we had to be all in. But the savings had been whittled away and just weren't enough in today's dollars. So Dad took out a huge loan for the money to renovate the place. I was back from college, and we worked on it together. We got pretty far and even officially registered the house as Cedarwood Spring Inn."

"You did a wonderful job," Anna said quietly.

Jake gave a small shrug. "Thanks. But we hadn't totally finished when the recession came along in '08. And the value of the property dipped, and people weren't doing big events. Not around here anyway, and without better publicity and a track record, we couldn't attract people out from the cities. We were up to our ears in debt and no way out. And then ..."

"What?"

He took a deep breath. "And then, of course, my marriage hit the skids." His voice was rough.

Anna visibly started. "I hadn't known you were married."

"No need to get into it all. But it's just that the problems with the inn were part of all that went wrong. Margaret's family was in the hotel business. She had this plan to add it to their franchise. Brand it, all that kind of thing. I tried, but it never felt right. It was around the time my mom got sick."

Anna turned toward him, her face full of sympathy. She reached out, lightly touching his sleeve, before pulling her hand back to her lap. "Wow, Jake, Iris had mentioned some of this to me, but not all of it. That's so much for you to go through. So much loss."

As his chest warmed at her touch, Jake realized he was suddenly on tricky emotional terrain. Really tricky. For whatever crazy reason, he'd just passed some kind of tipping point he hadn't seen till he reached it. The inside of the truck felt muggy, and he tugged at his collar.

"Yeah, well, the point is that I had to take out another loan to finish off the work. And it's all ended up just being Iris and me. And a great property. And a one-eyed cat." He tried for levity.

"That explains why this week is so important." Anna watched him.

"Exactly." He left it at that. They had reached the Filling Station, and he was just as happy to leave the sad ghosts of the past out of further conversation with Anna.

Jake pulled up behind where her BMW was still parked along the street. "Well, at least it looks like nothing else hit it," he said, getting out of the truck and walking around the car. "The auto-repair place is a few blocks down. But before we go, let me check in with Haven and see if the storm did any damage. OK?"

"Sure. No hurry. I'd like to see her too."

As soon as they got inside and the door closed behind them, Jake could tell something was off. The door had been unlocked, but the lights were out. He reached over and flicked a switch. Nothing.

"Haven?"

He heard a noise in the dark kitchen, and Haven rushed in

through the swinging door, looking teary. Her chin-length brown hair lay in disheveled wisps. "Jake! Anna! This is awful!"

"You lose power?" Jake asked, looking around the room.

"Lightning hit a transformer right by the café," she said, looking around in obvious distress at dark tables of the usually cozy, inviting room. "It fried all the circuitry in here—all of it! The outlets, all the kitchen equipment. I had the repair guy come by—it's why I didn't call you yet. I wanted to find out how much damage had been done first." She looked at him fearfully. "I know how important this week is."

"It's OK," Jake said, fighting a shot of anxiety. "What did he say?"

"That's just it." She paused, briefly pressing her fingers to her eyes. "The ovens, all three of them, are pretty messed up. It's going to take getting an electrician in here, and with other problems around town, he's not sure when he can get here. And the wedding is in five days! Jake, we have to get the desserts all made—and the wedding cake! It's the one thing everyone will see …" She broke off as tears oozed up again.

"I'm so sorry, Haven," Anna said, stepping toward her.

Jake raked his hands through his hair and tried not to show how amped up he was getting. "Don't worry, kiddo," he said, his voice tight. "We'll figure something out. Let me think about it. But right now, I need to help Anna get her car over to Seb's. Can I check back in with you later? You gonna be OK here?"

"Of course," Haven said. "I'm cleaning out the fridges and taking stuff over to a friend's so at least the food won't go bad."

"Good idea. Hang in there." He gave her a quick hug. "See you in a bit."

As the door swung closed behind them, Jake walked back to the truck, his stomach clenched. Telling Anna about the mortgage and Margaret had been showing way too many cards—what had he been *thinking*? And now it was clear exactly how vulnerable it all was. Everything could succeed or fall apart, just as easily as a storm and a transformer.

He had already been through so many losses. He was so close to turning it all around, and the idea of having this week start to fall apart was bad enough.

The only thing that would make going from not just defeat, but actual slow-motion humiliation, was having Anna—beautiful, successful Anna who had tumbled back into his life right at this moment—witness the fall.

Anna drove her car slowly, carefully staying close to the taillights of Jake's silver pickup as it led her down Main Street. She glanced briefly at the shops they passed, where people were busily cleaning up debris and reopening storefronts. There was the bookstore—she almost said "Yay!" out loud at the thought that it had survived all these years. Then the courthouse and the library, and what looked like a spiffy gourmet grocery store.

As she peered at the buildings, stitching together fragments of memories from the past with the new images she was seeing, her phone vibrated in her handbag. She'd managed to push aside the anxiety that was gaining steam around the pilot, which had meant avoiding Rubin. She needed the space. Even if she hadn't made it to Silverwood—thank goodness they gave refunds for weather problems—somehow she had stumbled into something that was, maybe, even better.

Last night with Jake and Iris, seeing how great the old inn looked, and for that matter, everything here in town, which was in much better shape than she'd expected—for a moment it felt like time had stopped.

It might not be the direction she'd started out going yesterday morning, but maybe it could still do the trick of letting her disconnect and reset. Well, she'd definitely reset; her whole sense of time and place, which normally barreled ahead like the West Side subway, was now weird and elastic. Whether that helped with "disconnecting" remained to be seen.

The phone buzzed again. Odd how you can hear a vibration. Not so odd how she could ignore it. In fact, that "ignoring" muscle felt like it was getting good exercise.

They reached the garage, and Jake waved for her to pull into a parking place along the side of the low building. She locked her car and came back around to his truck. "It'll be OK here?"

"Of course. It's Cedarwood Spring, not New York. Speaking of Cedarwood Spring, next stop is the farm-supply store—need to check on Tom." He raised his eyebrows. "You'll get to see your old digs?"

Anna felt a rush of nostalgia—and apprehension. The good parts of the past kept being neck-and-neck with the not-so-great parts. And the last time she'd been in the place, she'd been Annie.

"This will be interesting. I spent so much time there growing up. But I haven't been there in years."

"What do you remember?" Jake kept his eyes on the road.

She looked over at him, appreciating the question. What *did* she remember? Lots of good moments with her papi, for sure. "OK, let me see … to tell you the truth, I loved how it smelled, wandering up and down the aisles. Even playing there when I was little. The smells of different bags of grass seed, of fertilizers, of mulch. I would pretend it was a little village." Smiling, she pictured the aisles, which led to an image of seeing Jake there when he'd stop in after school or on Saturdays. Would he remember it the way she did? She tested the waters. "You came there a lot in high school. I don't know if you remember."

"Of course I do." He glanced at her then back at the street. "Why wouldn't I?"

She shrugged. "I don't know. A farm-supply store doesn't

seem like the kind of place that would be memorable to most teenagers."

"Well," Jake said, pausing. "It was to me." He pulled up in a parking space and paused. "Ready to check it out?"

Something in his voice told her that she wasn't alone in this visit to the past, but that she had a friend whose hand she could hold, figuratively speaking. "Sure."

The front of the store was still generally the same: wide glass windows punctuated the low one-story building, with heavy bags of seeds and soil bearing sale signs alongside samples of iron patio chairs. But she could see the stone had been repointed and wooden window frames upgraded to smart, black-metal outlines. The sign was still the same, though: Cedarwood Spring Feed & Seed. A light lump rose in her throat, knowing her papi was no longer inside. Which made him feel doubly invisible.

As they walked in—the light and smell still as she remembered—Jake called toward the back. "Tom? You back there?"

A stocky fifty-something man with a short red ponytail emerged from one of the aisles, reaching to shake Jake's hand. "Hey, Jake! Good to see you. Everything OK out at the inn?"

"It's alright, thanks." He lightly set his hand on Anna's shoulder, which once again helped her feel she wasn't alone. "Tom, there's someone I'd like you to meet. This is Anna. Anna Diaz. Her father used to manage this store for years."

Tom's smile widened. "Of course, Jorge! He did amazing work, built this store up into the best in the county. It's an honor to meet you, Anna." He shook her hand warmly. "I came on here after your dad retired. I hope I've been able to do him credit."

Anna smiled, feeling a small, sweet ache in her throat. "Thanks, Tom, that means a lot. Papi and I spent a lot of hours here together." She glanced around. "Mind if I wander around a bit? It takes me back."

"Of course. Help yourself. I need to talk to Jake about the

prep for the wedding. Especially with the storm, we've probably got some work to do to make sure we're on track."

Jake was watching her carefully, and she was grateful to be under the care of his gaze. "Go say hello to some memories," he said softly, turning back toward Tom.

Their voices became more removed as she retreated down first one aisle, then another. Yep, smelled exactly the same. Only now there were electronic screens here and there with videos and information about the merchandise, and the old cash register she'd been so expert at using was replaced by a small, neat scanning device.

As she wandered out the back into the outdoor area with large soil and seed bags, she felt a pang. The picture of her papi working long hours become more and more vivid, often invisible to the men who came and went, buying supplies and talking among themselves. He was always training her to do the buying and managing of the store, excited to show her how it all worked. He was proud of it, as well he should have been. And, she realized, his life could so easily have become hers.

After all, that had been the plan. She'd watch the kids who had other things expected of them hanging out at the library, talking about college, going skiing, driving around town. Kids who somehow always seemed inside of something that she could only look at from the outside. They seemed a world apart.

So she'd tried to grab onto the only expectation her parents seemed to have of her, the only they'd thought was realistic: that she'd go to work in the store. She'd tried, helping her papi as best she could. But he could see—they could all see—that her real passion wasn't being in the store; it was being in the kitchen. Instead of having her hands in gloves and soil, she'd wanted them bare in flour and butter.

So she'd split her time and herself between the store and home before deciding it would be the kitchen she'd take into her future—and not the store. Her papi had been wistful. But he and her mom had never said no.

The phone vibrated in her bag—again—bringing her back to the store as it was now. She pulled it out, knowing there was no more avoiding Rubin.

She paused in front of several stone birdbaths and wooden birdhouses. It was a strange combination—Rubin's voice in her papi's old store. Anna and Annie.

"Hi Rubin, how's it going?"

"Finally, you answered. You're still alive!" Rubin turned everything into high drama. "How's it going?"

"It's good, thanks."

"How's the car?"

"It's waiting for the guy to get in on Tuesday to assess it."

"Tuesday? Well, how far is a train station?"

"Next town over. But I need to stay to get my car. And anyway, I'm actually getting the break I needed, Rubin. It's all good."

"As long as it's not too long. Sierra's in touch with me—she knows you were trying to get away so she didn't want to bother you. But Anna, we need your help. There's stuff that's not coming together the way it should."

"Like what?" Anxiety sat like a microchip in her chest.

"It's all the stuff that you have to advise us on—like exactly where you'll be for each stage of a recipe, so we can plan lighting and camera shots around it. And there's some problem with permits? I couldn't get it straight. But you need to talk to her. We have to get this moving. We have a show—it just needs a place it really belongs."

The chip of anxiety ballooned. The images of her young-girl self, disheveled curls back in a rough ponytail, working along-side Papi vanished in a poof. And her mind's eye immediately lasered in on the space for the pilot they'd been setting up in Soho.

"I thought the permits were all set," she pressed nervously.

"You know this crazy bureaucracy in New York. Some paperwork wasn't filed right. I'm gonna kill Sierra's assistant. Anyway, what's your plan?"

Anna glanced back into the store, where she could see Tom and Jake still talking by the front door. For reasons that weren't clear, she felt torn—though between what exactly she couldn't have said. She was balanced precariously, teetering between old and new, between what's she'd left behind and what she really wanted.

Except that … for some crazy split second, she wasn't sure what it was she had left … and what it was she really wanted.

She took a deep breath and almost ended up coughing as the pungent smell of mulch stung her nostrils.

That did it. At least her life in New York was a known quantity—and that felt more solid than the confusing mix of old memories and new desires that was swirling around her right at that moment. The devil you know versus the devil you don't.

"I'll call Sierra right now. She or anybody else who needs me can call me anytime. I'll do better at grabbing a call when it comes in." Shoot. So much for disconnecting and resetting. But if that's what it took to get her café, then so be it. "I can start solving problems from here. Don't worry, Rubin—I'm on my game."

"Atta girl." For once, Rubin's tone lightened. "This is going to be sensational. Once everybody sees that it is, then they'll launch the series—with you, my dear, as the star. Talk soon. Lots of hugs!" He rang off.

Anna stood quietly, holding the phone in her hands and staring into a middle distance somewhere among an array of bird feeders.

"Anna? Anna!" She jumped as Jake's voice replaced Rubin's, and felt so totally different. Again, two realities colliding. She'd kept them so clearly apart for years, thanks to both time and distance, but with this insane detour things had taken, it was suddenly hard to keep them that way.

"Coming," she called.

As she quickly strode back past bags of birdseed and dog food, Anna's gait became more determined—more like she was striding the blocks of Soho than the aisles of her papi's old store. She might have gotten rerouted to wait out the storm, but she couldn't risk rerouting her focus. As she walked past the shadowed memories of her father lifting bags and hauling equipment, Anna remembered more than ever of how hard she'd worked to push wide the boundaries of her life.

Yep, it was great to be back in Cedar Spring—better than she would have imagined, if she'd ever stopped to try to imagine it.

And yep, she was still plenty attracted to Jake Petersen—just as much now as back then. History did have a way of repeating itself.

But attraction was one thing. Acting on it, another.

She'd be back in New York soon enough.

As Jake drove them through town, stopping in to check with other folks after the storm, he found it all to be the strangest sensation.

On one hand, echoes of Annie from years ago, her sweet familiarity and easy presence, seemed so close that it almost felt like time travel. It seemed he could happily have wandered the aisles of her dad's old store with her once again, making jokes about the bags of gerbil food and their teachers at school. Then they could have hopped in the truck—his father's old Chevy—and driven out to the farm stands to say hi to their friends there, munching on whatever was fresh at the stand or whatever goody she'd made with her mom the day before. She'd seemed to admire him in those days—which, come to think of it, had probably meant more to him than he'd realized. It had been like his own oxygen supply.

On the other hand, it was as if he were with some totally new amazing creature, who brought new ideas into the tiredly familiar footpaths of his life. Someone who could see him—and his screw-ups—with startling clarity. And he really didn't need any of that right now. He had gotten so used to taking care of everyone—it was a persona that worked for him—that he had no idea how to be around someone who didn't even need his help at all.

Besides, she didn't need to admire him anymore either; she'd surpassed him.

Jake's eyes scanned the edges of Main Street. He was glad to see the town was coming alive again, and it gave him some easy conversation topics as they slowly drove through. The quirky antique shop, Collectibles, had its welcome flag hung back out. The bookstore had its awning opened, and employees were setting up sidewalk tables where they'd stack on-sale books. Workers were hanging potted impatiens and begonias in yellows, pinks, and fuchsia from the classically arched, iron lampposts that lined Main Street from City Hall on one end to the entrance to town on the other, past the shops, the library, and the little central park with the gazebo and fountain.

Once they reached City Hall, he parked and they strolled down the sidewalk, peering through windows, remarking on spots new and old. Jake watched her cautiously in his periphery, and her voice seeming to sparkle as they chatted with shop owners: the florist, the Chinese-food hub, and then the Bread-and-Butter Bistro that especially seemed to impress her. They roamed the aisles, pulling off artisan pickles, local mustards, and grain-fed meat from nearby farms. Before Jake realized it, he'd forgotten the looming stresses of the week and felt almost—*almost*—at ease.

Come to that, when was the last time he'd felt even "almost" at ease?

As they reached the park, Anna gently pulled his arm as she paused before the rounded fountain.

"It all feels so different than it did the other day." Her tone was reflective.

Trying to ignore the spark of heat that came from her touch, he pushed his hands into his back pockets. "Well, that was Cedarwood Spring at its worst. This is what Cedarwood Spring does best: charming small town, full of great spots. And great people." He hoped his voice wasn't betraying how good it felt to wander his hometown with someone he'd long ago talked himself into believing was just a fixture of his teenage life. That the warm memory had only ever belonged in that one, brief phase of life.

And then anyway, of course, she'd left.

Anna stopped at the fountain's edge. "Well, it's good to see that some classics are still here," she said, smiling as the water bounced and frolicked. "Ha! I think there are still some pennies down there that I threw in."

When she took her hand back from his arm, Jake missed the feel of it. "We tossed in a few together."

"Yeah. I was always wishing ..."

"For? You never told me."

"Then it wouldn't have come true!" Anna smiled, turning back toward the water. "I think it was usually about getting out of town. Being successful, feeling freer than I felt here."

"Shaking off the dust of the town?" His voice was understanding.

"Something like that. But you never wished for that, did you?"

That seemed so long ago. "No, not that."

"Then what? What did you wish for?" Her voice betrayed a real curiosity.

What he'd always wished for was more of a feeling than a thing, but still, he tried: "Probably something about succeeding too—only it was about the farm. And being 'someone' in town. Figuring it out. Living up to …"

"To what?"

He smiled down at her upturned open face and felt like she would understand. "What people felt like they saw in me, I guess."

Her eyes briefly clouded as they both paused. "Well, maybe we both got our wishes. You think?" Anna always had had a way of cutting right through to the big questions.

But as comfortable as it was being with her, this one again felt too close for comfort. "Still figuring it out." He stepped backward. Part of him wanted to keep showing her more of Cedarwood Spring and what it had become—in other words, he knew, he wanted to keep showing her his life. At the same time, another part of him wondered why. "Come on, let's get to the Filling Station."

After all, he thought as they walked, she had an amazing life that awaited her—as soon as her car was fixed. A life that had nothing to do with fritzed electrical circuits, or worrying about whether the right color tablecloths had been ordered, or mulching the gardens out back—or wedding cakes by a newbie baker.

So crazy—why couldn't she have landed back here when the inn was totally up and running and a raving success? Why now, when it was all so precarious?

But of course, she was leaving in a few days anyway. Again.

As they neared the Filling Station, he could see that Haven was already outside, picking up twigs that had littered the small plantings lining the large front windows rimmed in sleek dark metal. When she saw them, she stood up straight, brushing hair from her eyes with a smudged forearm.

"Hey guys. Thanks for coming back. I hope I didn't seem too

upset before. It's just that the electrician had just delivered the bad news."

"Not at all," Jake said, bending over to help her. He kept his voice light, in contrast to how he felt. "So what are you thinking? About having the desserts and cake ready by Friday. What's a good backup plan?"

Haven sighed and shook her head, reaching down for another twig. "Well, I've made some headway. I found some people who have good kitchens—one is even professional-grade, the one over at Albert's."

Anna nodded. "That's terrific, Haven. It's hard to get top-level kitchens. I'm sure people will pull together."

"They're all being great, they're fine with my borrowing them this week. I can get the desserts made—the tartlets, petit fours, things like that. I've made those things tons of times and I know them like the back of my hand." She paused, standing straight again, looking at both Anna and Jake appealingly. "But the one thing I'm nervous about is the wedding cake ... I mean, if I'm not in my own kitchen. I'll be running around to other people's kitchens. The wedding cake's ... different. I'm new to it. And it takes a lot of space, and none of my friends have that kind of space. Albert does, but he's using most of it for his own stuff for the wedding."

Jake forced down the anxiety in his gut. Think, think, how could this work? He could call over to some bakery in the next town over. But the whole pitch to the Abbotts had been that the talent would all be local since they were so high on supporting the businesses in town—most of which Abbot Senior had his fingers in one way or another. So they would know.

Besides, it was the whole branding behind the Cedarwood Spring Inn. He had staked his future on it—and lost his marriage to it, more or less.

Maybe Iris would have an idea, or maybe she could even

help Haven handle it. She always helped him get unstuck—one of her favorite words.

Stressing Haven out further wouldn't do either of them any good. Jake put his arm across her shoulder and gave a light squeeze. "Just keep focusing on those desserts and getting the electrician over here. Let me go home and talk to Iris. Don't worry," he added valiantly. "We'll figure something out."

Haven's smile was genuine. "Thanks, bro. Thanks, Anna. Let's talk later today."

Jake lifted his hand in a wave as they turned to head back toward the truck. "Sounds good," he called out.

But it didn't sound good to him at all. Not at all.

CHAPTER 4

"Everything looks so different than it did a couple of days ago. Like it's a completely different place. Isn't that amazing how fast it can transform?"

Anna cupped her coffee mug as she drank in the scene through the front living room window. It was Memorial Day, and the world was dry once again, and the flowers in the front courageously and staunchly raised toward the sun as if the sky would never pelt them again. Birds skittered and chatted among the treetops.

They had all just finished one of Iris's carefully made breakfasts of local strawberries and cream scones, and Anna and Jake had made their way to the front of the house while Iris cleaned up. It felt good to move slowly and take in the day one action at a time. So different from her usual pace. She could sense Jake standing beside her, not too close but not too far, and caught fresh, clean musk.

She smiled warmly at him. "It really is beautiful here, Jake."

He shifted closer—haltingly, it struck her. Still, he spoke casually. "Now that the water's dried up, mostly, and I've cleaned up the limbs, I can really show it off. You've gotten to see the town a bit. If you, uh … have a few minutes now, I can show you around the grounds. You'd said you never really saw it all before."

She knew the morning's onslaught of calls from New York would begin any minute—holiday or no holiday. And she felt a renewed commitment to taking them.

Still, she didn't quite feel ready to leave the beauty of the moment, and she wanted to steal a few minutes more with Jake. After all, she'd be gone soon enough and wouldn't be seeing him again. And that thought suddenly felt like a dark cloud on the horizon.

"Sounds great," she said emphatically. "I've seen the barn from my window, but I'd love to see inside."

"Ah, but there's more than just the inside to see. You have to come out and walk the land. That's the only way to get to know a place."

"OK. Let's walk the land." She set her mug down emphatically on the end table beside her phone, which she touched lightly, just to see how many missed calls there were. She felt his eyes follow her.

"I know you're busy," he said almost brusquely.

"No problem," she said assuringly, slipping the silenced phone into the back pocket of her dark-rinse jeans. "Plenty of time. Let's go."

"OK, then. This way." Once outside, Jake led her down the front path and stopped at a waist-high sign at the edge of the front flower bed, deep red with contrasting gold letters: "Welcome to Cedarwood Spring Inn – Built 1872." Gladiolas sprang around its base.

Anna touched it. "I know I saw this yesterday, but it wasn't here before. I mean … years ago." She didn't really feel like adding, *when I came here in a delivery truck with Papi.*

"Good eye," Jake said, unaware of her silent comment. "That was part of what Mom and Dad and I did. We wanted to transform the place and still claim the history. And—I hope—a place on the map. We put this up about five years ago. And ..." He pointed toward the delicate vines clinging to the front of the stone house. "We grew clematis all over the stone. It's a little early in summer for it to look this good, but we were lucky with a warm April. And the flower beds here in front—Iris started some of them from seed, but mostly we got the plants from a greenhouse in town so they'd be in full bloom for the wedding."

Anna looked appreciatively at the well-structured garden plots framing the flagstone walkway. "This is the perfect welcome as wedding guests arrive. It invites them to walk further."

"Hope so. The weather looks like it'll be perfect. Come on. Let me show you around here." Jake's voice warmed up, and in it, Anna could hear his love for the place—and she realized he was showing her more than the inn. He was showing her his life.

Suddenly aware of how precious the time seemed, how she might not get much more with him, Anna realized that more time with Jake was exactly what she wanted—as inconvenient and out-of-the-plan as that was. She wanted to draw him out, to hear more of his voice, to see him move. "Lead the way."

She followed him to the right side of the house where cedars clustered in low, cool light. A wrought-iron archway framed the entrance to a winding flagstone path that slipped its way among the cedars toward the back of the house. Jake reached out and touched the archway as they passed through it. "Jacob made this with a local blacksmith when they were building the house."

"So you can touch history?" Anna asked, doing the same.

He paused and turned to her, the crinkled squint at the edges of his light-blue eyes. "Yeah, pretty much. You can touch history." He turned and kept walking, his straight pale hair combed smoothly toward a small wave in the back. She flashed on that view from years ago, when there'd been no hint of gray in it.

Oblivious to her thoughts, Jake strode purposefully in his work chinos and faded blue oxford-cloth shirt.

As she stepped after him on the path among the cedars, Anna felt magical. She'd forgotten how much she liked plantings and the smells of earth. All she had now were a few large pots where herbs nestled in her apartment. She ran her fingers lightly along the webby needles of the cedars. "I feel like looking for fairies among the branches," she laughed.

Jake chuckled ahead of her. "I think Jacob believed there might be a few around. So look sharp."

Ah, playfulness. Nice. "You know, Jake, you always were quite the teaser. You're still not as tough as you look."

He threw back a mock-serious glance. "Me, tough? I'm a cream puff."

"No, that's my department."

"So you should know one when you see one."

"Ah. Touché."

They rounded the back of the house, and Anna recognized the view she'd seen from her window. But now it beckoned to her with an imperative she couldn't have felt from a distance.

A flagstone patio created a gracious space out the back door of the inn, and along its edges were raised beds of flowers and herbs set amid winding pebble walkways. The space half basked in warm sunlight and half in shade, under a string of small white lights that crisscrossed overhead. Some of the trees were still in flower—purple, white—amid what was now mainly new-spring green.

"What kinds of trees?" she asked, pointing.

"Dogwoods, mostly." He shot her another playful glance. "You used to be able to nail the name of every single tree around here. Lost your skill set, Diaz?"

"I guess I have." She giggled, then paused thoughtfully. "You know, it actually makes me kind of … sad. Just a little. I was really good at that. Like Papi."

Jake paused too, hooking his thumbs in his pockets and jerking his head toward the house. "Iris has a big book of all the local vegetation. You can check it out. Don't worry—people change, it happens."

"True. But not totally." And for some reason, she suddenly needed to believe that some things hadn't changed about her … and Jake.

His eyes twinkled. Twinkle-crinkle, as she was beginning to think of it. "You *are* still an Eagles fan, right? I mean, you didn't switch over to … the *Yankees*." He dragged out the last word with a sarcastic drawl.

Laughter fluttered up her throat, as she lifted her right fist to punch the air in what had always been their team cheer. "E-A-G-L-E-S, Eagl-l-l-les!"

"Whew. Glad to know there's still morality in the world."

"There is. And it's right here," she said, admiring the patio. "The patio will be perfect for the guests. And the gardens are amazing. I'm so used to buying from greenhouses, local ones," she added hastily. "But in my Brooklyn apartment—no rooftop access—I don't really have much green space myself."

"Well, now you do," Jake said, sweeping his arm toward the garden beds.

"Tell me about the plants?" Anna knelt beside one.

"These were mostly Iris's planning." Jake stood beside her, and Anna was once again aware of—distracted by?—how powerful his presence was, though she knew that he wasn't aware of it.

"It's what she calls a sensory garden," he went on. "Purposely made for different colors over the summer, different smells, and even different sounds."

"Sounds?" Anna asked incredulously, teetering as she tried to stand back up. Jake quickly reached his hand down, and she automatically grasped it. Its strength pulled her up and, she had to admit, she would rather not have let go.

But she did. "How can gardens have sounds?"

Jake chuckled. "By the birds and bees it attracts. And of course, the herbs are ones she uses all summer in cooking."

"Everything's pretty vibrant for this early in the summer."

"Exactly. She began them inside from seed so that the gardens would look more complete early on." He glanced at her significantly. "The Abbott wedding was already on the dockets—they reserved it last fall. We've kind of been gearing up for a long time."

"Good job," Anna murmured, as he led her among other raised beds toward the back.

As they stepped onto where the flagstones became a brick path leading down toward the barn, Anna instinctively sucked in her breath, struck by the view before her. The low trees around the gardens and patio gave way to an open, gentle grassy hill sloping down to the barn, the old brick path carving out the way. Now she could see more clearly the large bronze star that hung over its wide door, to the left of the high opening where—she knew from all the years of work with her father—hay bales could be moved in and out of a loft.

She pointed to the star. "The classic barnstar. Wow, that's deep in my memory."

Jake nodded. "Yeah, part of life around here."

"I always assumed it meant good luck, but I never really thought to ask. Is that true?"

"That's the lore. Who knows …"

As they headed down the slope, she heard a gentle sound that was more than simply the breeze. "Jake, I feel like I hear water. Running water?" She looked at the edge of a stream she could see flowing just behind the barn.

Jake smiled as he drew her off the path and began high steps through the thick grass in an arc toward the back of the barn. "*That's* why you have to walk the land. Otherwise, you'd never see—"

Anna followed his sightline, stepping carefully among the tufts of grass, curiously scanning to see what was behind the barn. As they reached the back, a small waterwheel sprang into view, creaking and churning from a weathered wooden stand.

"Jake!" She turned to him, her hands flying to her mouth. "I never knew you had this back here. It's wonderful."

Jake's eyes crinkled proudly as he looked from her to the wheel and back. "Yep. Jacob built this too. He and his brother. And the bridge." He pointed beyond the wheel to where a small wooden bridge arched low over the stream.

Anna could only stare enchanted as the small waterwheel slowly churned around and around, dipping water and then releasing it back down into the stream. In spite of herself, she made a little skip toward it, feeling like a child dancing among flowers. Jake sauntered more slowly after her, smiling proudly, hands in the front pockets of his jeans.

"So … you like it?" It sounded like he simply needed to hear her say it again.

And she was glad to. She looked up at him in wonder. "I *love* it! Has this always been here?"

"Yep. Or at least an earlier version of it. Believe it or not, the spring used to be more of a gusher. When old Jacob got here 150 years ago, it was bigger and spread out into some kind of pond. We figure that based on diagrams he drew of the property. Either that, or he was just really optimistic."

"Must run in the family."

Jake grinned and ducked his head. "He built this wheel—he knew how from his own Dutch upbringing—to get water into the barn. It broke decades ago, and the spring calmed down into a small stream. The wheel was part of what Dad and I dreamed of —bringing it back to life. We talked about it for years. Planned it. Drew our own diagrams. Then … we finally did it. Of course, we used newer timber in most places, but it still has some of the original wood. And this whole system is where the runoff from

the drains around the barn comes. But let me show you what else
we did."

His voice was excited as he reached down and pulled her
hand—which, like so much else now, felt both totally natural and
stunningly new. Anna let him guide her back toward the front of
the barn where the two front doors stood open. As they stepped
inside, he let go of her hand. "It'll take a second for your eyes to
adjust to the dark. But it won't be dark on Friday."

Anna peered around, her pupils adjusting, and saw the clean,
finished interior, as polished as any event space in New York, yet
with rustic touches like the wooden beams lining the white,
vaulted ceiling. Large clear windows lined the sides and the back
so that the green beauty of the fields gleamed like Impressionist
paintings, and she could see rooms off to the side up front—
restrooms, storage, she assumed. The floors were restored wood
—maybe a laminate, she knew, but rich and sturdy.

"Tom and his crew are doing setup, and Pete and Tina are
doing a fantastic job of planning the design and flowers. It's all
on schedule to put together tomorrow and Wednesday. At least
the storm didn't screw up the timing. We'll have lights strung
back and forth—" Jake gestured from where one loft ran along
the left side to another along the right—"and the caterers will
have their things all along the edges."

As he talked energetically, Anna smiled and nodded, but part
of her was also simply watching him—this man she had known
so well and yet was meeting for the first time, his stubbornness
and fears and hope, all charmingly channeled through his planning and details and explanations.

"So ... what do you think?"

Anna realized he'd paused and was looking at her impatiently. "After all—you do these kinds of things all the time."

"True, but not as the manager," she answered. "It's one thing
for me to do my work in the kitchen. It's another thing for somebody to create the space where all of this can happen." She

noticed that relief moved his expression, and suddenly, she wanted to reassure him that everything would be terrific—and somehow, and completely irrationally, she wanted to protect him from anything that might go wrong.

This old friend, this new friend, whichever he was—she just wanted to see him succeed.

"Jake, you've done a terrific job." She turned squarely toward him. "Well done. It'll be splendid, I have no doubt."

His smile was both broad and shy, as he hooked his thumbs into his pockets again. "Thanks. That helps." His eyes caught hers and lingered. Then, as if remembering himself, he turned and gestured toward the door. "But look. I've kept you long enough. I know you have things to take care of. Up in New York."

Anna's heart inched down from its high. She knew she should be happy to call New York and work on … whatever needed working on. Still, a shadow of loss passed through her. "Sure, right. Thanks for the tour."

"You're welcome. After you." He held his arm toward the door, once again more formal than familiar.

As they reached the brick path and started up the grassy hill toward the gardens, the patio, and the inn, Anna paused and looked back toward the barn and the fields beyond. Jake stopped, following her eyes.

"I'd forgotten how special it is here," Anna said, taking in the ducks that puttered across the water and the graceful hills that lay beyond. Vees of birds dotted the sky in their pilgrimage back north. What this place had become moved her—and so did the man beside her who had given everything he had to it.

She turned back to him. Something in her instinctively wanted to reach for his hand, but something else just as instinctive said no. She crossed her arms and looked at him squarely. "You've done great work here, Jake Petersen. You have a lot to be proud of. I think you got your wish."

Jake blushed and looked at his feet. "Thanks. I do love it here." He squinted toward the sloping fields. "A long way from New York?"

He really seemed stuck on New York. She watched his silhouette for a split second, tracing in her mind the slight curve of his nose and rise of his cheekbone. Still grizzled, she noticed. "Well ... yes and no."

"I'm glad you got to see it—before you went back." There was an edge in his voice, and he pushed himself straighter. "Come on, time to go. Iris and I have to figure out how to handle a wedding cake."

And, predictably, her phone buzzed. His eyes jerked toward her as she quickly pulled it from her pocket and glanced at it.

"It's Sierra," she said apologetically. "The director. I—I really have to take this. Go on up without me. I'll see you back inside."

Wordlessly, Jake gave a terse nod and headed back up the hill. Anna watched him disappear as she tapped her phone. "Sierra, hi, how are you?"

The woman's voice on the other end of the line was warm and excited, if a little nervous. "Anna, it's good to hear your voice. Rubin tells me you got waylaid in the storm?"

"I did. But ..." She looked again to the stream, feeling as much as hearing the regular churning of the wheel, which was just out of sight behind the barn. "But it's turned out really well. Actually, I'm back in my old hometown, believe it or not. It's strange, but not bad. I'm going to stick around here for the week instead of trying to get to Silverwood. I'm staying with ..." She glanced up the hill. "Uh, with friends. So how's everything with the show? Rubin said there was a problem."

Sierra's laugh was wry. "*A* problem?! Try dozens of them. The point is having the team to solve them. That's why we need you." Anna felt a twinge. "One of the permits for the new space where we're going to shoot—where we need to make up the

Love Bite café for you—still hasn't come through. We've still got three weeks, but I don't like cutting it that close. And I'm having trouble figuring out the placement of everything in the kitchen. After all, it's the center of the whole set. We have to be able to get good shots of everyone—especially you—when you're doing your thing. We have to make sure everything you're doing has a good camera angle. That has to drive the whole show."

So what 'had to drive the whole thing' were *shots* of her mixing and beating and folding—but not her *actual* mixing, beating, and folding themselves? For the umpteenth time, it struck Anna as backward. She shook her head silently.

"OK, how can I help?"

"For now, my assistant is working on the permit problem. But for the set, I'll email you sketches. Can you print them and brainstorm some ideas? Get creative, play with it. Then draw in your suggestions and scan them and shoot it back over to me."

"Sure, OK. I just need to see if there's a printer here."

"There's no printer where you are?" Sierra sounded dubious.

"I'm sure there is." Anna glanced nervously at the inn. Surely, they had a printer. Or at least someplace in town would. "I'll text you when I know, and then you can email them. Anything else?"

"Yes. Rubin didn't seem clear on when you were coming back."

"That's because *I'm* not clear when I'm coming back. I got a bashed headlight during the storm, and my car has to be fixed." Though as Anna looked across the little valley at the rippling grasses, she was again grateful for the delay. After all, she didn't know when she'd be back looking at the lazy waterwheel that Jake and his dad had built. If ever.

Sierra's voice cut into her reverie. "I'm glad you're getting a break, Anna. You needed it. Just be sure to do something fun. Something that you really love."

Anna frowned lightly, feeling slightly sarcastic. "Like what? It's not like there's an indoor pool or a sauna around here."

"Not that stuff, silly. Do what lights you up, makes you happy. Like what you used to do as a kid."

"As a kid?! I used to bake. And work in my papi's store. That's it."

"Yeah, well. Just keep an eye open for whatever chances come up."

"Thanks for that totally useless advice," Anna said, her voice teasing. After all, what could she possibly do here that would light her up?

"It *is* a pickle," Iris said thoughtfully, leaning back against the sink and drying her hands. The white ceramic plates from breakfast stood clean in the dish rack.

Jake had been sitting on a stool at the center island, the top of his head bowed down and clamped in his hands, in what he knew —because Iris often told him—was the archetypical Petersen-male end-of-his-rope stance. As Anna came in through the back door, he glanced up and quickly shoved his hair into place, or so he hoped.

"You know," Iris was saying, "putting your head in your hands that way is what your granddad, and your dad, and now you have always done when—"

"What's up?" Anna asked inquisitively, her soft dark curls framed by the sunlight behind her.

Jake dragged his eyes from her and shot his grandmom an annoyed look. She didn't need to start talking about him like he was just somebody's kid or grandkid. This was his farm now, and he didn't need to hear about them. "Nothing's up. I just need to figure out this last piece for the reception."

"It's true, a wedding cake is a very special thing," Iris was saying slowly while gazing into the middle distance, as if talking out loud to herself—and ignoring Jake, it felt to him. He hated it when she did this. It usually meant she was up to something.

"Of course it is, that's the point." He tried to keep his temper even.

"It's not just anyone who can do it. It takes a real pro," she continued as if he hadn't spoken. "Especially under this kind of stress. I mean, it would have to be started in a day or two, I assume. The frosting, at least. Right, Anna?"

Anna gave a startled glance, as if she only just realized that Iris was directing something toward her—which Jake only just realized as well. Wait, whoa … surely, Iris wasn't …

"Yes, that's right," Anna was answering. "It's a complex operation, if it's going to be large enough for a big group, and then on top of that, it has to be foolproof. You can't goof it up. It's harder than the wedding dress! A dress just has to look good. The cake has to taste good too."

"Mm, mm," Iris said thoughtfully, as if turning something around in her mind.

"Isn't there someone in the next town who could do it? I mean, I know people in the city, but—"

"Thanks, but we're fine," Jake cut in, his ire and embarrassment rising. "The idea is that it's local. Iris …" He turned back toward her, forcing his expression to be as emphatic as possible. "Are you sure you can't do it?"

Iris shook her head firmly. "I don't have the strength these days, and I've never made a cake on that scale. You know me. Sometimes a recipe works out, sometimes it doesn't. But maybe …" Her eyes drifted to Anna in an inquisitive way that struck Jake as perfectly natural … and completely orchestrated.

"Grandma, what are you—" he said, rising from his stool.

"Shush." Iris flapped her hand toward him as she turned to face Anna with a gentle expression. "Anna, I know this would be a huge favor. And you landed here in the middle of our lives without planning to at all. And you have so much you're taking care of in New York. This is our problem, not yours. But I was wondering. If Haven and I promised to help you out, do you think … Would you be willing to …"

Jake froze, as if watching something fall and break that he just couldn't grab in time. He saw Anna's eyes widen and her mouth move, as Iris continued.

" … to take charge of the wedding cake?"

Jake stood up fully, trying to reign the moment back under his control, which seemed to have been temporarily lost. Asking Anna, the darling of New York baking, to keep the wedding reception at his inn from going off the rails? There had to be a better way. "Grandma, that's not necessary—"

Again, Iris held up her hand to him and kept talking, her head tilted kindly. "But if Anna would be willing, then it's just the perfect solution. And we'll make sure you get full credit. And it works out better for Haven, since all the pressure won't be on a first-timer. She can learn with training wheels, in a way." Iris chuckled gently, then looked soberly at Anna, who seemed to be answering Iris with a thoughtful expression.

"Anna, I know you're not the one who needs this," Iris said. "It's us. You'd be helping us out in a crisis."

"But Grandma," Jake started, not sure what to say, "I told them we'd be using local people."

Iris turned to him. "Anna *is* local," she said. "It would be perfect."

Anna seemed to have finally registered what Iris was asking, her elegant posture asserting itself and her face slowly brightening. "Iris, that's a good idea. I was hoping to help out in some way around here. And this is a way I can do it. I count as local." She smiled warmly. "I know it's a real make-or-break moment for you. And we don't want it to break."

"Oh, thank you," the older woman exclaimed, reaching spontaneously for a hug. "That's wonderful. It means the reception will be the very best it can be. And Haven can be an apprentice in the process. I'll go let her know. She'll be thrilled."

As Iris's footsteps padded happily into the living room, Jake and Anna quietly faced each other, Jake trying desperately to grapple with the new and totally unexpected turn of events—though it was perfectly in keeping with the fact that everything was unexpected that week.

"But I know you're … you're leaving soon and you have so many things to think about with the show and all," he attempted. "You really don't have to worry about taking care of our problems here."

Anna's smile was warm; she seemed on another wavelength. "Don't worry, Jake it's really no problem. I've made more wedding cakes than I can count. Besides, Iris and Haven can help me a lot. And it just so happens that Sierra—that's the director—just called me at the barn saying I need to do something fun, something like when I was a kid. I think baking a wedding cake will do the trick." She paused, looking down, and Jake wondered what was going on inside her head. "Who knows. Maybe playing around in the kitchen when there's no camera around might actually be good for me. All the stuff for the show —it's about sets, and how everything is laid out for the right camera shots. And getting permits. That's why Sierra called in the first place. Good heavens, can you believe I've even been told to 'love the camera'?" She shook her head ruefully and began pouring a glass of water. "I know this sounds crazy, but it's starting to seem like the show is about everything *but* the baking."

This would be easier to swallow if it felt like there was something in it for Anna—and not like he was just a charity case. "So using our kitchen to make the Abbott wedding cake lets you actually get in some real baking?" Jake raked his hand through his hair.

"I think so," Anna said. "It will feel good to get back into a great, homey kitchen like this and do my thing. And a wedding cake is something people don't ever forget."

"That's true. The Abbotts won't forget it, that's for sure." Then he looked up quickly and caught her eye.

She sipped and set down the water glass. "It's OK," she said quietly. "Making the cake doesn't mean I need to deal with them much. After all, they just know it's being made by somebody local, right?"

It felt like something else needed to be said, but Jake wasn't sure what. This had happened fast. Too fast.

So he just nodded again, feeling like he could get this new angle under control, as long as Haven and Iris were helping her. That would make it seem like it wasn't too far outside of what the plan had been in the first place. Besides, he couldn't come up with any other solution. This seemed to be the only way out.

So why look a gift horse in the mouth, Petersen? No need to be ungracious. "I can't tell you how much it's helping … um, the inn. Haven can give you the specifics of the order. I think it was pretty traditional," he said, then added hastily, "and of course, we'll pay you for it. Whatever your normal fee would be."

"Oh, no, I couldn't accept money," she said quickly, holding up her hand.

Jake's pride and demeanor darkened briefly. "Why not? I don't want you to do it out of charity or anything. We're doing fine here. We're getting back on our feet. I've got it under control."

A shot of empathy transformed Anna's face. "No, I promise," she said more slowly, "it's not charity, Jake. You've done so much here since I knew it before. And it's so unexpected that I'm here anyway. And I don't know when I'll be back." She briefly averted her eyes, then looked back at him. "This is my chance to contribute something to … to an old friendship." She gave a small smile that struck him as a little bit strained.

Jake eyed her warily. Part of him wanted to believe her, that this worked for her too, but the bigger part of him was still busy being angry at Iris for putting him in this position. The big event that they'd been working toward for months, just days away. And even more to manage now than he'd anticipated, thanks to the storm—making sure the food was terrific and everything fell into place, and the centerpiece of it all, the cake, being juggled at the last minute. All while knowing that the Taggarts reviewer would be standing there with pen poised in hand. It felt like he was walking a fine line.

But what made the line into a tightrope was something more. It was that the woman who was keeping the wedding cake from crashing to the ground, the one who could ensure the Taggarts review was top-notch, at least for the cake, was the one person he didn't want watching him fail, if it came to that. And yet … that was the one person he kept wanting to be near.

Not that Iris realized all that.

Or did she.

Sometimes his grandmom knew just too damn much.

"Oh, Anna, I can't thank you enough!" Haven threw her arms around Anna, almost knocking her backward where they stood in front of the inn later that afternoon. The two of them teetered into Jake, who caught Anna from the back, lifting her to her feet with muscular arms.

Anna glanced back at him, blushing. "Good save," she said. He smiled down at her, momentarily struck dumb by the feeling of holding her—even from the back.

"You're the one who's saving us," Haven continued. "It really means a lot. When Iris called and told me, I couldn't believe it. Now I can focus on the other desserts and know that the wedding cake—the centerpiece—will be done by a real pro.

And … I'll get to learn from you?" she added, looking hopefully at Anna.

"Absolutely. I'm happy to show you the ropes." She took a deep breath. "Actually, it feels nice to be paying it forward like this. And it's always better when someone doesn't just tell you how to bake something. You have to get your fingers in the batter. Sort of like … you have to walk the land."

Her playful glance toward Jake gave him a rush of warmth. "Sort of like," he said, smiling.

"I can't wait," Haven said. "When should I come over?"

"Well, the wedding is Friday. Thursday I'll do most of the baking, including the buttercream icing—lots and lots of buttercream." She wiggled her eyebrows mischievously. "Then Friday morning we do the final assembly, and you can see how to really make a wedding cake happen. So, see you Thursday morning? Bright and early?"

"It's a date," Haven said. "Wow, I can't believe we have Anna Diaz on the team! You know so much. Hey, I know what! Give us advice, in general. Like, what do you end up most worried about when you have a big event you're baking for?"

The warmth inside Jake from the feel and look of Anna evaporated. Geez, was there no end to this? It would be easiest for him to handle if they could keep Anna focused on the cake. He could take care of everything else.

"Ah," Anna was already answering, holding up a finger, as she seemed to do with charming regularity whenever she had a point to make. "Timing, that's the devil. Making sure your stuff is coordinated with the caterer—that's Albert?" she asked, glancing from Haven to Jake. "I've seen things go from being spot-on to coming off the rails, just because all the pieces weren't coordinated. Want me to make some suggestions? To make sure it goes off smoothly? I've got lots of ideas."

"Definitely!" As Haven plied Anna for more details, Jake raked his hands through his hair; at this rate, he was going to rake himself bald. Sure, he wasn't *perfect*. But wasn't he doing a good enough job with this whole thing anyway? After all, he'd gotten them this far, hadn't he? Haven had asked for advice—but he definitely hadn't.

"I can't imagine what a glamorous world you work in," Haven was saying—even more annoying, since it brought to mind yet another an image of Anna surrounded by fawning, accomplished men.

Anna laughed, oblivious. "It sounds more glamorous than it is. But yeah, actually, it has its moments."

"I bet you can't wait to get back."

Jake's mouth turned downward as his thumbs hooked onto his belt loops. He didn't need to hear this again. His voice was level as he cut in. "Haven, we've taken enough of her time." He looked at Anna with what he hoped was pointedly casual professionalism. "You'd said you had work to do?"

"Yes," she said with a touch of confusion. "Actually ... I, um, need access to a printer. Sierra's sending something I need to download, work on, then scan and get back to her. Is there a place in town, an office-supply place where I can pay to use a printing station?"

OK, that did it. She thought he was so out of it that he didn't have a printer? Before he could answer—or more to the point, decide how to answer—Haven broke in. "Oh, Jake and Iris have a great outfit here—state-of-the-art. Don't you, bro?"

Jake nodded, jutting his chin toward the inn. "Sure. State-of-the-art." Hadn't he just shown her enough of the renovations for her to get that?

"And she can use it ... right?" Haven's voice was slow and pointed. Uh-oh. Now he was in trouble.

He cleared his throat. "Right, of course. In my office—it's off the coatroom in the back, behind the dining room. You'll see the login posted by the monitor—the whole team uses it whenever they're here. Help yourself."

"Thanks," Anna said, but her look was curious.

What, had he grown a second head? "No problem. Should be pretty straightforward."

She nodded, glancing back to Haven. "OK, then. I'll get to it. See you later."

Haven watched as she disappeared into the house, then turned squarely on Jake, hands on hips. "What's the deal, dude?"

What was it with the women around here today? "What are you talking about?"

"You were just curt with her."

"Curt? I offered her the office. What's curt about that?"

Haven crossed her arms and rolled her eyes. "Don't play games, Jake."

Jake took a breath, knowing there was no good reason to be mad at Haven. Or Anna, for that matter.

"Sorry. Just feeling … I guess tense about the wedding."

Haven eyed him thoughtfully. "But you've been tense for weeks. You don't usually treat people that way. What gives?"

Jake dug his toe in the ground, feeling ridiculously seventeen again. "Not sure." Though actually, he did know. He wanted to look to this gorgeous woman like he was in control, right as he seemed to be losing more and more of that control—to her, come to think of it. And she then was going to disappear back into her own success in the city as soon as her car was fixed. Like she had years ago. And … he wanted to be closer to her.

This totally didn't make sense.

"You know, Jake, she's not Margaret."

Jake looked up, startled.

"Anna. She's not Margaret. Just the fact that she's in this hospitality biz too, and really good at it, doesn't mean it's a battle you're going to lose."

Jake felt his arms relax, even as he felt a flicker of embarrassment at his young pal's ability to see in him what he hadn't been able to see himself. He gave Haven a half-smile. "What is it with you smart women?"

Haven grinned and linked her arm into his as she led him toward the back of the house. "It's that we want you to be happy. Jake, I think there's something there with Anna. I don't know what it is. But don't let your memories scare you away from what's here now."

Jake sighed, resigned. Best just to end the conversation. "Got it."

"Promise?"

"Promise."

"Great." She pulled her arm free. "Now—go talk to her. You have to make nice."

Jake's office looked—predictably—like, well, Jake. Anna ran a finger along the weathered wooden table that served as a spare, elegant desk beneath the long window facing the back gardens. Haven had been right—the setup was super, and the printouts she'd made on his printer looked great. It would be easy enough to draw in her suggestions for where things should go. She just needed to imagine it …

But try as she might, she couldn't. New York, Soho, some café they hadn't even finished setting up—let alone the idea of a reality TV pilot—all felt a world away.

She set the printouts down, forgotten, and tilted her head to scan the titles of academic-looking books flanking either side of the window—always, ever looking toward the barn, she thought. Hotel management, mechanical engineering, business finances. Book after book after book. And spiral-bound notebooks and binders framing the large window.

She eyed the binders more closely. *Floor plans '08. Floor plans '09. Renovation specs '10. Contractor blueprints. Permits.*

Anna ran her finger lightly along the spines. Wow, this was essentially the map of Jake's journey with this place—the problems, the solutions, the money ... and probably a lot of invisible things that were written in between the volumes. And in between the lines.

She lifted a finger to pull one of the notebooks off, then paused. Even if Jake had said the whole team used this space, it felt oddly like trespassing. If these past days had shown her anything, it was how much pride Jake had, and she would never violate that.

Instead, she glanced over at the dark-green wall to her left, plain and clean above a long empty desktop affixed to the wall. He left everything clear for the team, she noted, picturing her own messy, flour- and recipe-laden cooking spaces.

At the end of the desk, one framed document in particular leaned against the wall, as if set there by chance. There were no nail holes in the wall. Anna walked over and looked closer.

"Cornell University, School of Hotel Administration, is pleased to award the Master of Management in Hospitality to Jacob Daniel Petersen, Summa Cum Laude."

Anna stood up quickly, her hand flying inadvertently to her chest. She'd had no idea he'd gone to Cornell. When they'd both headed off to college, he'd gone to a private school in Philly, and everyone had just assumed he'd come straight back and carried on the inn. As had she.

Yet even as she thought about it, Anna knew it had always been a loose thread dangling in her memory. Never finding out whether that was what had happened. To be honest, as she'd pushed away the life she'd tried to get past, she'd pushed Jake along with it. Then as small steps of success began to be bigger ones, she'd been too afraid to look up. Or back.

So he'd gone to Cornell. That explained all the academic tomes. And it explained a little more of his pride—not only in the inn, but in how he seemed to take it on himself to be the one to save it.

She picked up the frame and held it closer. He too had pushed the boundaries. And summa cum laude. He'd pushed them really well.

"Oh, here you are."

Anna jumped, turning. "Yes, I …"

He walked toward her, eyeing the diploma in her hands. She set it back down quickly.

"Did the printer work out OK?"

"Fine, yes. Thanks." Anna felt a flush of embarrassment, but at the same time, she couldn't forget what she'd just figured out. Better to be direct.

"Jake, I'm sorry, I didn't mean to be nosy. But I was looking around at your books, and then I saw this." She pointed to the diploma and shook her head. "I never knew you'd gone to grad school. And in hotel management at Cornell. That's really something. There are lots of people in my work in New York who either went there … or tried and couldn't get in."

Jake gazed around at the books, his face softening. "Yeah. After college. I wanted to … I don't know, do better than anyone had before at managing this place. To up the game. If I was supposed to carry the legacy forward, then I needed more firepower."

Anna nodded as it dawned on her that her old friend had been carrying a bigger burden back then that she'd realized. "It's quite a legacy."

"Yeah. The thing about legacies is that they come with plenty of expectations but no how-to manual. I could see the inn would need something big to bring it into this century. Something more than Dad or Granddad had done. But I wasn't sure what. So this seemed like a good idea."

Anna felt a wave of empathy. "I'm sorry, I never thought to

ask. We've talked about my life, my work up in New York, my reality show. But I didn't ask you …"

"It's OK," he said quietly, as if he wasn't used to talking about himself. He moved closer, and she felt her heart rise. *You're thirty-five, you're thirty-five, not fifteen*, she thought. Jake gestured around the room. "Want to know more about all this?"

She nodded, grateful for the save he'd given her. "Yes, I would."

"It was back in '06 that Mom and Dad and I started working on all this stuff for real. They'd talked about it for years, but I'd gotten back from Cornell, and I knew it was time to do something. All kinds of things were wrong."

"Of course, all the stuff that can go wrong in such an old home. Papi and I saw a lot of that." But of course, living in a two-bedroom apartment, they'd never had to deal with it firsthand, she thought, mentally trying to keep up with what Jake was saying as she began to see the inn in a new light.

"Then you know the problems that can be visible," he continued. "The exterior, the barn, the windows. But the stuff you can't see is what's a ticking time bomb. Structural things, the foundation, things below the surface."

Anna smiled and glanced down. "You said a mouthful there."

Jake gave a faint smile. "Yeah, too much to bite off and chew. Anyway, we started going beneath the surface and assessing everything with contractors …"

As he paused, pulling out one of the spiral notebooks, Anna hesitated, then took a leap. "Jake, I don't want you think that I haven't wondered … about you. What you were doing. *How* you were doing. And I know I could have gone online and all that. I'm sure there are old high school networks on Facebook. But I kind of … got burned by all that." He had spilled a lot of details; she owed him a few. "For a while, I was really just keeping my head in the game up there. And I think it felt like if I looked back, I would lose everything I was gaining. And then once my career started happening, it was a boyfriend, Carson. I thought we were serious. Then I found out through an accidental Facebook tag that led to another posting, that led to another page … well, I'll spare you the details. But that's how I found out he …" She glanced down, aware she'd gone into the deep end. All she could do now was swim. "He was seeing someone else. The point is just that I felt burned by all the online stuff, learning about people's personal lives. So there were double reasons never to look back." And double reasons that looking back toward you would have been painful, she added silently.

His eyes lingered on hers. "Sorry you got burned. And you never looked back here? Never?"

Anna couldn't quite read his face. She exhaled, smiling slightly, feeling emboldened by his own revelations. As the conversation deepened, it began to feel like a comfortable old space she could rest in. And the more truth she could tell, the easier it would be too isolate the parts she couldn't tell him. Not now.

"Never say never, right?" she said. "Some things, some … people … were in my mind. I always thought back to you. Our friendship in high school was more important to me than I can explain. It helped me get through. And this crazy, accidental detour back here, I'm realizing it all over again. I know I may not be here long, so it … it wouldn't be right if I didn't tell you that."

A small nod. "Our friendship was important to me too."

"I've missed talking to you, actually." Anna's giggle was shy. "Sometimes I even imagined what we would say. Can you believe that?"

"And what would we have said?" His gaze was level.

Anna felt the pink rise into her cheeks again. She hadn't meant to bring them quite this far. Her fantasy life was definitely where she was drawing the line.

"Oh, you know, just catching up. Like this." She gestured

toward the books. "It looks like you did a great job. And then you came straight back here?"

"Pretty much. After Cornell, I had offers for jobs, good ones."

"New York?" she couldn't help asking.

His eyes crinkled in that way she was becoming undeniably fond of. "Yes, among others. It was tempting. But that's when Mom began to get sick, and I decided to come back here right away. And then I ended up …" She saw him swallow. "… getting married. I guess one thing led to another."

Anna held still. The moment felt tender, and she held it like a baby bird.

"Then way too fast, what everything led to just seemed like … loss." He wasn't looking at her anymore, but out the window at the greening fields. "Margaret Sneed—that's my ex—was from this big business family, in hotels."

At the familiar name, Anna nodded.

"Oh, right, you knew her too."

"Knew her? No. I saw her. I don't think she ever spoke to me." Anna tried to avoid a bitter tang to her voice. After all, this was someone who had married Jake. Her Jake. Hard to get her head around the idea. A flicker of irrational jealousy …

"Yeah, that was Margaret. Her whole family, really. They meant well. In fact, once I really got out from under it, I sort of felt sorry for her. You know? She felt as much pressure as I did. They were trying to get me to manage this place as an affiliate for their chain. But pretty soon, I realized—it wasn't about me or the inn."

"It wasn't the legacy you'd imagined?"

He eyed her, shaking his head quickly at the memory. "Not in any way that felt right, you know, in my gut. It was just about her family's vision for something apart from me. She didn't get … this place. She tried. We both did."

He suddenly seemed vulnerable. Anna's mouth was dry, but

everything in her yearned to say something, anything, so that he didn't feel alone. "It's hard to know these things when we're in the moment. Lots of times … you can only learn once you've got a little space to look back."

Jake seemed to struggle to meet her eyes, and when he did, she felt it.

"Yeah. I learned that I drove away parts of myself in order to fit in." He quickly looked back out at the fields and gave a rueful smile. "And after it was all over, I swore I'd never do that again."

"I understand." More than he knew.

"Your ex?"

Anna simply nodded. They'd already covered enough tender ground.

"Thanks." Jake let out a low whistle and looked around. "Well, enough of this. How are the plans coming?" He gestured toward her printouts.

"Fine, I guess." Her voice was flat.

"Doesn't sound like it."

Anna looked at the diagrams, suddenly loathe to pick them up. "It feels too far away from … me. I look at all these angles and directions for how the café is going to be set up. It's not really about all the stuff I love to do."

He raised his eyebrows. "So then, what would help? After all, this is supposed to be time off for you. What would be fun?"

Suddenly Sierra's advice—which had seemed useless—popped into her head and now seemed absolutely spot-on. She pushed the diagrams aside. "I know! Have a few minutes?"

He nodded.

"OK, you." She pointed a slender finger toward his nose. "Meet me in the kitchen in half an hour, mister."

"Ta-da! Mexican Wedding Cake cookies!" Anna announced proudly. She stood at the old worktable in the center of the kitchen, the afternoon sun slanting through the windows, counter-top lamps glowing, and held her hands out toward the assembly of ingredients. Her hair was gathered in the back in a loose white chignon, and silver bands gleamed on two of her fingers.

Jake eyed her, affectionately, it seemed to her. "I love those —haven't had them in years. And you're going to make them? Now?"

"Why not? I checked with Iris earlier—nothing else going on here now, dinner's already prepped in the fridge. I've got all the stuff. Come on, Jake, let's have some fun."

Maybe it was the buzz from being in the barn with Jake, maybe it was Sierra's phone call. But whatever it was, Anna was feeling downright impish—and how long had it been since that happened? What's more—probably adding to the playfulness— she could feel Jake watching her. And to be honest, it felt pretty comfortable.

She hummed happily as she began strategically separating out bags of sugar and flour from bowls and spoons.

"You're right," he said, tracking her movements. "There's enough work this week. Time to play a little … can I help? After all, I am the manager of this place."

"You can't manage an artist." She was enjoying the old familiar feeling of teasing Jake Petersen. Sort of like never forgetting how to ride a bike.

"Ah, good point. So I'll sit at her feet and learn."

"Well, not my feet!" Anna laughed. "You'll get flour all over you. The stool will do just fine, sir."

As she leaned over the bowl, creaming the butter and sugar, then mixing in flour, the two of them chatted comfortably as the old friends they were. Anna realized Sierra was right: it had been awhile since she simply did something she loved—and even longer, as she watched Jake smiling, bantering, and grabbing fingers full of dough from his stool, since she did it with someone she … liked.

Liked? No, that was too much like a thumbs-up.

So if it wasn't "like," what *was* she feeling for Jake?

She glanced down at the bulk of dough they'd created. Better to pay attention to what she was doing. After all, she had a reputation to uphold. "OK, so, last step," she said, spreading confectioners' sugar thickly across a small plate. "We bake them, then while they're still warm enough, we roll them in the sugar."

"I think you've got your recipe wrong," he teased. "Doesn't the sugar fall off?"

She bopped him on the shoulder. "Not if you time it right, dude. Has to be just warm enough so that the sugar clings to the cookie—but not so hot it melts. Like I said before: timing is everything." She pulled a pan from the oven and, using a spatula, lifted the cookies onto a rack covered in waxed paper. "Now, these will start to cool while I'm getting the next pan ready." She pushed his hand back as he playfully reached for another piece of the dough.

Anna slid the pan into the oven, loving the fragrant heat that met her face. There were so many sensual parts of baking. No wonder she missed it.

"OK, almost ready." She lightly held one of the baked cookies, inspecting it with mock-seriousness. "I think we're there. Here, take this one and roll it lightly … like this …" She stood beside where he sat, reaching her right hand along his arm and guiding his hand as he rolled the small warm ball around in the sugar.

His grin was broad as he looked sideways at her, his broad shoulder brushing her arm. "This has to be more fun than football."

Anna laughed over his high school obsession. "Well, it's certainly less dangerous." She touched his small scar delicately. "Right?"

"Hey, don't get sugar on me," he said, ducking.

"Sorry, I'm sure I have it all over me." Anna suddenly thought she must look like a sugary mess. She tried to glance at her reflection in the glass oven door. "Do I look OK?"

Jake set down the cookie and slowly stood up so that he faced her. "Hmm, let's see."

Anna's heart flipped a beat—deliciously hoping he'd come closer.

Which he obligingly did. "You look great. Just a little bit right … *there*." He pointed to her left cheek.

"This happens way too much," she said, awkwardly reaching the back of her forearm to her face. "I try to get it off and end of making it worse. Help me?"

Apparently it was exactly what he was planning to do. Jake lifted his hand, let it hesitate in the air, then quickly touched away the sugar from her cheek.

As he pulled his hand back, smiling a bit foolishly, he put his finger to his own mouth. "Mm. Sweet."

Anna's breath caught in her chest, and she knew that if her eyes were beaming as much as her heart, it was a total giveaway. "Yes. It is. Thanks … for helping me."

He set his hand back down slowly and turned to look at all the action on the table. "Hey, oops, forgot—more cookies to roll."

"Oh, no, and more to get out of the oven!" How could she have spaced out? Well, she knew how—by having Jake's finger on her cheek. Enough of that. She had work to do—even if it *was* play. And felt pretty great.

He rolled dough while she finished the last pan, talking comfortably about the preparations for Friday as the stress seemed to temporarily ebb. It was nice, Anna noticed, simply to be talking and planning with this man—her old friend, her new friend. Maybe it was the sweet heat from the cookies, but she warmed to it more and more, hoping she wasn't crossing any lines.

"I can't wait to do the cake, Jake, this'll be fun," she said, pulling the last pan from the oven.

"It'll be great, I'm sure. If it's half as good as these cookies." Jake gave a brief smile, then averted his eyes toward the back door, seeming to change gears. "Anna, this has been fun. But ... speaking of getting ready for Friday, I guess I should get some things done out back. Deliveries start tomorrow."

As she watched him turn, his broad shoulder framed by the back door that led down to the barn, Anna suddenly knew she wanted this wedding cake to be the best she'd ever made; no, what she wanted was for this whole thing to be the best it could ever be—for Jake's sake. She should be able to use all her skills toward that end.

"Jake, wait. Before you go. Just so I'm sure about the timing of everything—the wedding ceremony is at the church at three?"

Jake nodded. "Yep."

"And probably about an hour, so we can count on people beginning to arrive here not long after four?"

He nodded once more.

"OK, so I'll be here." Maybe this was another chance to help manage things. "I can help with whatever you need while you're at the ceremony. Anything in particular you want me to keep an eye on?"

Jake seemed to hesitate. "Thanks for offering, but everything will be fine. Iris will be here, and Albert and Tom will oversee all the setup. We're good."

Anna's heart took a little hit. For just a moment, it had been sweet to feel needed, like she was part of the team. Somehow she had just assumed she'd be helping with the reception—geez, she hadn't even thought to ask.

The old ghost of being the outsider beckoned from the edges, slowly crooking its finger at her.

"Should I, um, not be here for the reception?" She nervously pushed a curly strand behind her ear and avoided his gaze.

"What?" Jake's eyes widened, as comprehension crossed his face. "No, no, that's not what I meant." He stepped toward her, his tone apologetic. "Of course, you should be here. But the ceremony—somehow I had assumed you wouldn't want ..."

Despite the heat of the kitchen, the heat that she'd been hazily enjoying between them, she felt an old chill and braced herself. Jake paused awkwardly, as if thinking something through. Then quickly, his demeanor changed; he turned fully toward her, which made her own heart skip a beat, and cleared his throat. "Anna, I want you to come to the wedding. With me."

Anna paused, sugary hands in midair. "Really, you want me to come to the wedding? At the church?" She felt like the little girl inside was the one actually asking the question. It probably sounded like it too. "I don't know if I should go there." Again, the little girl spoke.

"What? Why not?" Jake looked at her curiously.

Anna had no idea how to tell him how vulnerable she felt at this moment, teetering between who she thought she'd been before, when she'd watched Jake's crowd from a distance, and who she hoped she was now, in her own crowds in New York. Like Cinderella at the stroke of midnight, she feared he would disappear. Damn those old fairy tales.

And besides, it was one thing to make the wedding cake for the Abbott family behind the scenes. Going to the wedding would put her right out in front. With Jake.

"I don't know. It's ..." she began haltingly. "I haven't seen people here since ... well, since I was Annie."

His eyes narrowed. "Ah. So you're afraid that's who they'll see?"

She shook her head. "You don't get it, Jake." She set her hands lightly down onto the table. "I'm afraid that's who I'll *be*."

"And what would be wrong with that?"

Anna blinked. "I … I don't know. I guess, I always felt like I didn't belong with … with everyone else." The truth bubbled up of its own accord, and she knew it was probably the spike of anger at the Abbotts that pushed it to the surface. "I never knew what to say. Your friends never looked at me the way they looked at each other. My hair was too curly, my skin was too dark. My parents weren't like anyone else's. Then all of that happened with my father with the gardens at the community college. And … Mr. Abbott. He might treat me like I'm invisible again. Like he did Papi."

Jake was still, and she couldn't quite read him. "I knew there was that stuff with your dad. But I didn't know it was that bad for you back then."

Anna felt a shot of embarrassment, suddenly realizing she'd gone too far with her explanations. "I'm sorry," she said quickly, retreating inside. "It was just … teenage stuff."

"Sounds pretty grown-up to me. Anna … Annie …" He intentionally caught her eyes. "You've done great work, and you should be proud. And that girl I remember? She was never invisible to me. You want to know what I saw back then?"

Anna wasn't sure if she did, but hopeful curiosity got the better of her. "Sure."

"I saw someone who was smart. And kind. And fun. Someone who really listened when I talked. Someone who was creative and who saw what was going on, instead of the stupid teenage sleepwalking everybody else was doing. Including me."

Anna's heart went from being a stone to being a butterfly. "Really?" Suddenly she could see her old self in her mind's eye, and that young girl didn't seem like anyone she needed to run from.

"Really. And now … Anna Diaz. Come with me to the

wedding. I've, um …" Jake glanced down at the barn and back. "I've got everything under control here. Just come and enjoy the wedding. You deserve it."

"I'd love to." Anna's hands instinctively came together, the tips of her fingers shyly touching her sugary mouth. She could go to the Abbott wedding, she could be with Jake, and they could see the real Anna. She could show who she really was, and they'd finally see her.

"And Jake?"

"Yeah?"

"I can't thank you enough."

"For what?"

"I think you know."

CHAPTER 5

F riday morning dawned bright and clear, with a western breeze puffing up from the swirling acres of early-summer grasses. As Anna surfaced from sleep, bathed by pale-yellow light from the double windows, she began grinning. It was like Christmas morning, and she hadn't felt that way since many, many Christmases ago. Excitement and anticipation were brimming in her chest, and she wasn't sure it is was about teaching Haven how to assemble the cake, or the success she hoped for the inn, or … Jake.

Well, if it was about Jake, she told herself quickly, it's just about wanting him to be happy, like she would with any of her friends. Surely, it wasn't about the fact that he'd asked her to go to the wedding with him. That she—Annie—was going to a wedding with Jake Petersen.

The smile never left her face as she cleaned up and pulled on the distressed jeans from yesterday and a fresh V-neck tee— she'd shower later, after everything was ready. They'd gotten all the baking done yesterday, so the cake could be put together this morning before she needed to dress for the wedding.

And thank goodness, she'd even managed to hastily fill in

Sierra's diagrams, quick slashes of the pen pointing to where the optics would be best for showing her fingers in dough. Good heavens, she'd be more worried about how her fingers looked than by what they were making. By the time she finished, she'd had the clear, if unwelcome, thought that it had been much more natural to play in the kitchen with Jake. But what the heck she was supposed to *do* with that thought … wasn't so clear yet.

Anna looked in the closet, grateful she'd automatically thrown in a sleek pale yellow dress when she was packing, plus white shoes she'd totally scored with on consignment online. After all, she'd been going away for the Memorial Day holiday, and weren't white shoes the thing to wear? Good thing it hadn't been her usual city-wear black, she thought, giving herself a little thumbs-up.

"Anna?"

Iris's voice echoed down the hall. Anna glanced once more in the mirror—no makeup yet, her hair in a loose topknot, but she'd take care of all that later. She opened her door.

"On my way!"

"Good, my dear. Coffee's ready, and the big day's here!" Iris sounded more excited than the vibe she'd been giving off all week.

When Anna got down to the kitchen, Haven was already there, her face shining. "Hey there, cake woman! I can't wait to get started."

Anna pulled up a stool to the table with them. "OK, well, lesson 1 for the big day—don't rely on all the sugar to get you through. Believe me, I learned that the hard way."

"Licking buttercream off my fingers isn't probiotic?"

"If I could find a way to make that happen, I'd make a fortune. No, you have to do it the old-fashioned way. A solid breakfast, with plenty of protein." She spread almond butter on one of the bran muffins Haven had brought with her. "By the way, these are excellent. You're good at this, Haven."

The younger woman beamed, her sleek, simple hair swinging over her face from its side part. "I hope so. It means so much to have someone like you say that."

Anna looked thoughtfully at where she'd taken a bite from her muffin. It was odd—and sweet—to have someone back here in Cedarwood Spring feel like her opinion mattered so much. As close as the old memories had felt during this curious detour, Haven was a good reminder that this really was a different time of life. And of Cedarwood Spring.

Anna hoped the wedding and the reception would show them all it was a different time of life. And who she'd really been all along. Her heart did a hopeful flutter.

Speaking of which ... "Where's Jake?"

"Who knows?" Iris said affectionately. "Somewhere on the property. He's been up since dawn doing everything from sticking extra plants into the flower beds to going over and over the final setup in the barn. He'll tire himself out soon enough."

"This is so important to him," Anna mused, then fearing she had betrayed the leaning of her heart, added quickly, "for all of you."

Iris took it in. "Yes, it is. But I want it most for him. He's got something special. I loved my husband dearly but Philip didn't have that fierce drive that Jake has. The drive you have to have to turn an old place like this around—but not so that it makes him important. He does it so that it's bigger than he is. He's humble that way."

Anna had the feeling Iris's words were particularly directed at her, for some reason she couldn't quite fathom. But whatever the reason, Iris had nailed it—nailed what Anna had always sensed about Jake, even way back when.

Sure, he'd always had charisma and a classic handsomeness —now with aged ruggedness around the edges—that make it seem like he should be on top of the world. But something else about him always showed that Jake Petersen saw life as a level playing field. Something that kept his feet obstinately on the ground. Like in how doggedly he held onto his vision for the inn and how he insisted it included local friends trying to find success there. Her heart swelled a bit in admiration.

"My only worry," Iris continued, "is that he's trying to do too much. It's too much to be the one managing everything for an event like this one—and all the others we hope we'll be getting if this takes off. I think he believes that he has to do it himself, that it's all on his shoulders. But if things go well, like we hope, he's going to have to learn another way."

The few seconds of silence among the women felt like it was another voice in the conversation.

"Well, he sure has helped me," Haven spoke up. "It's why I always call him my god-brother. I don't think I could have gotten the Filling Station off the ground without him. And he knew how much I wanted to get into event catering and baking, and he had enough confidence in me to offer me the wedding cake." She cringed and laughed simultaneously. "That could have ended up a disaster, but thanks to you, Anna, it didn't. Imagine—having one of the best pastry chefs in the country right here to save it for us."

"Speaking of which—" Anna said, putting her hands flat onto the work surface of the island. "Let's do this!"

"Where is everybody?"

Anna was standing at the sink washing the last of the equipment they'd used that morning to assemble the cake. She glanced up, startled. "Oh! You scared me!"

"Sorry." Jake grinned shyly as he came into the kitchen from the coatroom door. Like Anna, he was still dressed for work, the sleeves of his worn, burgundy cotton shirt rolled up over his forearms. He felt like a nervous wreck, making sure everything was in place on such a high-stakes day—geez, there were so many things that could go wrong and it was up to him to make sure none of them did.

Most everything had gotten back on track after the disruption of the storm. Tom, Pete, Tina, and everybody had really come together. He was proud—and he'd be sure to tell them all that. And then, of course, Anna saving the day with the wedding cake. That had come together too. He'd have to tell her.

Not that he'd fully made peace with the whole thing. She'd been really nice about it and all—said over and over it would be fun for her. The cake would be great; it was still "local talent," broadly speaking. So it had finally started to feel like he was steering the ship again—which he could make clear to the Abbotts and to the Taggarts reviewer. They all had to see he was for real—and maybe now, it would be the truth.

It's just what Anna had briefly said about seeing the Abbotts again—good heavens, even making their cake—that made him the smallest bit uneasy; he wasn't sure where to put it down inside of him.

Returning his thoughts to the woman at the sink, he had to admit in the midst of all of this that there was something pretty damn simple and wonderful about walking in and seeing Anna at work, crumbs and buttercream smeared here and there on her pale pink T-shirt, her soft, thick waves pulled back from her face. The place somehow felt … complete.

"I've been in the barn with Tom and his crew making sure everything's just right." He jerked his thumb behind him. "Only just had a chance to get away. Where's Iris? She OK?"

"She's fine, she just went upstairs to rest," Anna said, turning off the water and reaching for a towel. "Haven made one more run into town to pick up the last of all the goodies she's made. Sounds like she did a good job."

"Super. How'd it go with the cake?"

"It went great, thanks. Want to see?"

"Love to. Where is it? I need to make sure everything is … um, all set." Jake glanced around the kitchen.

Anna smiled mischievously. "Hmm. So you do, do you? Alright then. Close your eyes."

"What? No way. Where is it? I said I need to see—"

"Hey, Petersen, I said close your eyes!"

Jake looked suspiciously at her, unsure what she was up to, and not so sure this was the time for a game. He glanced at his watch. "OK, but make this quick."

He crossed his arms over his chest and closed his eyes, feeling oddly vulnerable—which also felt unexpectedly good. He sensed Anna moving closer to him, smelled her freshness and the sweetness of the cake. Nice combo.

Suddenly, he felt the dish towel pulled gently over his eyes and jumped. Her giggle rose behind him. "It's fine, it's just how I can reach your eyes," she said. Her hand pressed against the middle of his back, and Jake realized she was holding the towel lightly around his eyes and leading him from behind. Which also felt good.

"Straight ahead," she ordered.

"Yes, ma'am." Might as well give in.

Jake walked slowly toward the dining room, feeling awkwardly like a stranger in his own home. Anna kept pressing her hand against the small of his back, guiding him through the door and into the room. Then she caught the worn cotton of his work shirt and pulled him to a stop.

Her voice was teasing as she dropped the towel from his eyes. "OK, does it pass muster?"

Jake opened his eyes to the sight of the simple, spare dining room. A few strands of ivy and camellia blooms lay strewn on the sideboard, waiting to be taken down to the barn. The long wooden table was gleaming in the morning light—with probably the most extraordinary cake he'd ever seen standing at its center.

"Anna, this is … this is *stunning*," he murmured truthfully before he could even think, slowly pacing around the table as Anna stood, smiling proudly, near the door.

Its five layers were perfectly proportioned, their pale buttercream sides carved into what looked like thick crinoline made into white sashes around the waist of a wedding dress. Atop the highest layer was a rounded setting of buttercream camellias modeled on those that were clustered around the room and would be at its base once they moved it down to the barn.

He stopped when he reached Anna again. The cake was amazing, and he had to say, the relief he felt at this big task being complete—and perfect—was pretty great.

But how do you say 'the cake looks amazing' in real pastry-chef language?

"Thank you so much," he tried, stymied, and hooked his thumbs on his belt loops. "I've never seen anything like it. People are going to *love* this. You took this problem that could have been a disaster, and you took the bride's dream of something classic but one-of-a-kind, and you made it all work." He paused, watching her.

Anna grinned and blushed, playfully curtseying. "Thank-you-sir. But ..." She held up a finger mischievously, "... like I said before. It's no good if it doesn't taste as good as it looks. Here—I saved a piece for you before we assembled it." She reached for a small plate on the sideboard. "I knew you would want to make sure everything was right," she said pointedly, eyeing him.

She'd nailed that one too. "OK, OK, you win. I have no doubt it's great, but ..." He pointed to the frosted cake slice on the plate and made a frown of mock-concern. "... for proper procedure, I should go ahead and taste it. I mean, just to make sure I'm doing my job as manager of this whole outfit. I have to be able to speak authoritatively on the subject."

Anna mimicked his mock-frown. "Absolutely, Mr. Petersen, I think that's protocol." She lifted the plate, then looked around quickly. "Shoot, no fork. Um … here, this will have to work. 'Scuse my fingers. They're clean, I promise." She delicately picked up the piece with two long, slim fingers—one with that thin silver band that kept catching his eye—and brought it to his mouth.

As Jake opened his mouth to bite the cake, his eyes met hers, and for a split second he felt almost paralyzed. There was something so close and exciting about having her lift it to him.

And then just as quickly, he had a fleeting visual of the only other time a woman had done that for him. It had been his own wedding cake, and it had been Margaret.

But with the next beat of his heart, the burst of sweetness in his mouth and Anna's shining eyes brought him firmly back to the present. This was Anna, not Margaret, to quote Haven. And it felt pretty good.

And tasted great. Like, really great. "Mm, wow, that's amazing!" He looked wonderingly at the ceiling, again feigning concern. "What's in it that makes it taste a little different? I think I need another bite."

Anna grinned and lifted the cake to him again. "I did a little bit with extract—almond, and one more … well, I won't tell you exactly what. A chef has to have the occasional secret. I am a brand, after all."

OK, two could play at that game—and having fun with Anna felt so good, Jake wasn't *quite* ready to stop. He gently took the saucer from her, setting it back down on the sideboard and wiping crumbs from his mouth with the back of his finger.

"OK, Miss Big Shot pastry chef. I'm a brand too. Or at least, I'm gonna be. And now it's your turn."

Her eyebrows shot up inquiringly. "Oh? My turn for what?"

"I have a secret too, but you can't taste mine. Come on."

Jake instinctively reached for her hand. As he led her swiftly through the kitchen to the back door, he had to admit he liked having an excuse to hold onto it for a moment. Reluctantly releasing it, he opened the door and steered them across the gardens and down to the barn.

"This is great, Jake!" she said, pointing toward the series of small lanterns hanging from looped poles that lined the old brick path. "These will be perfect tonight. The lanterns will lead people to the barn. Footsteps of light." She stopped abruptly as the barn came fully into view, pointing. "And look! The barn door and the patio. Jake, it's beautiful. Just the right way to welcome guests into the space." She instinctively walked faster down the path, Jake chuckling behind her, and they scanned the garland of ivy, white flowers, and small white lights that lined the top of the wide door and dangled down its sides, shifting lightly in the breeze. Urns of boxwood and sprays of dark branches entwined with white flowers were set out along the edges of the brick patio in front of it. Even in the sunlight, they could see the twinkle of the tiny lights woven among them.

"Thanks," he said, keeping up with her. "But that's not the secret."

"No? Is it inside?"

He could hear the anticipation in her voice, and he enjoyed it so much he almost wished he thought for a second about how to prolong this. He could draw it out, take her around back first … but no, better not to get too far off the path, literally or emotionally.

"Yeah, it sort of is inside. Well, it *is* the barn. Wait here." He stopped her where the path opened out to the patio and strode up to the door, opening it slightly.

"Tom?" he called into the barn. "Ready for the big reveal?"

"Ready!" A voice answered from inside.

Jake turned back to Anna. "Time for you to get a taste of your own medicine." He circled her, putting his arms around her shoulders from behind and covering her eyes gently with his hands. It was startling to feel her this way—held and guided by his arms. He was starting to really get into this thing of coming up with reasons to touch Anna.

She giggled and instinctively put her hands up to his.

"Just go slow and walk straight ahead into the barn," he said, close to her hair. "I got you, don't worry."

"I'm not worried." Her voice was almost a whisper.

Tom pushed the door open, and Jake led Anna across the threshold, stopping inside. Glancing around quickly, he let himself feel proud—they'd done good work. All morning. And for weeks. All leading up to now.

And though a week ago, he'd had zero idea that he'd be standing here with Anna Diaz, it now felt like he couldn't imagine doing it without her. And he didn't want to.

"Hit it, guys!" Tom said.

With a loud click, the lights came on in the dim of the barn, and Jake pulled his hands from Anna's eyes, stepping up beside her. "What do you think?" he asked, both sheepish and proud.

Anna's eyes rounded, and her hands flew to her mouth as she turned around and around, taking it all in. "Jake, this is … magic. The cake's just cake, but this is magic, pure and simple! It's heaven!" She walked further into the barn, hands upturned, as Jake savored watching her every step.

Tiny, sparkling ferry lights crisscrossed from one side to the other, making a canopy of light that illuminated both the graceful height of the angled ceiling and the polished floor below. Long, narrow tables were set the length of the barn and covered with white damask—Pete and Tina had said to make sure to use the real thing. Ivy intertwined with white lights was strewn down the middle of the tables sprinkled with white roses and baby's breath. Each chair had its own setting of pale pink plates. Pale pink glass cake stands whimsically dotting the tables held champagne flutes.

Long willowy bare branches wrapped in small lights lined the walls, making it into a magical forest. The dance floor in the middle was bare, reflecting the glow from the lights. Pete and Tina's staff were bustling around, putting the finishing touches on the tables along the perimeter of the barn, where Albert and his crew would later put out food.

"Great work, Tom," Jake said, nodding with satisfaction.

"Hey, buddy, it's teamwork. Your choice of the tables and setup were great. Pete and Tina just left—this might be the best design I've seen them do yet, and I've seen most of their stuff. Do you know them, Anna? Peter and Tina, PT Design?"

"Not yet, but I'd love to."

"Yeah," Jake said, proudly, nodding at Tom. "It doesn't get better than the local people. Pete and Tina only started up a couple of years ago. They moved out here from New York ..." He quickly looked away from Anna, feeling a small shadow pass even under the bright twinkles of light.

"Really?" she asked, interested.

"They had been in Brooklyn. But they wanted more space to build a business and wanted to be somewhere they could use the local greenhouses. And other natural stuff, like the branches."

"Those are called design elements," Anna said teasingly.

"Ha!" Tom guffawed. "I think they're called 'whatever blew down in the storm!'"

"That works." She smiled, looking around before turning back to Jake and Tom. "Guys, it all works. This is beyond the events I usually do in New York. They're all going to love it. Even the Taggarts' guy," she added, glancing encouragingly at Jake.

Jake couldn't stop himself from smiling. "I hope so. And like the lady said, it's no good if it doesn't taste good. I sampled everything at Albert's yesterday, and it's almost as good as the wedding cake."

"Which will go ... where?" she asked.

"I thought right here," he answered, pointing to where they stood, "right where the guests first come in here from the patio and the walkway. It will help them feel like they've … arrived. Speaking of which …" He glanced down at his watch. "Shoot, it's later than I thought. We have to 'get to the church on time.'"

Anna held up an OK sign with her fingers. "Meet you in the living room in an hour."

~

Anna stood in front of the full-size oval mirror. In it, she saw past and present, who she was now and who she'd thought she wasn't anymore, all in one image.

She smoothed the front of her pale sleeveless dress, noting how nicely the darker skin of her neck rose gracefully from the cowl collar, her bare dark arms by her sides. She checked her hair—even without the stylist who was always there before interviews, she had to admit she'd done a good job, with the usual fullness of her hair tamed into a sleek bun. She'd gone with minimal—or no—makeup all week, which, she realized, had felt fun and natural. But now was time to kick it, and as she checked out her eyeliner and elegant brows, she had to say: she'd owned it!

And even though she wasn't going to be in front of any cameras, it still felt like something of an interview—a life interview, maybe. This was going at Jake's side to a big-ticket wedding where she'd surely see many of the people she'd known —or at least seen from a distance—growing up. Would the Abbotts see her, know who she was? What's more, would they know she'd made the cake? Would they see who she'd become —and who she always was?

The week had gone way off track, and yet she couldn't say it felt like it had gone wrong.

She looked into the mirror at the room reflected behind her. The simple, elegant wooden furniture, the bright midday light on the white walls, the faded picture of Iris and Philip back in the

'60s hanging on the wall. The room told a story. And for the first time, she felt like she was part of that story—though exactly how, she wasn't quite sure.

But the feeling of belonging was unmistakable. Maybe, she realized, because it had been so rare.

Exactly how long was that feeling going to stick around? Only one way to find out.

Anna slid her silver bangles onto her arm and silver-and-diamond studs into her ears. She started to reach for the perfume she usually had with her, but paused, seeing once again the locally made lavender body cream, and instead smoothed that up her arms and onto her shoulders.

She smiled once more at herself in the mirror. Here she was in Cedarwood Spring, with Jake, and she felt like … Anna.

Wow, what a weird combination.

"Anna?" Iris knocked on her door. "I think Jake's ready. You don't want to be late."

Anna opened the door.

"Oh, don't you look lovely, and what a perfect dress," Iris said, clasping her hands, before turning to bustle down the hall. "Now I have work to do. See you when you get back."

"See you soon," Anna replied, picking up her small white purse and pulling her door closed behind her.

Jake stood in the living room, glancing alternately at his watch, then out the window at the delivery men, and then back at the stairs. It felt both old and totally new to be waiting to take Anna to a wedding—not as Annie and Jake years ago, which never would have happened. It wouldn't have occurred to him to step so far out of his social circle for such a special event. Which, he was beginning to understand, Anna had read more clearly than he had.

But this was as Anna and Jake *now*—and it felt like it was totally happening.

He looked nervously back out the window, watching an ice delivery van pull up. Why did he almost feel like … a groom?

Behind him, he heard the light tap of heels on the wood of the stairs and swung back around. His breath caught, and he straightened and faced Anna as she reached the last steps where she paused.

Jake's jaw moved slightly before he found words. "Anna … wow. You look amazing." Between the cake and Anna, he was using that word way too much. His life didn't usually operate at the level of amazing so there'd never been cause to unpack it. Time to check out Iris's thesaurus.

He took in the curving silhouette of the pale yellow dress, the sleek white pumps, and above all, the face, the face he'd known years ago, then seen on videos and interview clips, and now in his living room looking back at him. For years, she'd seemed so far away, yet here she was … Annie. Anna. Stunning.

She smiled and blushed slightly. "Thanks, Jake. I've heard lots of wows before, but that one meant a lot." She appreciatively checked out his black tux, well fitted and sleek, and his clean-shaven face, where, he hoped he'd avoided any nicks. "You look dashing. Not that I didn't like the unshaven look."

Jake grinned, resisting the urge to rake his hair back. "Yeah, nothing falling down in my face for once. I can clean up."

Anna paused. "You always could."

Their eyes met, and Jake knew it was time to move. "Ready to go to the church?" He stepped forward, reaching for her hand, and led her to the door. Outside, still lightly holding her fingers, Jake steered them toward a sleek, newish gray compact, clicking it open with a fob.

"Where are you going?" Anna asked, confused.

"To the wedding." He gave a half-smile and pulled open the passenger-side door. "Your carriage awaits."

Her laugh sounded as silvery as her bracelets. "I didn't know you had this. I was ready for the truck. I think I kinda miss it," she added teasingly.

"There's a time for truck—and a time for this," he said, closing her door and coming around to his side. Climbing in, he glanced at Anna.

"Thanks for coming with me to the ceremony. I, um … I feel better with you there." It might sound silly, he thought, but twenty years ago, he'd always felt better when she was there. Why not just claim it?

"I feel better with me there too …" She seemed to hesitate, and he waited. "You know, Jake … this past week … it's totally what I didn't expect."

"Oh come on, you purposely came out when an electrical storm was predicted and made sure you were right at Exit 13."

"Right, right." She smiled down, then back at him, her eyes earnest. "But seriously, it's not what I expected. And if you'd asked me, I would have said it wasn't what I wanted. But … it's been a nice surprise. I always pushed away memories, thinking they were past. But this helped me see that that girl is still part of me …" She took a deep breath. "And that that's a good thing … make sense?"

"I think so. At least, I think I had to do something like that—make peace with everything I've, um, been." He glanced out the windshield. "But of course, most of what I've been is right here. And you get to head back out of town again." At that moment, he wanted more than anything for her to say, *No, I've changed my mind, changed my life*, and somehow magically she will stay right here.

But all she said in a flat voice, was "Of course."

He started the car as she smoothed her dress.

The church—an old stone structure with wooden additions out on either side of the nave, and old, clear, wavy-glass windows looking out into the summer green—was full and fragrant. As Anna sat listening to Rev. Claudia Turner's voice, which felt abstractly comforting, she was aware of Jake breathing beside her.

Most of this week, they'd seemed to be out doing something —or if they were alone together, it had been in the truck with both of them in some version of work clothes. But now, sitting in the focused quiet of a moment in the church, dressed with care, and smelling his musky, soapy clean, his tux fitted and polished over his tall frame, she felt more aware than ever of the man he had become—quirky, stubborn, honorable.

A man, she realized, whom she admired. A lot.

His hands were clasped calmly in his lap, and he seemed to be listening intently to the service. Without turning her head, she managed a quick scan of the side of his face before clearing her throat and focusing on the couple standing at the front.

The flowers at the altar matched the roses and baby's breath she'd seen in the barn, and the sunlight from the large, clear window behind the young pastor framed Sarah Smart's simple dress and veil so that she almost glowed, contrasting with the classic firmness of James Abbott's black tux. The bridesmaids and groomsmen stood angled up toward Rev. Claudia.

Anna could make out the heads of the senior Abbotts in the front row, watching attentively. She and Jake had slipped into their seats just before the procession, so there was no reason they would have—or should have—seen her. This was their day, not hers, and the thing with Papi and the gardens at the college happened so long ago. The memory of Mr. Abbott still stung, she knew that. But she also knew that was about her story, not his, which only underlined that there was a little unfinished business for her there.

Well, surely this whole detour back home, seeing Jake, making an unexpected cake, and showing up for who she really was … that would wrap up any unfinished business so she could go back to the city freer than when she left it. Surely, that was the reason all this had happened.

"And now," Rev. Claudia was saying to James, pulling Anna out of her reverie, "repeat after me the vow over the rings. With all that I am."

"With all that I am," James repeated to Sarah, sliding the ring onto her finger.

"And all that I have," the pastor continued.

"And all that I have."

"I honor you."

"I honor you."

As Sarah repeated the same vow to James, slipping the ring onto his finger, Anna felt almost overcome with a powerful sense of yearning that she had thought she had successfully battled into submission years ago. But the beast reared its head again.

What beautiful words—"with all that I am and all that I have, I honor you." There was something about it that was both strong and vulnerable that spoke to her as never before.

All that I am, she thought. That would mean all the stuff that looked so good on a day like today, when she felt at ease and accomplished in her "Anna" skin. And it would mean all the "Annie" pieces that had struggled and pushed and felt invisible —the parts that her ex, Carson, had so painfully rejected.

As Rev. Claudia asked them to stand for prayer, Anna remembered having dared to hope for something this real with Carson. "With all that I am and all that I have." When she'd found out he was seeing someone else, that daring opening inside her had closed back up. Real quick, and real tight.

But as she listened, she realized that hope hadn't vanished

quite as fully as she would have liked. Anna sighed, unsure of whether she was grateful or annoyed to see it was still there. And to see it right when she was standing by her old high school flame … now a magnificent man. Shoot. How inconvenient.

She knew she should be saying the prayer's responses along with everyone else, but she couldn't help but listen for Jake's voice instead of her own. After all, she'd never made it to the altar, but he'd actually stood up there himself. What had he dared to hope for? She knew nothing about it.

"You may kiss the bride!" the pastor said jubilantly, breaking into her thoughts.

The organist began the classic Mendelssohn recessional, and everyone around her began clapping and hooting. Anna came back to the present, feeling simple joy at the sight of the couple who now held each other in a victorious embrace.

Suddenly, everyone seemed to be hugging or shaking hands. Jake turned to her, and they met each other's eyes. He impulsively reached his left arm around her shoulders and gave her a light sideways hug. Her right arm came up around his waist to his back, aware of its broad masculinity, and hugged him sideways, her head brushing against his shoulder. It felt right.

Then—he released her, blushing. "Now we have to scram and beat all these people back to the inn. Here goes!"

CHAPTER 6

Anna stood on the patio, relishing the feeling of the satisfaction of a job well done. Her eyes traced the old brick pathway to the barn, then the dark-blue horizon that melted into a few pale clouds still backlit by the long-gone sun. The whole event seemed to have gone off smoothly—and, she was pretty sure, the cake had been a splendid part of it.

She'd hovered more than she should have—she knew—as caterers had moved the cake from the dining table down to the barn where they set it atop a small round table at the entrance. Then she'd hovered just a tad more, checking over every inch of the cake for any near-invisible imperfection. Why had she been so nervous? After all, it's not like her name was on a placard stuck in the top of the cake ... then again, it felt that way.

And then she'd headed back up to the kitchen where she'd tried to take out all that nervous energy by helping the catering staff, though truth be told, they didn't seem to need it. And the warm closeness she'd felt with Jake at the church seemed to have dissipated, as he darted in and out of the kitchen, checking with Albert and keeping the sequence of courses moving.

And of course, there had been a lot of introductions—or reintroductions—of Anna to others who remembered her from the past, with Iris, Haven, Tom, even Jake in the midst of his anxious management, being intentional about it. To her surprise, everyone remembered her genially as part of the high school class, and some—even more impressively—knew what she was doing now. She began to let herself feel the glow of being admired right here in Cedarwood Spring. A clash—or a convening?—of hitherto separate worlds.

It was only when Mr. Abbott cruised across the patio to stop in quickly and say something to Albert that Anna felt that glow retreat briefly. Whether Iris noticed or not, Anna wasn't sure, but the older woman stepped forward from where she was monitoring the cases of wine and called Mr. Abbott over with the naturalness of an everyday encounter, introducing Anna with the usual "Surely you remember Anna …" Her anxiety briefly spiked, but he gave only a nod and a perfunctory mention of her father being such a fine manager of the store—Anna could tell he didn't remember much else. Albert called to him from the back door, and he turned, but not before adding, "I hear you're doing great things in New York. Congratulations, young lady," as he shook her hand.

Iris glanced at her significantly as she went back to help a waiter select a wine bottle, and Anna quietly considered the back door Mr. Abbott had headed into. So he knew who she was now. And the moment had been no time to mention her father and the community gardens. Somehow, she didn't feel the need to. It was enough that he had seen her, that he knew something of who she was—and where she had gone in life. Anna's defenses, which had been at the ready, slowly backed down. Her awareness of the gap between Annie and Anna seemed to be only hers. She began to breathe again.

Dinner and dancing were winding down at this point, and guests wandered in and out of the barn along the path, their footfalls lit by the dotted glow of small lanterns along its edges.

From the patio, Anna could glimpse the interior of the barn through its wide door; lights crisscrossed back and forth above the narrow tables, where a few guests lazily, happily lingered over plates of half-finished desserts.

At the center of the entrance, she could just make out the wedding cake—or what was left of it. She had to admit, it might have been her best—especially lucky since she'd been working in an unfamiliar kitchen. Haven had been a real help. Come to think of it, it had been pretty terrific showing the younger woman the craft of a wedding cake. Felt a bit like she was paying it forward—helping someone else who was also working hard to break out and do her thing. That had felt good. So good, that part of her wanted to do more of it.

A lot of things this week had felt unexpectedly good.

Anna pulled out her phone and scrolled through pictures people had already posted from the reception. As she saw picture after picture tagged with glowing comments, all @cedar-springinn and #cedarspringwedding, she felt oddly proud. For a split second, she glanced up and wondered if it was her place to be proud. After all these years, did she belong "enough" to be proud of the inn?

She shook off the feeling. Dammit, she'd feel proud anyway.

"Anna, there you are!" Haven was coming out of the back door from the kitchen, wiping her hands on her apron. Iris was behind her.

"Hi! Just enjoying the view," Anna said. "Come join me. You've both been working so hard."

"Whew, this was huge!" Haven said, slipping an arm around her waist as they both looked out over the scene.

"And," Iris said, joining them on the other side of Anna, "an unqualified success. Congratulations, gals, I think this was everything we were hoping for. I'm bushed."

"Listen, I do these kinds of things all the time," Anna said.

"This was top-of-the-line. It doesn't get any better. You should be proud."

"You should too, you were the ingredient we needed," Haven said, giggling at her pun. "People couldn't stop talking about the cake. It's so cool I got to help. I feel like now I can really do this on my own. But still …" she added wistfully, looking back toward the barn and the fields behind it. "I wish you could be here all the time."

Without taking her eyes from the dark sky, Anna felt a pin prick in her heart. All the more reason, she thought, to be careful with whatever desires about Cedarwood Spring had begun to pop up inside her like the baby's breath in the barn. As much as she'd enjoyed—was that the right word?—this little getaway, it was soon going to be time to get back to her life, and the show, and Rubin and Sierra, and the unfinished Soho space for the pilot episode.

Though even as she thought about the pieces of her life in New York, Anna realized, it didn't feel all that clear that her life wasn't here too. Exactly where she'd thought it did not belong. This was unhelpfully confusing, she thought wryly. Not to mention impossible. Why think about what wasn't even an option?

Just then a silhouette looming up the path materialized into Jake, emerging from the dark in front of them. "Hi, ladies."

Haven let go of Anna and ran to hug him. "Congratulations, Jake—you did it! It was great."

Jake smiled, giving her a quick hug back. "I think congratulations are due all around. Good work, everyone. And Anna," he said, glancing over to her, "we were lucky to have you on the team."

She'd heard it from lots of folks by now, but it sure felt nice to hear him say it.

"Oh, *I* know," Haven exclaimed. "We need a picture! A team selfie!"

"Absolutely," Iris said, coming to put her arm around Jake on one side and Anna on the other. Haven, shorter than the others, stood in front of them and held up her phone. "Perfect, I can get all four of us. Smile!"

She clicked several shots, then inspected them. "Now Anna and Jake—I want a picture of the two of you!"

"Oh, well …" Anna began awkwardly, but Iris stepped to the side, pushing the two of them together. "I do too. Come on, Jake … Anna. For old times' sake."

Anna stepped up against Jake's shoulder and felt his arm slipping naturally around her waist. Sort of like at the wedding. That had been twice today. She could make a habit of this.

"Perfect," Haven said, checking the shot. "Oh, that's a keeper!"

"Can you text it to me?" Jake asked.

"Me too," Anna added, feeling a quiet gladness that Jake so quickly said he wanted a picture of them—together. In fact—had they ever had a picture of them, in the recesses of days long past? She scanned her memory, not coming up with anything. Then again, she hadn't been quite so photogenic then, hair always crazy and clothes that came from consignment in town, not online in this hip, new era of reuse/recycle.

"Done! I want to run back to the barn for a sec and get a few more down there. So I can remember the exact setup for our *next* event!" Haven disappeared down the path.

"And I," said Iris, "am going to see how the caterers are doing cleaning the kitchen and then put my feet up for a bit. You can manage out here, Jake?"

"Absolutely, Grandma," Jake said, giving her a peck on the cheek. "You've been a champ. Go in and take it easy."

As the door closed behind her, Jake turned back toward Anna. For the first time all day, Anna felt like the week's bustle had finally melted into a satisfying arrival, though exactly where she had arrived, she didn't know. How can you arrive when you're not home?

She focused instead on the man in front of her. "You really did do a brilliant job, Jake. I see these kinds of events all the time, and in some pretty posh places. You totally aced this one."

Jake inched his way into a brief smile, and Anna figured he rarely let himself enjoy a sense of success. "Thanks. I ... I feel good about it. Now I just have to figure out how to do it this well every time."

Anna nodded. "You're right, it's all about getting a whole system down. But you can do it. And I'm ..." She paused. "I'm just happy I got to see all this. Reconnect with the town and ... and you. It meant a lot to be part of your team. More than I knew." She tucked her hands in her back pockets, and her voice softened. "Thanks to the storm."

She expected him to turn and head down the path back to the barn, but to her surprise, Jake's eyes held hers without wavering. A smile flickered across his mouth, then quickly faded, and his face became even more unguarded than Anna had seen it since that afternoon at the wedding when their arms had briefly found each other.

The heat of anticipation shot through her, and her breath quickened.

Then—unexpectedly, but somehow insanely naturally—he turned toward her fully, reaching up lightly to touch her jaw with his finger, his other hand moving up to gently hold her shoulder.

"To storms," he said in a rough, quiet voice, almost a whisper.

Her own voice was a whisper as she fully faced him, overpowered by the end of the evening and the feel of Jake's finger on her cheek. "To storms."

He tilted her face to his and haltingly leaned in to brush her forehead with his lips. She felt his breath as he moved his lips lightly down her nose. He pulled back only slightly to look once more at her. Then, his eyes closing, he gently filled the remaining space between them and leaned down, touching his lips against hers.

For once—on neither his part nor hers—there was no retreat. Until—

"Jake? Jake?" Haven's voice came up the path in the dark.

The spell broken, they pulled quickly apart. Anna cleared her throat and crossed her arms, smoothing her hands up and down her bare skin. Her mouth hummed with warmth. She could still smell his skin, and it smelled crazy good.

"Yeah," Jake called back. "I'm here. What's up?"

Haven reached the patio and spotted them toward the side. "I think Mr. Samuels from Taggarts is leaving and he wants to speak with you first," she said, slightly out of breath. "Can you come down to the barn? Like, right now? He's ready to go."

"On my way."

Jake only met her eyes for a second before disappearing down the path.

Back in the glow of the kitchen lamps, watching the caterers clearing out the last of their equipment, Anna knew the glow had to be coming as much from her as from anything else. It felt as insane as last weekend when she found herself inexplicably in Cedarwood Spring riding in a truck in a rainstorm with Jake Petersen.

Had that only been a week ago? How was that possible? Time had both raced ... and stopped.

And now, just like then, she felt like she needed to repeat the reality over and over to herself. Only this time, it wasn't riding in a truck. This time it was ... overlooking a romantic party at his inn on a magical night. Jake Petersen kissed me.

Jake Petersen kissed me.

"*You're* looking dreamy." The voice of the caterer cut into her admittedly dreamy thoughts. A sweaty fortyish man, his white shirt wrinkled with the evening's end, was loosely folding used towels. "I'm Albert. I know Jake introduced us but we haven't gotten a chance to chat much tonight. Been pretty busy."

"It's been terrific."

"I've followed your work for the past couple of years up in New York. You're really good. Local girl conquers the big city. It's cool to meet you."

Wow, could tonight *get* any better. Anna touched her cheeks, sure they were flaming. "Thank you, I'm so flattered. You did a great job yourself tonight. The food was amazing, and your staff are really professional. Are you based here in Cedarwood Spring?"

"I'm originally from a couple of towns over. But I run the business right out of Cedarwood Spring, down on Main Street. Called Purveyor. You should stop in anytime and give us some advice. We do events for miles in any direction and run into all kinds of situations." He gave an eye roll. "I mean, *all* kinds, if you know what I mean."

Anna laughed—it was fun to be talking shop right here at Cedarwood Spring Inn. "I'll bet. You and I are in the same biz, after all, and I know the crazy stuff I run into."

"It's true. I can't imagine all the stuff you've seen. You learn to cover your butt pretty quickly." He winked.

"Totally." Anna pointed to a tablet that was leaning up against one of the boxes on the worktable. On it ran a video feed from the front door of the barn. She could see people walking by the videocam. "Is that part of cover-your-butt? Or just research?"

Albert gave a quick laugh. "Probably both! Learned the hard way. I was doing a wedding on the other side of the valley. I was busy avoiding a disaster in the kitchen with some cream puffs about to go wrong. The guy who was my runner—the one who's supposed to keep an eye on the eating area—stepped outside for a smoke and totally missed the fact that they were ready for the big entrance of a flambé. Everyone was applauding—and no flambé. I barely saved face, and I swore I would make sure that didn't happen again."

"Hey, that's a great idea. I can think of cool things to do with that in the plot of my new reality show." Though as she said it, the words felt unsettled.

"I think I saw something on that. Where are you doing it?"

Where, indeed. "That's just it. We have the concept, I have the dream. But we haven't settled into a home yet. So to speak. But they're supposed to be finishing up with a place in Soho, back in New York."

"A café without a home?"

Anna raised her eyebrows. "That pretty much says it all."

"Oh, it'll work out fine. And if it doesn't, then come back here. We could use you!"

Anna's heart gave a frisky flip. Dang, if only that were possible. But how, where? And wasn't she stuck—no, obligated—with the TV show?

Her eyes wandered back to the video feed on the pad.

"I've always thought it could make a good plot twist. You could use it in your show," Albert said. "Here—I'd muted it, but it actually picks up conversations pretty well." He tapped the screen. "Now if you'll excuse me."

He headed back out the door with a tub of platters to load onto his truck, and Anna leaned in, fuzzy from the wedding, the wine—and the kiss.

She smiled to herself, watching the video on the tablet with an almost distracted attention. Oh, there was Jake, right near the camera. And he was talking to Mr. Abbott and Mr. Samuels, the rep from Taggarts.

Anna jumped a little and leaned closer.

This was important. A good Taggarts rating would make such a difference. She could hear Jake's voice and tapped the tablet up to full volume, crossing her fingers for him. She could just hear them above the background din.

"So you're the manager of the venue?" Mr. Samuels was saying.

"Absolutely. Success or failure, you can hang it on me." Anna smiled again at the rough, low sound of Jake's voice and all that she knew was behind that statement. She silently cheered him on, watching fondly as he made his characteristic sweep of his hand through his hair.

"Well, I'd say a success. I want to make sure I understand how it works here. When we publish a review, people have to know they can count on the product being good—and unique. I've heard you're all about local sourcing—talent, materials. Is that what makes Cedarwood Spring Inn stand out?" Mr. Samuels stood with pen poised over paper.

There went his other hand through his hair. "Definitely. It's about being local, and about being excellent—both. Our whole message is that you don't have to sacrifice one for the other. We have the very best subcontractors, people who are the best of the best. But also people who are local. We really believe in supporting the local artisans, farmers, and ..." he paused "chefs."

"That's why we had the reception here," Mr. Abbott chimed in. "It's where James and Sarah grew up, and there's no need to go somewhere else for top-of-the-line quality. It's part of the new Cedarwood Spring business model."

Hmm. Was it really? Or was it just Mr. Abbott's old, settled habit of inserting himself into local business? That would explain a lot.

"Indeed," Mr. Samuels agreed. "I'm especially impressed with the high quality of every ..." He gestured around the barn. "... every single part of the event. The food, the lighting, magnificent. The use of long tables instead of round ones. And then ..." He gestured significantly, just off camera to where Anna knew the wedding cake was.

Her eyes widened. Oh, the cake—*her* cake! Did he like it?? She leaned in.

"And I have to tell you," Mr. Samuels went on, "as good as everything was, that wedding cake stood out as the real center-piece of the evening. So delicate and subtly flavored, and those white frosting flowers on the top just stunningly crafted. So that was made by someone local too?"

Someone "local"? Yes, of course she was local! And she'd never been prouder to be. She strained to hear Jake's answer.

He paused and cleared his throat before replying, averting his gaze from Samuels's face to look down. Anna frowned. Not a good sign.

It was Abbott who started in: "Jake only works with the folks we see here in town. A real hometown effort. You know, the people you meet on the street, in the café. In fact, it was that sweet gal who runs the Filling Station who made it, right? The one who makes all the great muffins? Jake wanted to give her a chance, didn't you, Jake?"

There was a pause, during which Anna's stomach recoiled. She could only see the back of Jake's head—and the telltale hand that ran over it.

"Yes, sir, absolutely." His voice sounded weaker. "Haven. She runs the Filling Station on Main Street—she made all the desserts."

"Ah, spectacular, spectacular. Well, give her my compli-ments, would you? I wouldn't mind tasting a wedding cake of hers again. Especially if she'd be working for your venue, I'm glad to especially recommend it for wedding receptions." He clicked the pen closed and slipped it into a shirt pocket. "Well, I'll be off now. I've got a bit of a long drive back. But it was worth it. Thank you again."

Anna slowly eased down onto one of the stools, her heart shrinking into something very small.

"Thank you, Mr. Samuels, Mr. Abbott. Have a safe drive home!" Jake's voice seemed distant.

Anna blinked around the empty kitchen, its light dimmed and a few remnants of the evening still here and there.

Surely she hadn't just heard him lie about her—about who she was and what she was capable of—to an important reviewer, a man who could influence her career as well as his. Surely, he hadn't just ignored the fact that she, too, was local, or had been. That she had been part of the team all week, working and planning and helping.

Surely, surely, Jake had not just out-and-out lied. But she had heard it. She wished to heaven she hadn't. But she couldn't kid herself. He had lied by omission, sure. It's not like he'd said she *didn't* do it.

But still, his words, 'a local woman.'

Like. She. Wasn't.

The old Annie inside of her bristled and ducked. Once again, like Papi, her talents, her work, were … invisible. And in front of Abbott, no less.

She felt a little sick. Talk about a plot twist.

"Hey, you OK?" Albert reappeared at the kitchen door, folded towels in hand. He frowned lightly. "You looked so happy a few minutes ago. Now you look like something … happened."

Anna nodded slowly, avoiding his eyes. "Just got some bad news about … about a friend."

"Hey, I'm sorry about that. And at the end of such a lovely evening. That's too bad." He leaned over and tapped the tablet screen blank. "Well, this is the last thing left. Time to take it and head out. I've got a couple of staff who'll come by tomorrow morning to pick up the last of the stuff. It's been a big day. Get some rest."

"Thanks. You too."

As the door closed behind him, Anna looked around the kitchen in a daze. Tears suddenly began to well up behind her eyes. Oh, no, I can't do this. Not here. Jake will be back in any minute.

She quickly picked up her phone and quietly slipped up the stairs.

◦◦◦

I should rise above this and get over it, Anna repeated to herself resolutely, as she laid out the dark-rinse jeans and white T-shirt she'd had on last Saturday. After all, she was kind of eavesdropping on the tablet—though it happened so fast, she didn't mean to be.

But "getting over it" didn't seem to be happening.

There was a mew at the door and the gentle rattling she'd come to know as Putz pushing his paw along the door jamb. Anna smiled gratefully and let him in, pushing the door closed behind him. This funky one-eyed cat was yet another thing that had become part of her in the space of one scant week. Boy, she'd miss him in Brooklyn.

As she stroked the cat's head, Anna kept straining painfully to put things together that just didn't go—like mismatched puzzle pieces whose edges didn't fit.

On one hand, Jake had just betrayed her. Even after this amazing week when they had slowly begun to open up to each other and—geez—she had just helped him out of a major pickle, he'd simply denied she'd done it. Or that sure was how it felt.

I mean, sure, I totally get the emphasis on local, she thought. Good heavens, it's what I do. It's the basis for my own café, my concept. But maybe that's why it hurt all the more; rightly or not, she was some version of local, and right at that moment, with Mr. Abbott standing right there for heaven's sake, she needed him to need *her*—and to show it. To say who she was and what she'd done.

On the other hand, she had to admit, Jake had taken her in

when *she* was the one in a pickle. How many guys in New York did she know who would take in a high school pal they hadn't seen in years, give them a dreamy place to stay, and involve them in their lives for a week? Not many.

And then ... there was the kiss.

The one that brought past and present together in what was probably the most breathtaking, barely-there kiss of her life.

Anna looked out the window toward the barn that was slowly darkening inside as Tom's team dismantled the lights. And the past week flew before her eyes. She remembered that first night here, looking out into the storm, straining to see what was behind the old inn. Then having Jake show it all to her, the gardens, the stream, the waterwheel. Explaining the nooks and crannies of his home—which were, of course, the nooks and crannies of his life. Then today, the feel of his hands over her eyes, his breath so close, about to reveal the magical place the barn had become. And then the kiss as they looked down at it all together.

She sighed and turned back toward her room, her heart dashed with sadness. Damn, that was the thing about magic. It was ... magic. Not the real thing.

It was going to take her a long time to sort it all out. These past days, she'd felt closer to herself as a kid than she had in years. And if you'd stopped her on the streets of New York and asked her if that would be a good thing, she would have sworn it would've been disastrous. And yet something in her gut told her that that *was* a good thing, in ways she'd have to figure out down the line.

But down the line it would be—not now. She shook her head unconsciously. The only thing she needed to do now was leave. Her time here was done, and whatever in her had irrationally, and completely unrealistically, wanted something magical to swoop in and transform reality, this was not, as she'd already sternly told herself, magic. It was life.

The kiss and the betrayal both hung raw in her heart. The detour was over. It was time to get back to work. She'd sort out whatever needed sorting once she got back to the city.

Anna picked up her phone slowly, casting about on the small wooden desk for the business card of Seb's car repair.

"Seb? Yeah, hi, it's Anna. I'm sorry it's so late."

His voice sounded easy on the other end. "No problem, I just got back from the party myself. Everything seemed to go great. Is Jake happy?"

Her heart squeezed. "Definitely. Seb, you'd mentioned my car was ready. I should have gone ahead and made arrangements with you, but with so much going on, I forgot. Can I pick it up and pay you tomorrow morning?"

"Sure, of course. We offer car service for people picking up their vehicles. I can have my assistant drive out and pick you up."

"That would be a real lifesaver."

"Time?"

She didn't want to see anyone tomorrow morning—it would be easier that way. She glanced out the window where she could still see shadows moving around on the grounds, cleaning up and escorting the last guests to cars. Tomorrow Jake and Iris would be so exhausted, they'd surely sleep in.

She could escape early. "Would around six be too early?

"You don't want to get some rest after that big shindig?"

"No, no, I … I need to get back home. You know, things to do." She tried to sound light.

"OK, 6 a.m. it is. I'll tell Marv to look for you out front."

As she hung up, her words rang in her head: I need to get back home. Back home.

When she closed her eyes that night, lying back in the simple, luxurious bed that had cradled her all week, images from the town, the inn, and Jake mixed in with bits from Brooklyn,

Sierra and Rubin, and her TV café that didn't yet have a home, like some strange sidewalk-chalk drawing.

"Home" seemed to hover everywhere—and nowhere.

CHAPTER 7

R ain spat into Jake Petersen's face as he stood at the back door, looking beyond the threshold to the garden. Beyond it lay the barn and the fields, sodden with the morning's unexpected rainfall.

Perfect, he thought. Rain had brought her to me, and rain took her away.

If nothing else, he appreciated the symmetry.

Of course, he appreciated a lot. Last night had gone off without a hitch. In spite of his usual tendency away from optimism, he was hopeful about the Taggarts review, compulsively checking his phone for news of the posting even though he knew it would be a few days till he got word. That's what Samuels had said.

And the whole team had gotten the last of the stuff from last night cleaned up this morning really well. Tom and his staff had been champs, and so had Albert and his crew, and Pete and Tina, and of course Haven and …

Anna. Jake realized he was staring right at the place where, just the night before, they had stood.

And he had kissed her. And she had barely kissed him back.

Not that she'd had the chance. Haven had shown up, he had to go talk to Samuels. And then somehow, after Jake had gotten through wrapping up everything at the barn and all the cars had purred back down the long driveway, he'd hurried back into the house, anxiously hoping to find her there. But she'd apparently gone up to bed. And he'd spent too much of what remained of the night going over and over what he would say to her this morning. Got almost no sleep until just before dawn, when he'd fallen into a heavy doze.

And when he got to 'this morning,' Anna was gone. No chance to say anything.

What the heck had happened? The edges of his mouth tugged down, as he glanced at the dregs in his mug. Of course, she was gone. Her life was in New York, she was here accidentally, so he knew she was going to leave—like she had years ago.

Still, it seemed to be shockingly fast. And no goodbye. Just … gone.

Why? Wouldn't she at least have had breakfast, talked about how it all went? They'd talked about every detail that week. What could have made her check out like that?

He quickly scanned the day before. Starting with the wedding, all the way up to … the kiss.

It was the kiss. It had to be the kiss, he thought. I shouldn't have tried it. Anna's a glamorous, gorgeous woman who didn't come back to Cedarwood Spring to have some guy fall for her. I'm sure she has plenty of those in New York. No wonder she hightailed it out of Cedarwood Spring … again.

Of course, he hadn't given her a chance to say one way or the other, since that was right when Haven had come to tell him about Samuels. And he'd headed down to the barn to do his big pitch about how unique the place was, and how the team was local.

Local.

As his memory scanned beyond the kiss, down at the barn

and his chat with Samuels and Abbott, Jake suddenly memory freeze-framed on the last thing he'd said to them. 'Who made the wedding cake,' Samuels had asked. Not that Jake wouldn't have immediately answered that it was Anna, and that she was local, only local-makes-big.

But Abbott had, as he will, jumped in to make a business pitch for Cedarwood Spring. Not that he blamed him; Mr. Abbott had done a lot to make Cedarwood Spring what it was. He wasn't a bad guy. And Jake had indeed told him Haven was making the cake—and it simply hadn't come up in those last hours before the wedding that Haven would have "help."

So in the moment, standing right in front of Samuels and Abbott at the final moment of judgment—or so it had seemed—Jake had buckled. Said whatever would close the conversation seamlessly so he could jet back up the hill to Anna. Not that he'd lied, exactly—Haven had been involved. But still, it was only at this moment that the full impact hit him: it hadn't been the real truth, a real truth that mattered because of what he knew it meant to Anna. Thank goodness, she hadn't heard it. Well, hopefully it would all get lost in the mix.

Still … something moved uneasily in him.

"There you are, darling." Iris's voice cut into his thoughts as she came through the kitchen to the outside door. She put her hands on his shoulders from behind, giving him a squeeze, and looked around past him to the barn. "You feeling OK about everything? Did Tom get it cleaned up before the rain came?"

"Yeah, yeah, of course. They all did great. You did too, Grandma. Thanks." A gust of wind blew rain into the doorway, and Jake led them back to the kitchen, pulling the door closed. He gave a small snort in spite of himself—or maybe *to* spite himself. "What is it about Saturdays and rainstorms around here?"

Iris looked at him gently. "That's right, it was just a week ago we had the big storm. And we were so worried about damage."

Jake nodded, pouring himself some more coffee.

"And as it turns out, the storm didn't hurt us at all. It helped us. It brought us Anna. Wasn't that a lucky stroke." Iris's voice remained light.

Without looking at her, Jake frowned and slid onto a stool at the worktable, dangling a spoon in his mug. The lamps in the kitchen gave it a comforting glow against the gray that was outside, and there were only a couple of boxes of Albert's remaining catering supplies.

Now it looked like it had been before. Just as warm, familiar, and inviting, everything clean and cared for, like Iris kept it. Like it had always been.

Except that now it felt incomplete. There was something hollow about it. Something missing.

Jake glared into middle distance. "She left pretty quick." He looked up at Iris. "So she didn't talk to you before she left?"

Iris eyed him, shaking her head. "My answer is the same as it was the last time you asked me. No. I didn't see her. And I got up pretty early—my body was on the same time clock it always is."

He stared into his cup, trying to mask the range of feelings knocking around inside of him. Not that he could identify all of them. But pain was definitely in the mix.

"I was kind of surprised she'd left without a goodbye, but I'm sure there was a reason," Iris said. "It was good having her here all week, and in some way, it felt like she belonged. Don't you think so?"

Jake shrugged, even as something inside of him was saying, hell, yes, it felt like she belonged. A flicker of anger sprang up.

But this is crazy, he thought. She doesn't owe us anything.

"Of course, we knew she'd have to go," Iris continued. "After all, she lives in New York. And Jake?" She met his eyes. "The fact that Anna had to leave, for whatever reason, doesn't mean it's like Margaret."

That flicker of anger he'd felt now popped into a full flame. His post-flower-child grandmom had an irritating way of cutting to the brutal chase. And this time she was chasing something he wasn't sure he felt ready for, something Haven had mentioned as well.

"Margaret," he snarled. "What does she have to do with anything?"

Unruffled, Iris got up and put water in the electric kettle, flicking it on. "Maybe I should be asking you that."

"What are you talking about, Grandma?" He knew he sounded irritated. But anything to keep the issue at bay.

"I mean, the fact that you and Margaret hurt each other when you were both really young doesn't mean that Anna's doing the same thing. Oh, I know it might look the same on the surface. The kind of work they're both in, how they're both successful. But that doesn't mean it's the same underneath. Of course she was going back to the city. But not for the same reasons Margaret did. And it doesn't have to mean the same thing."

"Remind me again why this is even a topic?"

Iris opened the tea tin emphatically. "Because you're clearly unresolved about Anna. And maybe she is about you too. You don't know, and you don't know because you haven't asked her. The fact that she left doesn't mean that it's the end of the story."

Jake cast a baleful look toward her. "Is this one of your feelings talks?" He was annoyed but at the same time didn't want her to stop.

"Yes, this is a feelings talk." As if to emphasize the fact, Iris pulled out a favorite teacup and put some loose tea in the old flowered teapot.

Oh, no, not the teapot. The point of no return.

But maybe that was a good thing. Somehow it felt better that she was asking these questions. There had always been a deep wisdom in Iris, and Jake grudgingly knew he needed it. Like medicine.

"You get lunch?" she asked.

"Not hungry."

"I see." As the water boiled, Iris pulled a plate of plain ginger cookies from the cabinet. "I kept these aside, just in case we needed something basic after all the fancy goodies yesterday."

"Aw, Grandma, you're the best." Jake reached for one and crunched the edge of it.

Iris poured the hot water into the teapot, the steam temporarily fogging up her glasses. She looked at Jake, raising her eyebrows over the whited-out lenses, and they both laughed —a long-standing joke between them ever since he was a kid.

"Feeling better?" she asked as she sat back down. Putz jumped up onto the table, and she stroked his head before shifting him back down.

"A bit."

"Good. So now you can answer my question."

"Which was?"

"Even though Anna's gone back, how are you going to find out what's next in the story?"

"How do you know there is a 'next'?"

"Because I can see it's not the end. Jacob Daniel Petersen, I know you. I don't know Anna well, and I don't know why she left without saying goodbye to any of us. But I do know that if you don't try to find out, it's not like it's going away. It's not like you're going to just forget this week. Something changed. You can't go back." Iris reached back and authoritatively tightened the low ponytail that held her soft, white hair.

Jake looked at her fondly. "Grandma, you old fox. You know how to nail it, don't you?

"Yes, at my age, I'll take credit for that," Iris said, taking a first sip of steaming tea. "The mistakes we make when we're young … that's fine. They get us to grow. Like you and Margaret. But the mistakes we make when we're older … you don't want that to be the mistake of thinking the past will only repeat itself."

"The mistake I made with Margaret was trusting her." Jake's voice had a bitter edge.

"No-o-o," Iris said, looking heavenward. "The mistake you made with Margaret was more like just not paying attention to what she wanted—and what you wanted. You were both so young, neither one of you probably even knew. I think you always felt pressure to keep up with the family and she looked like a way to do that."

"You mean, to live up to the Petersen lore?"

"That's it. I loved your dad like crazy. He was a great son. But I'm not sure how helpful he was to you, helping you learn how to carry the weight of this place and know where to go with it. You were always expected to somehow rise to everything on your own. It's not like there was a map to get there."

Jake nodded slightly, trying desperately to stifle the lump that suddenly rose in his throat. "He was always pushing for this place to be better, but it never felt clear how. It never felt like enough. Then we finished fixing the place up right when the recession really hit, and everything seemed to tank."

"Mm-hmm. It's my guess that when you proposed to Margaret, you jumped a little too fast, just to try to do the right thing. To stabilize. And thinking back to the pressure her family put on her, maybe she said yes for the same reason."

Jake hesitated, watching his grandmom. He'd come this far —why not clarify a bit of misinformation. "Grandma?"

"Yes?"

"There's something I don't think I ever mentioned about that."

Iris raised her eyebrows.

"I didn't ... I didn't actually do the proposing. She more like said that it would be a good idea, and I thought, why not." He gave a dry laugh. "To be this old, divorced, and I don't even know what it feels like to propose to somebody."

"Well, knowing Margaret, that makes sense. She was a take-charge gal—it was one of her talents. And as for proposing to someone—the right someone—it just means that that's simply an experience you still have to look forward to. The fact that she was the wrong person doesn't mean it was the wrong idea."

Jake gave her a grimace and took a sip of his coffee. "Where do you come *up* with this stuff?"

"Life. But what about your life, Jake? Back to my point. Isn't that space still there? The space you had thought Margaret would fill?"

Jake shifted on his stool. This was uncomfortably close. "OK, OK, I get it."

"Do you? Then talk to Anna."

He looked startled—how had she ingeniously circled back around to Anna?

"Oh don't look so shocked," Iris said affectionately. "It was pretty clear to see."

"What was?"

"The two of you. There's something special there, Jake. There always was, even years ago. And you've been stuck in life lately. Don't get me wrong. You've done a wonderful job with the inn—you really should be proud of yourself. And now, hopefully, it'll launch. But there's some piece of your life you've never really gotten back to … since Margaret."

Jake felt his defenses spike. "The inn is my life, Grandma."

"That's fine, as long as it's not your whole life. You need to get unstuck. And I think Anna's the unstick-er."

Jake sighed heavily and looked balefully at her from underneath his sandy brow. "And how exactly is that supposed to work?"

"Well, that's the question, isn't it?"

~

She'd only been back in the city a few days, but it felt like longer. If was as if some strange time warp meant that the woman who had headed out to the Poconos on Memorial Day weekend in her BMW was no longer the same woman who now sat in a hip Midtown bistro.

She had walked into the looking glass.

Make that a fun-house mirror.

New York was gray and strangely cool for June. But then, Anna thought, as she gazed out the restaurant window at nothing in particular, everything felt gray and strangely cool. And not "cool" in the good way.

She glanced at her black-leather watch. 1:20. They were supposed to have met at one, but then Sierra and Rubin were both chronically late. And she was still chronically early.

Note to self: Break the "early" habit and start being late, or I'll never get anywhere in this biz.

She shifted in the sleek chair of the equally sleek restaurant —one of the spots where her business contacts seemed to be seen, though that too changed with distracting impermanence. Her heels, snug black pencil skirt, and Dolce & Gabbana jacket (bought online second-hand, but who knew?) felt familiar and comforting. The bustle of waiters and the buzz of clientele were almost frenetic, as if whatever they said over lunch would have to propel them through a long tiring afternoon.

"Darling, there you are!"

Even when she was expecting Rubin's voice, it always made her jump. She turned as he hurried up, looking like his job was his biggest pain and also his biggest love. Anna knew it was both.

She reached up for a quick hug, as Rubin gave big, wide air-kisses with a "mwah, mwah." It was always a weird combo of stressful and reassuring to see Rubin. He reminded her of something out of *The Producers*, his bald pate shining and his large fashionable glasses perpetually sliding down his nose.

He slid into a chair opposite her and started pulling papers out of his ubiquitous zippered pouch. "We've got final paperwork for you to sign off on, and, well, just sign." He started sorting through the top sheets. "When did you get back?"

"Last Saturday. Where's Sierra? I thought she'd be with you."

"She is—stopped in the Ladies. Ah, there she is."

Sierra hustled over to the table, learning down to give Anna a hug. "Hey, girl, it's so good to see you!"

Seeing her friend reminded Anna how much she'd missed her. Sierra was only a few years older than she was, but like Anna, she'd really worked her way up. And somehow, Anna thought, watching Sierra settle in making yummy sounds over a menu, she'd never seemed to become jaded or cynical about the whole media biz—which would have been as easy for her as a Black woman as it could have been for Anna as a Latina.

Yet here they sat, rising to every challenge. In fact, Anna thought fleetingly, Sierra had probably risen to challenges that Anna never even knew about.

The waiter came by and took their orders—multiple appetizers were always what Rubin insisted on. Said it was better for midday protein. As the waiter hustled away, Rubin picked up his phone, pushing his thick glasses pointedly up, and peered down the end of his nose as he began scrolling through.

"So, my dear, it's good that you're finally back." He looked at her over his glasses, then back to the phone. "Now—I have about a half-dozen interviews lined up. Just need to confirm the times with you so I can set everything up with the stylist. I got

Henna—you liked her, right? She did fabulous things with your hair before."

Anna nodded yes, remembering briefly how it had felt to let her hair do its own thing back at the inn. She'd changed it with her moods, to be sure, but whether in a chignon or down loose around her shoulders—fleetingly she flashed on Jake's hand there, then pushed the thought aside—it had felt comfortable, sexy.

"Hey, Anna, I said to look at these and confirm the times for me," Rubin's voice broke into her thoughts. "Or do you want me to forward this to you?"

"Oh, sorry," Anna said, gathering herself and reaching for his phone. "Sure, let me take a look."

Sierra was watching her thoughtfully. "Feel like you're having to jump back in quickly?"

Anna looked at her gratefully. "Yeah." She scrolled through the note on Rubin's phone, squinting a bit.

He didn't miss it. "Glasses, baby, in your future. But we have to get good frames—check with Henna when you see her. Or—" he looked at her pointedly—"it's never too early for laser treatments."

Anna sighed. This was all feeling like more than she could process at once. "I'm fine, Rubin, for now. Though, thank you for your concern. These all look fine. Looks like the first one is tomorrow morning. Tell Henna I'll see her then—at your office?"

"Perfect," he said, abstractly scrolling through emails. "These will take most of the next few days."

Anna looked down at her lemon-slice-laden glass of water. "Oh, I ..." It was only as he said that that she realized she needed something else.

"What? We've had to delay these past bits since you were hanging out in the boonies. We gotta get back on track."

"What's up?" Sierra said gently, ducking to catch Anna's eyes.

Anna shrugged lightly. "Definitely, we're on for the interviews. I just thought ... I thought I'd spend a little time in the kitchen."

"Why?" Rubin asked incredulously, pulling off his glasses.

"Just puttering. You know—getting ready."

He shook his head, pushing his glasses back on. "You don't need to get ready in a kitchen—you need to get ready with the stylist. Not that you don't look fabulous—you always do. But she needs to get settled with some possible looks for you—different ways of doing your hair, and of course the clothes. The *clothes*!"

Anna flashed back to the jeans and T-shirt she wore puttering happily around the worktable in the kitchen at the inn. Pushing Putz off the counter. Sipping Iris's tea. Listening for Jake's footfall.

She cleared her throat and refocused on Rubin. "Of course. The clothes."

"And then hair and makeup," he continued. "There's fabulous stuff Henna can do with your coloring—remember, she specializes in makeup for darker skin. You're going to be a knockout, and it'll be so great for more women to identify with you. You're really pushing the envelope."

Anna looked at Sierra pleadingly, though what she was pleading for, she couldn't have said.

Sierra took the cue. "Rubin, you're right. Anna's a great role model, and it's great to have a stylist who knows how to show how terrific our skin and hair are. But there are lots of ways she has to get ready for the shoot. Appearance is only one of them."

Relief shot through Anna. "Thanks. And Rubin, thanks for all you're doing. I'm not saying it's not important, and it's all we've worked on for months. I just ... miss baking."

Rubin looked up, a frustrated expression on his face. "Didn't you get enough of that out in Cedar Bluff or Cedar Boonies or whatever it is? Isn't this what you want?"

Anna's eyes flickered, which Sierra registered.

"Of course it is. I'm super excited. I want to help other women. But I also need to do it ... as me."

Rubin looked at her blankly.

"I think some kitchen time is a great idea," Sierra broke in. "It'll help me with blocking out the shots. I got all the mockups you did in ..." She glanced pointedly at Rubin. "... Cedarwood Spring. Thanks again for doing that on top of ... time with your friends there. Now we need to walk it through. Can we do it in the kitchen of the new place? It's almost all set up, just some final arrangements and permits, and the show will have a home."

"Home," Anna echoed her, feeling that now-familiar tug of Cedarwood Spring.

"Home. Love Bite café." As she said it, Sierra visibly winced a bit at the name, and Anna giggled in spite of herself.

Rubin looked baffled. "What's funny?"

"The name," Sierra said, laughing. "It gets me every time."

"Hey, it took a night of major margarita drinking to come up with that. It was no small feat! I trademarked it."

"And we love it," Anna assured him. "Sierra, thanks, sure, that sounds like a good plan. Is everything there at the restaurant, the way we'd organized it?"

"We have most of the camera equipment, and lighting rigs —" Sierra began.

"No, no, I meant ..." Anna glanced down. Case in point. "Flour. Sugar. The creamery butter and eggs from the place upstate, the French salt, yeast, the extracts from that cool couple in Vermont ... you know, the stuff the show is really made of."

Sierra laughed. "I like that. The show is like a cake."

"It *is*. And real cake has to actually be at the center of it all."

Rubin kept his eyes on his phone but mumbled audibly, "That's not *all* the show is."

Sierra ignored him, shuffling through papers in her large leather bag. "Let's see what's there. Here's the invoice for the food we ordered."

Anna took the sheet from her, glancing down the list. As she quickly scanned the vendors and items, her heart sank even as her anxiety spiked—not a good sign. She looked back up at both of them. "It's not my list. I mean, some of it is. But there are some substitutions." She looked pointedly at Rubin, who kept his eyes on his phone. "You said you'd make sure it was followed exactly, Rubin."

"Sorry, I gave that to my assistant. I guess he punted when he couldn't find it."

Anna suddenly felt the urge to run her fingers through her hair—geez, even when she wasn't with Jake, she still carried him inside. "Did your assistant order from the wineries, distilleries, and coffee roasters that I gave you?"

Rubin averted his eyes. "Uhhhh. I think so?"

Anna set the paper down and took a deep breath. "Guys, I love you, and you know I think the concept of the show is cool. But the whole idea of my being able to take a break was that you'd be able to get this final stuff ready." She leaned back and expelled a shot of breath.

Sierra glanced at her watch. "Anna, the ingredients are important—I totally agree. Let me ask my assistant to help with whatever the last pieces are." She looked pointedly at Rubin. "But in the meantime, I do need to get in the kitchen with you and a camera and at least start blocking it out. Can you deal with these ingredients for now, since they're already there? While we're working on getting the right stuff?"

"Sure, of course," Anna said quickly. She hadn't meant to hang Sierra up—it was just that the show seemed to be getting farther and farther from ... well, from her. And it felt really lousy to be disappointed by the things her friends were excited about. The gap seemed to be growing. "Most of what I wanted is there anyway. It was just a few substitutions. No problem. When do you want to do it?"

"Soon as possible."

"Anytime at the Soho café space is fine." Anna patted Sierra's arm. "After all, that was the deal. We said I could get away, and when I got back, I'd be all yours."

"Well, if this doesn't sound too crazy, how about this afternoon? I'm heading over to the restaurant anyway to see how the permits and setup are going. I just have to stop by the office first. Meet you over there after that?"

"Sounds good."

"Now, speaking of food, let's eat some."

Hmm. "Love Bite." As she wandered through the dark seating area of the empty, half-equipped café toward the kitchen, Anna felt a frustrated affection for Rubin. It had seemed like a good idea at the time. Not that it wasn't cute and catchy—but the name of the place had started to sound more like Rubin than like her.

She ran her fingers along the chair backs, hearing Sierra's voice recede behind her. She was talking to the manager about the permitting, and Anna tried to block out the fact that Sierra's voice was sounding uncomfortably animated.

Oh well, not her problem. What was her problem was making sure the kitchen felt like home. Like … the inn.

Home. There was that pesky word again.

As she walked into the dark kitchen and felt the wall for the light switch, Anna tried to physically shake off the image of the kitchen at the inn—or more to the point, shake off how it had felt. It was a nice vacation. But it could not become her point of comparison for anything else. It was only a detour, and you don't mix up a side road with the right road.

Ah, there was the switch. She flicked it on.

The kitchen lit up before her, glaring and bright from what she realized were already the studio lights installed around the room. The stainless-steel worktables in the center gleamed glaring and cold. Anna scanned the counters and the large multibay sink. No lamps along the edges, no way to create different moods for different times of the day.

She tried to imagine the space filled with people—with staff and crew and camera equipment and lighting and scaffolding. What they'd planned all along. And she felt like she didn't belong.

All the plans—nothing wrong with them, and maybe it did all belong right here at Love Bite. It just didn't feel like she did anymore.

Man, this was *really* inconvenient. And what other possible options even existed?

Feeling a yawning emptiness inside, Anna instinctively reached for her phone and flicked through the pictures with her thumb till she came to ones she'd taken of Iris at the sink, Iris smiling over a fresh pan of scones, the farmhouse-style way the old white dinner plates were stacked on open shelves, Putz sniffing at something on the counter. Anna smiled. She'd said she took the pictures to remember how the kitchen was set up— something she liked to do with kitchens she visited. But as she slowly swiped to the pictures of the barn, the gardens, and … the selfie of all four of them Haven had taken and texted her, she knew she wished she could not just remember it, but be there. Again.

And then the picture Haven had taken of her and Jake.

She'd worn out her phone screen swiping through those all week, always ending up at the one of her and Jake.

Anna sighed, setting the phone down and looking around

once more. With a sinking heart—and this time, no anxiety, just an icy calm—she realized: This feels soulless to me.

A kitchen without a soul. That was startling close to a life without a soul.

The sound of footsteps made her turn abruptly. Sierra emerged from the dark seating area followed by a couple of beefy guys she had introduced earlier as cameramen who'd agreed to help her map out angles.

"Ready to go?" Sierra's voice was terse.

"Yeah, sure. Everything OK?" Anna asked. It felt like everything was getting a little edgy.

"Sure. I just wish the manager would get on the ball to get this permitting wrapped up." Sierra set her hands on her hips firmly and motioned around the kitchen. "But right now, this is what we're doing. Guys?"

As they began mapping out where cameras would be set up and where key staff—or actors, as Anna still thought of them—would be, Anna moved around the kitchen, pulling out the ingredients, which were not the ones she'd ordered, and trying to make it feel like a groove. Flour, sugar, metal measuring cups, and stainless-steel bowls all came off shelves and hooks onto the worktables in the center under super-bright lights.

She tried to pull together basic dough—for cookies, no big deal—so the crew could set up the angles. But it felt stiff, and the tools—measuring cups, tablespoons—that were normally as natural to her as using a toothbrush felt alien in her hands. She missed the feel of the crockery, the weight of a ceramic bowl for hand mixing. She even dropped measuring spoons onto the floor, which she never did.

Several times, Sierra gave her a glance that seemed to say she understood, but that this simply needed to be done. Dutifully, Anna worked the dough, eventually pulling out of the oven a pan of light, crumbly sugar cookies that melted in her mouth.

"Think you got everything you needed?" she asked Sierra, as

she pulled the last sheet from the large industrial oven. "Were those diagrams I did for you back in Cedarwood Spring OK?"

"Definitely. We still have to do final setup for the seating area, but we can come back for that. The manager hasn't gotten that together yet either." Sierra looked heavenward. "OK, guys, it's a wrap. Thanks for coming out."

"No problem," one of them said, pulling a camera off a pivot. "Though it's kind of hard always getting the right shot. Anna keeps moving around so much. Hey, Anna—" She raised her eyebrows. "I know this is all about baking and everything. But could you maybe have some of the food already made—like order it in from somewhere? Or make it in advance. Just some of the basic, uh, stuff. It would be less complicated that way, and we can get straight to the action with the staff and customers."

Anna stood dumbly, still trying to process the question. "Bring in ready-made food to a bakery-café so that the show is less about baking?" she repeated slowly.

"Well, yeah," he said absently, missing her irony as he wrapped a cord between his thumb and his elbow. "This show could end up really big. You would never have to worry about baking again."

Sierra quickly took the reins. "No, definitely not. This is about what Anna does so creatively in the kitchen. We'll make it work, guys."

"Got it." He gave a thumbs-up as the two men headed back through the darkened restaurant. "See you tomorrow."

"Yep, see you tomorrow." Sierra turned back toward Anna, who still stood, blinking. "Sorry about that, girl. They're pros at camera, but they don't always get the creative thinking behind a show."

Anna shook her head slowly. "It's no problem. They're just doing their job. So are you, you're doing a great job. And so is Rubin, actually. You're all doing exactly what you're supposed to."

"It sounds like there's a 'but' coming?"

"I don't know." Anna frowned lightly. "I've been excited about this, and we've all worked so hard on it for months. It would make such a difference for my career, and yours and Rubin's."

Sierra slid up onto the counter, her legs dangling off, and pulled her water bottle over. "Hmm. Anna, you do know that's not enough of a reason to do something like this ..." She gestured around the kitchen. "... this big. Hell, the camera equipment outnumbers the baking utensils. What's up with you? It's great to have you back—but it doesn't really feel like you're really ... back."

Anna leaned against the work island, smoothing her now-floury black skirt and missing her jeans. "What do you mean?"

"I mean, it feels kind of like you left some part of you back in Cedarwood Spring."

"You're right, I think I did too." Anna flashed a sharp look at her. "That's ironic. I worked so hard to get out of there because it never felt like I belonged, like I was invisible. And now I've built a world in New York where I'm super visible—" she jerked her head toward one of the cameras—"and it feels like part of me is back in Cedarwood Spring where I thought I never wanted to be."

"So you felt like you weren't seen back there?"

Anna nodded.

"Well, you may have felt that way. But it doesn't mean it was the truth." Sierra picked up her water bottle and took a swig. "Is this about the guy you were staying with?"

Anna looked at her, startled.

"Oh come on. I could tell when I talked to you while you were still down there. Something happened—something I haven't seen happen with you before. What's up?"

Anna sighed and looked down, picking the sugar from under

her manicured fingernails. "You're right. Something did happen. I just don't understand what it was."

"With him?"

Anna nodded.

"Name, please?"

Anna hesitated, then smiled. "Jake." It felt sweet to say his name. Not that she knew what to do with that feeling. In fact, it felt so nice, she said it again, with more oomph. "Jake."

"Good name. Solid." Sierra took another swig. "He's special to you, I can see it. You knew him from before?"

"Yeah, we were friends … really good friends … all through high school."

"Did you date?"

Anna shook her head vigorously. "No, it wasn't like that. He was part of the popular crowd. And I was …"

"Invisible?"

"Yeah. Just not to him."

"Wow." Sierra slid off the counter. "One of those deals. The good-looking nice-guy who noticed you in high school becomes the good-looking *interesting man* who notices you again … years later. Sound about right?"

"You pretty much nailed it."

"My guess is that you're interesting to him too."

Anna nodded again, wary of the pain that sat incongruously beside the pleasure of thinking of Jake. "I don't know. See … that last night before I left, something happened."

"Uh-oh, doesn't sound good."

"That's just it. At first it was—it was amazing, actually. We …" Better to go ahead and name it. "We kissed."

"Wow, lady. First time ever?"

Anna nodded weakly. First time in real life. But of course, the thousandth time in her imagination.

"Sounds beautiful. So what happened."

"Well, a friend, Haven, came up, and Jake had to go down to the barn. To talk to the rep from Taggarts."

"Taggarts was there? That's a big deal."

"Right? So to make the story short, there was a video feed I saw up in the kitchen, and I heard Jake …" Now saying his name felt painful. "I heard him tell the guy that someone else baked the wedding cake. A woman in town who helped me, really sweet gal. It was her first, and she was learning, but—"

"But it was the cake *you* made."

Anna nodded again, looking up at her, unable to go on.

Sierra let out a low whistle. "OK, I'm starting to get it now."

"Get what?"

"Why you're not totally back here in New York." Sierra glanced at her watch. "Oh, shoot, I'm due back at the office. But girl, you can't leave me hanging. I want the full scoop. I'll call you later. In the meantime …"

"In the meantime, what?" Anna wiped her eyes with the back of her hand.

"Why aren't you calling him? It sounds worth it, you know."

Anna frowned quickly. "I heard what he said—it was clear as day. He should be calling me to explain. Only … of course, he doesn't know I heard it." She shrugged lightly. "And anyway, I don't want a repeat of Carson. I just wanted to … get out."

Sierra nodded. "You and Carson dated a long time. I know I only met you around the time you broke up, but to be honest, when you talked about him, it never felt to me like you two were really connected. You can tell when somebody talks. But I've told you that before."

"Yeah, you have." Anna gave a dry laugh. "I just wish I'd figured it out sooner. About me, I mean. We sort of looked right, so I ignored that fact that it didn't feel right. Of course, the wake-up call was finding out that he was having heavy-duty business lunches with a gorgeous female colleague. Then when I confronted him …"

"What?"

"He said I was 'great,' but that he wasn't interested in my world. You know what else he said?"

Sierra shook her head.

Anna winced, knowing she'd never mentioned it before because it was too painful. She took a deep breath. "He'd said, 'You're just a cook.'"

Sierra's jaw dropped. "That's insane. I'm so sorry. What an idiot."

"Yeah, but you know, the thing is, *I'm* the one who felt like the idiot. I believed he had wanted me."

Sierra started putting a sheaf of papers in order. "You were not the idiot, I promise you. You gave him a vote of confidence. The fact that he wasn't worth it doesn't mean it was the wrong thing to do. Just the wrong person."

A spark of hope danced, uninvited, in Anna's heart. "You mean, it *could* work with the right person?" she asked, letting herself name what she knew had been lurking under the shadows of her sadness.

Sierra turned emphatically toward her. "Absolutely. Are you crazy? You're amazing, and lots of men would love to be with you."

"Oh yeah, like the guys over at the producer's office?"

"No way. Those guys will always be around, and they're more interested in what you do for them than for what they do for you. Trust me."

"I do."

"OK then. Someone like Jake who you knew, and who knew you, and now you're drawn together as the amazing people you've become? That's what I would trust."

"Really? How can I trust him? I wasn't sure if I should even try to talk to him again. I know I left in too much of a hurry. And it's all unresolved. But I guess I was waiting." Though something in her knew that talking to him again was inevitable.

"Waiting?" Sierra's hands went to her hips again. "So how's all that waiting working for you?"

Anna's heart opened even more, and the words tumbled out in a whisper. "It totally does not work." She looked at Sierra, daring to say the words she'd been pushing aside. "I guess I somehow wanted him to magically know I'd heard it, and for him to coming running up to New York and explain how it was all a misunderstanding."

Sierra's eyes narrowed. "I hear you. But it probably can't work that way. Too magical. He probably needs a little help."

"So you think I should talk to Jake about it?"

"You're the star of the reality show of your life. Write it the way you want it."

～

"Damn! That was my finger."

Jake was standing at the kitchen worktable, his old gray T-shirt smeared with butter and dusted with flour. His iPad was propped up against Iris's old flowered teapot and streaming something called *The Best Baking Show*. A ridiculously well-coiffed woman who looked as unperturbed as if she'd stepped off a runway was smoothly running through the motions of making what she promised were excellent chocolate-chunk cookies.

Which, of course, Jake had always loved. He just preferred filching them from Haven's display case.

"Now continue chopping the baking chocolate into small chunks of the size you'd like to bite into in your cookie—" Nursing the place on his middle finger where he'd accidentally nicked himself while trying to chop the chocolate, he leaned forward abruptly and hit pause.

"Chop chocolate, chop chocolate," he muttered to himself. "How do you chop chocolate? You're supposed to eat chocolate. And chop wood."

He set down the knife and reached irritably for the bottle of beer beside the iPad and took a swig. This woman was way too perky. He wiped off his finger and, on inspection, saw that it wasn't bleeding.

Geez, how did Anna do it? Once more, he tried chopping the small squares on the chopping block, but they kept popping out, with small fragments shooting onto Iris's clean kitchen floor. Frustrated, he set the knife emphatically down and picked up the beer just as emphatically.

"Jake? What *are* you doing?" Iris's voice startled him as he put down the bottle.

"Grandma! You're back early. Uh …" He looked down at the mess. How to explain that he had missed Anna so much he had temporarily gone insane and tried to see what baking was like. Anything to avoid actually calling her.

A wide grin crept across Iris's face. "You're not baking *cookies*, are you?" Her voice was as incredulous as her eyes were amused.

He looked down at the knife and the chocolate. Damn, again.

"Yeah, I, uh … thought I'd give it a try. You know, if we're doing more of it around here, I might as well learn more about it." Geez, that sounded lame.

Iris frowned amusedly. "You know, you've got lots of good bakers around here."

"Yeah, yeah, I just thought it was time I put my fingers in the batter—to use an expression." Anna's expression. Anna's *really* charming expression.

"Well, good for you." Iris gave a knowing look. "And how's it going?"

Jake winced inside. "Not so great."

"What show is that on your iPad?"

"I dunno, some baking show."

"Helpful?"

"No way. She says, 'chop chocolate.' But how do you chop

chocolate? I need a friggin' axe." Jake's frustration began to bubble over, though he knew it was as much about missing Anna as it was about proper chopping techniques. "It's ridiculous." He all but stuck the knife fiercely into the wooden chopping block.

"OK," Iris purred, gently taking the knife from him. "I can show you. Let me wash my hands first."

Jake irately picked up the beer and swigged again. "Not sure I want to know."

As if on cue, his phone rang in his shirt pocket, and he plunked the beer down, wiping his hands on his pants before pulling it out and glancing at it. It was a 212 area code—a New York number he didn't recognize. Anna's face flashed through his mind. Shoot, when was that going to stop happening.

"Yeah, Jake Petersen here."

"Mr. Petersen. It's Mr. Samuels."

For a second, he blinked, the name sounding both distant and familiar.

Into his silence, the voice continued. "From Taggarts?"

Sharp pinpricks of adrenaline shot through Jake's chest, his breath quickening.

"Of course, Mr. Samuels. Good to hear from you." He glanced pointedly at Iris, whose eyebrows shot up.

"I'm glad I got you. I wanted you to know the review process was complete, and the review is going live soon ..."

Jake held his breath to try to calm his heartbeat.

"... and I wanted to let you know directly. It's a 5-star."

Relief sprang through Jake's gut, and without thinking, he made a silent fist pump—thank heaven he wasn't on FaceTime. Iris mouthed "what," while Jake forced his voice to be calm: "Mr. Samuels, that's really good news. Thank you so much."

"You're welcome, and you deserve it. You and your whole team. You've put so much work and vision into the inn. We like it when somebody combines the local context with a very high level of service. Not easy to find. It's the best combination, and I wish you luck."

"I'll tell them all. They'll be so happy."

"It's especially impressive how you drew in the same people who serve the town every day. The caterer, the decor, and that wedding cake!"

In a flash, though he wasn't thinking of it even two seconds before, Jake knew the next thing he had to say. He took a deep breath, still feeling as if he were on a tightrope despite the news of the five stars.

"Mr. Samuels?"

"Yes?"

"When you asked who made the cake, it's true Haven helped. But at the last minute, we'd had a glitch with, uh … production. And someone was visiting and took the lead with the cake. Someone who is local—or was. It's Anna Diaz."

"Anna Diaz, I know her work in New York. She's from around here?"

When he met Iris's level gaze, Jake felt an inner prod and knew what he needed to say. "Yes, sir. We grew up together. She was an amazing cook then too, and her father ran the local farm-supply store. So she was … they were … part of the community. We were just lucky she was visiting back home right when we needed her. She taught Haven how to do it and everything—so Haven will be covering that for us going forward." He paused, then said something he'd finally understood with total clarity: "But Anna *is* local. She belongs *here*."

Jake stopped, breathing hard, waiting for the voice on the other end. Iris watched, her eyes wide.

When he spoke, Mr. Taggarts sounded bemused. "It sounds like I stepped in on an unfolding story. Places like your inn, your town, have real stories, Jake. It's interesting to see how Ms. Diaz is part of it."

Jake breathed a sigh of relief, looking at Iris with a thumbs-up. "You're right, this place does have a story. And it's still going on. Someone else very wise has said that to me too."

"Well, son, good luck finding the next chapter. And keep me posted. Don't forget—we'll be seeing you in the future to keep the rating updated. So be sure to keep up the good work."

"Yes, sir!"

Jake made sure the call was ended, clicked off his phone, and let out a whoop.

"Grandma!"

"What was the rating??"

"Five stars!"

Iris clapped her hands together. "Five? How wonderful! Jake, well done. Very well done."

"It was all of us, Grandma. You were amazing. We have to tell the whole team."

Iris touched his shoulder. "And I'm proud of you, Jake. I don't know quite why you were bringing Anna up to him, or why you didn't before. But you did the right thing. Now, Haven is right outside. She came back from town with me. I have to go tell her. And we can give Tom and the others a call. Haven!"

As Haven and Iris chatted and giggled, Haven calling Tom, then Albert, then Pete and Tina, Jake just leaned back against the kitchen door, hands in pockets, watching them affectionately. They'd really done it, all of them—finally. The vision he'd had years ago had come through ups and downs of every possible kind, and he'd dragged them all through it.

But the vision had survived. And it had happened. Maybe not on his timetable, and it took way more blood, sweat, and tears than he'd signed up for. But then maybe that was how visions worked in real life.

And Iris was right. He had done the right thing. Telling Samuels about Anna was making her story known ... when it counted. She might never know, or need to know, he'd done it. But he knew, and it felt good.

Except that—as he crossed his arms and let himself feel something close to peace—he couldn't quite get there. Something felt incomplete. Some piece was missing. And he knew what it was. It was Anna. She did need to know about the rating, even if he didn't tell her about the mistake he'd made with Samuels—after all, he'd managed to circle around and correct it. The question was just how to tell her—how to bridge the gap that she'd left behind when she left without saying goodbye. How to reach across that gap inside of him between his hurt pride at her having bolting and the ever-stronger desire to hold her just once more ...

"Everybody's coming to celebrate tonight. Albert's bringing dinner," Haven said after ending the call with Tina. "Sound OK?"

"Absolutely," Iris said, heading into the dining room. "I'll have everything ready for a crowd." The door swung shut behind her, and they heard the sounds of the sideboard's drawers opening.

Haven turned to Jake. "And I'll bring dessert. I just made a practice wedding cake using the recipe that Anna—" She stopped and shot her arms emphatically wide. "Of course— Anna! We have to call her! I still have her number from when I texted her the pictures of all of us." She paused, grasping her phone and tapping open the picture of Jake and Anna, looking with wide, almost bashful smiles toward the camera. She held it up to his face. "That was the night we all pulled this off. Remember this shot?"

Jake squinted and pulled back, slamming down the pain of seeing Anna's glowing face right beside his own. Right before he ...

"Of course I remember it." His voice was rough.

Haven lowered the phone, watching him. "Don't you think we should call her?"

Jake shrugged, feeling caught. "Sure, of course. Why don't you?"

"Well," Haven said slowly, "I think you should do it, Jake. She liked baking the cake and showing me how and everything. We had a great time together. But I could see—what she really wanted was to help you. You're the reason she ... she did it."

"Maybe." OK, there was that seventeen-year-old again. Come on, man up. "Sure, of course. I'll call her."

"When? This is a big deal." Haven's look was pointed.

"I know it's a big deal." Jake sounded annoyed, then tried to self-correct. No need to bug Haven with anything. He gave a half-smile. "It's everything I ever wanted."

Haven paused and slid her phone back into her pocket. Her voice was intent. "No. It's not everything you ever wanted, Jake."

"What do you mean?" Jake crossed his arms.

"There are other things you've wanted. And ... you should want them."

"What are you talking about?"

She shook her head and pursed her lips thoughtfully. "Nothing, really. It's just ... you know, work isn't everything." She eyed him cautiously. "I ... I'm not sure if I should mention this, but—"

"But what?" He was still feeling short with her—or with himself—he wasn't quite sure.

"I got some orders for breakfast platters, you know, muffins, scones, like that. To be delivered to the Sneed estate outside town several days next week."

A sense of déjà vu rippled through Jake's head. "Margaret's place?" Wasn't it enough that Haven and Iris had both brought her up?

"I heard that she ..."

"She what?" He walked over to the fridge and pulled out a pitcher of iced tea.

"Jake, I heard she got married. Up in New York."

Jake set down the pitcher slowly. The mix of the loss of the marriage and the now-unfinished business around Anna dissipated. He turned slowly toward Haven who watched him cautiously. "Margaret got remarried?"

"It's what I heard. I think the family is gathering at their estate outside town for some kind of vacation together. Jake, I'm sorry. Did I do the right thing telling you?"

Jake nodded, turning back to pour a glass. "You did the right thing."

"You OK?"

"Yeah, I'm OK."

"I don't think it's ever easy to hear your ex got remarried."

Jake pressed his lips together. "You know, I feel a little sad that we … we got it wrong when we tried. But she did her best. I'm glad for her. Glad she found someone." He glanced ruefully at Haven, then back at the glass of tea. "I hope they got it right."

"You did try, both of you. I'll bet she got it right. And, Jake …"

"Hmm?"

"I have no doubt you'll get it right too." She looked at him pointedly. "And maybe sooner than you think."

Whether Haven meant Anna or not, it was Anna's face that flashed unbidden back into his head, pushing Margaret easily into thin air. He took a swig of tea. "Come on, enough of all this. Go text everybody and tell them you're bringing cake. It's time to celebrate."

"You gonna call Anna? Jake, she deserves to know."

He set the glass down. "I'll text her first. Just to find out when would be a good time to call."

"You'd better, dude." Haven bopped his arm as she went into the dining room to help Iris.

Jake looked out the window toward the barn. Anna, whom he felt he owed some atonement to, even if she didn't know it.

Anna, whom he just plain wanted to laugh with again, to talk to again, the person he most wanted to tell all about the review. He wanted to hear what she said, how she laughed about it, what she thought.

Anna—who had headed right back to a life in New York and quickly, easily left behind the struggling little inn that surely paled in comparison. Without even saying goodbye.

He wanted more than anything to call her.

And it was the last thing in the world he wanted to do.

CHAPTER 8

Lower Manhattan glowed when the setting sun was behind it, peeping up over New Jersey and points west. From her long windows in Brooklyn, Anna could always capture a good chunk of the view—it was one of the reasons she'd eagerly put down a too-hefty deposit on this place the moment she saw it.

Home. She was sure it would be a great home.

As she looked at the layered rays, she was more aware than ever of the evening light that was stretching the days longer and longer toward the summer solstice. Why had she never noticed it like this before? Like some kind of nature-calendar that told you where in the year you were.

Anna absently picked up the electric kettle full of hot water, not really paying attention as she automatically poured into her mug. It was a hand-thrown mug from a potter she especially liked, a couple of neighborhoods over, here in Brooklyn. His stuff was always an amazing mix of having a real weight and yet also being thin and light. She loved how that let the heat radiate into her hands.

The afternoon at the restaurant with Sierra and Rubin had been tiring. Not like "a day of great work" tiring. But like "I'm totally tapped out" tiring. And Sierra had intuited that there was more going on for her than just a brief detour in a storm, and Anna realized it might help to talk about it with her.

Be the star of your own reality show, Sierra had said.

Wow, they should write that one into the script. Somehow it feels a lot scarier to be the star of your own show than to be the star of someone else's—but let's leave that one out of the script.

Anna settled over onto her couch, facing the rosy-orange light coming from the windows. She curled her legs under her, comfy in yoga pants, and pulled her sweater loose around her. She'd stopped by the studio and had a good vinyasa session earlier, which always helped.

Instinctively she reached down to stroke Putz, just as she'd been doing all week, and gave a bitter chuckle when she realized again that, of course, he wasn't there.

The days in Cedarwood Spring had changed her. They simply had. She wished it weren't the case and that she'd made it to Silverwood without ever turning down Exit 13—or that she'd made it to the local hotel and gone on her way after a day or two.

Or that if she had to be stuck at the inn with Jake, at least that he'd been some disinterested jerk, throwing ice-cold water over all the warm, fuzzy memories she'd had of him as some ideal. Then his comment to Samuels wouldn't have hurt. She could have written it off as being what she always knew Cedarwood Spring was and happily re-escaped back to the city.

That would have been helpful.

But no-o-o, it hadn't happened that way. It had happened in the very unhelpful way of seeing how charming the town was, how beautiful the bright green of the countryside was, how terrific Iris and Haven and Putz and everyone had been.

And how much she—what?—liked Jake? No, that's not it. All that conjured up was that annoying thumbs-up icon again.

Was "fond of" Jake? No, she was fond of Putz.

Was attracted to Jake? That would have to do.

Anna sighed. Until he hurt her by turning her back into the invisible girl she'd tried so hard to leave behind. And what felt weird was that he didn't know she knew. Did it matter?

And if it *didn't* matter, then why had the question occurred to her? Sierra was right: This was unresolved.

Her cell phone jangled brightly on the coffee table, almost levitating as it vibrated. For a split second, it felt like Jake went from being in her mind to being the phone call, and her heart fluttered with both hope and fear—because, she knew, she wanted it to be him.

Her eyes darted to the phone.

Sierra. Well, maybe they could at least talk a little more about it.

"Hey, what's new and different since about two hours ago?"

"Anna, I'm sorry I had to head out earlier. Did you get to the yoga studio?"

"Yeah. It loosened me up. But I'm still …"

"Your feelings still stuck? Even after vinyassa?" Sierra sounded almost teasing.

Anna tried to muster a smile but couldn't.

Sierra noted the silence. "You know, what you told me—the kiss plus what he said to the Taggarts guy. This means there really is something unfinished."

Anna felt dampness welling in her eyes, and she knew her friend was right. "Sierra, I can't make sense of it. When he … he kissed me, it somehow felt like … I don't know, like the truth. Like something I could believe. Maybe something I've wanted to believe from way back. It felt like I was in the right place. Where I belonged." These words weren't coming out right, but they needed to come out somehow—to hell with perfection. "And then when he wrote me off—that felt like a different truth. Like the old truth—that I *didn't* belong. I guess I don't know which truth to believe."

"You know, this afternoon I thought about what we talked

about. It sort of stuck with me too. And it sounds to me like life showed you a lot of powerful stuff last week, and you don't have enough information to sort it all out. Like I said, you need to talk to him. I know it feels risky, but I don't see how you have a choice."

The pump primed, Anna couldn't stop her words. "I keep trying to go back and pretend to myself that I didn't feel what I felt. Like I left it all behind when I pulled out of Cedarwood Spring and got back onto the highway—at Exit 13."

"But it wasn't that simple, was it?"

"No." Anna's voice was weak.

"Then it's not going away, and no amount of wishing will do the trick. If the pain of what you *think* Jake did is still there—and it wasn't something you just blew off—then it's telling you there's still a problem you have to unravel. But you've gone as far as you can trying to figure it out on your own. Anna?"

"Hmm?"

"You're going to have to ask Jake which truth to believe."

An anxious sob bubbled in her chest. "Is there any way around it?"

"I don't see how. You say he was a good guy—apart from the crappy comment. So give him a chance to explain it. He may give you a crappy answer. But at least you'll feel resolved. And you can head back down Exit 13 for good. If you know what I mean."

"Thanks. You're right." Anna took a deep breath. "Soooo … what's my next step? Do I call him?" Her heart fluttered again.

She heard Sierra take a deep breath of her own.

"Well, that's actually another reason I was calling. Anna, you know I went over to talk to the manager of the café space? About the permits and final certificates of the place? So we can, like, actually have a functioning café to film in—which is, of course, the whole point of reality TV. Your show needs a home."

"Yeah?"

"It's not coming through. The final permitting and the certificate of operation. I can't be sure it will be there in time, and we can't take a chance on not having a place for you to plant yourself."

Anna bolted upright, suddenly catapulted into a whole different emotional space. One quite unlike the cloudy space of thinking about Jake.

"What? You mean it still hasn't come through yet?"

"No, I mean it might not come through at all. At least not in any usable way for us for the deadline. For the solstice." A dry laugh. "There was a problem with the paperwork—and then apart from that, part of the plumbing didn't get finished. It's not up to code. It might squeak by. But you know how hard it is getting the infrastructure stuff done here in the city. We just can't risk the possibility that it won't, and we wouldn't have a kitchen for you to land in."

The bright vision of success, toward which Anna had been hurtling for months, began to darken into confusion. Something in her felt a shard of relief—but something much bigger panicked. They'd put so much into the show. If it didn't happen, what was she going to step off onto? Where would she belong? Panic rose in her chest.

"Is there really nothing we can do? An expedited process? Go into crisis mode?" Anna was up on her feet, pacing along her three tall windows, the backlit skyline now totally forgotten.

"We were already in crisis mode, babe. That's what Rubin and I have been up to."

"So what does this mean?" Tears that had been about Jake but were now about job security began to bubble. "Sierra, what should I do? I left my old job for this."

"Hey, Anna, calm down. I think there is something we can do. We need to secure a new place, somewhere we know is already set up with permits and is just waiting to have the pâtissière with the vision step in. And …" Sierra paused and took another audible breath. "That's what I meant about your next step with Jake."

"Huh?" Feelings from different places inside of her careened headlong into each other. "What does the café have to do with Jake?"

"I had an idea. I thought about what you told me about the inn—and Jake. I glanced at their website, and it's great. They've already got decent social media, it sounds like they have a solid team, and Jake must keep the place in top shape."

"Ye-e-e-s?" Anna said slowly, her mind still paralyzed.

"They're an established place with new furnishings," Sierra continued, "all ready for public display, and their certificates of inspection are up to date ..."

Anna's eyes shot wide. "You mean ... ?"

"Sounds like a great place to do a reality TV pilot."

"Ha!" Anna wasn't sure whether her chortle was one of excitement, hope, or insanity. "Shoot the pilot there? Shoot 'Love Bite' at Cedarwood Spring Inn??"

"I don't see why not." Sierra's voice was calm and persuasive. "They have everything we need, and it takes care of all our headaches in one fell swoop. It might help give the inn more publicity, and it sounds like they deserve it. And ... it takes care of your problem with your next step."

"Wh-what was that?"

"Now you can ask him what happened in person."

This was almost too much to take in. "What about the whole city-café 'Love Bite' concept? Marketing has already been branding it."

"I thought about that. We can brand it just as well with the whole countryside-in-summer concept. The café idea is still the same—a pastry or fresh bread from our world-class pâtissière and staff, and a drink locally sourced and coordinated to the time of day and the food they choose. In fact, fresh local ingredients will be a lot easier to come by out there. Why not do that looking out over a gorgeous countryside? Sounds better than watching Ubers honking at each other on Canal Street. And the marketing had been about the concept. They never really said much about where it was anyway. It happens a lot with pilots. Stuff gets changed around at the last minute, so PR is usually more about the concept than the specifics."

Sierra's idea slowly coalesced in Anna's mind, and for some crazy reason, she found herself nearly giggling—with relief, if also with what felt like a bit of insanity. And finally, planning-mind was kicking in. "What comes after the pilot? Do we stay there, or ..." Stay in Cedarwood Spring? What would have been unthinkable a few weeks ago now had a soft glow to it. She'd thought she had no options. But was this an option being served up to her?

"We don't have to figure that out right now. I ran it by the producer. He's fine with it being a sort of country-city thing where we come back to the city afterward if it all works out. The point is a successful pilot, something that really makes your whole café concept shine."

"Well, why not," Anna said weakly, holding up an open palm and letting the whole idea wash over it—and enjoying it. "Maybe it would work. It could be a solution."

"Sometimes you have to alter life a little," Sierra said. "Change up the ingredients, Anna. And my crew would love a summer week out in Pennsylvania Dutch country. We'll make it like a vacation. Besides, the solstice looks a whole lot better in the country. You can actually see what the sky looks like. Maybe we can take advantage of that at Cedarwood Spring too. It had just been a marketing concept. But now it can be better." She paused. "Now it can be the real thing."

"It is pretty gorgeous out there," Anna said softly, her mind's eye seeing the rolling patchwork fields that were out beyond the barn. "And the sky ..."

"Well, that's why you got away, wasn't it? Thank goodness you got rerouted. It may have saved our butts."

Anna's inner eye flitted from the rolling green fields to the man she imagined standing in the midst of them. The proud man committed to a vision. The man who could be as fierce and irate as he could be passionate.

The man who had somehow forgotten to say her name when he was talking about the wedding cake. Apprehension rose.

"Sierra, this could be cool. But you've already run it by the producer … and we haven't even asked Jake yet."

"Sure, sure, of course. But I know Jake's trying to take this inn up to the next level. So what's not to like about having you come in and help save the day?"

Though she couldn't put her finger on it, Anna knew that there might indeed be something he didn't like about it. There were moments when he seemed so gruff about her trying to help out with the reception, and at first, he'd even seemed to resist her doing the cake. And it's not like she didn't have mixed feelings herself.

The powerful draw of Jake. The hurtful memory of Jake. "So what do I do?"

"I think that's clear. You have to call him. To ask if we can do this—descend on the inn for a week of filming, which will mean—we hope—lots of customers and media coverage. There are logistics he'd have to handle on his end, but I can call him and fill him in, and I'll have my assistant stay in touch with him, and we'll get plenty of staff out there to do whatever he needs. If he says yes, then it puts you right back where you were when you bolted out of town. And once you're there, that's when you bring your other question to him."

"About the kiss … *and* the comment."

"Exactly. Isn't it nice when a plan works out." She wasn't really asking.

"This wasn't the plan, Sierra."

"It doesn't matter. It's the plan now. Let me know what he says."

"About the pilot?"

"About all of it."

~

Jake gazed at the quiet barn, overlaid with a black velvet sky and diamond-speck stars.

It was amazing how even when it was totally dark and silent, it still felt like it had life inside it. The gardens and fields beyond were dark; there was a gentle rhythmic slosh from the slowly cycling waterwheel. The paths where guests' feet had walked, accompanied by voices and clinking glasses, were now practically invisible without the lamps. But he knew them by heart.

That night had been a little over a week ago. But somehow it had changed everything.

He stood on the dark patio, letting the breeze instead of his hand ruffle his hair. He was sweaty from a day of working the front gardens with Tom's guys. Even as the sun had been setting, he could tell it looked great.

He took a sip of cognac from a small crystal glass.

The Taggarts review had only been out a day, but it had set everything in motion. They'd already had several calls about bookings, and tomorrow he'd be showing the place to a couple driving up from Philly. Soon as they secured a couple more big bookings, he was set to hire an assistant manager part-time.

Life's moving on, Jake thought. I just don't want it to move on without Anna. But she felt so far away. And he just didn't know how to start.

He'd told himself things had moved so quickly after Samuels's call that he had to tend to the review and the calls. But inside he knew … he didn't know how to begin the conversation with her. And that was because he didn't know exactly what he wanted to say. That they'd gotten the 5-star review that she'd been a clear part of making happen? Ok, great. But also that when he was talking to Samuels and Abbott that night, he hadn't been fully honest—and it was his own damn fault, not Abbott's? But that he'd cleaned it all up by correcting it with Samuels when he called about the rating, told him how Anna had grown up there, how she and her dad were part of the community. And … that she belonged there.

No wonder he didn't know where to start. It's because, in his head, it always ended up going too far. Where should he put the stop sign?

Shaking his head at himself, Jake turned to head back inside and saw the dim light from the kitchen framing Iris's silhouette at the back door.

"Jake? There you are."

"Sorry. Just coming in."

She held the door open as he walked past, then held out his phone to him. "It rang while you were outside so I picked it up for you." She glanced down, then back up at him and mouthed the words "It's Anna."

Jake started, looking at the phone as if it could bite. "Anna?"

"Shh!" Iris hissed quietly, nodding furiously and holding out the phone. "Talk to her," she said in a loud stage whisper.

Jake rolled his eyes. "She can hear you, Grandma." His heart had jumped from first gear to fifth, and his grandmom was acting like a matchmaker to a teenager. This was about as ridiculously uncool as he could get. So much for knowing what to do with his hurt pride.

"OK," he said, motioning Iris back into the living room. She gave him an annoying two-thumbs-up and disappeared. He heard her going up the stairs.

He sat down heavily on a kitchen stool in the dim light of the kitchen and took a breath.

"Anna, hi. So good to hear from you."

"Hi Jake. Hope I didn't catch you at a bad time? I know it's a bit late."

"It's fine. Iris, um, went up to bed. I'm having a nightcap."

"You're in the kitchen?"

"Yes."

"With Putz?"

That was kind of her: a nice icebreaker. "With Putz." The cat had leapt onto the island, and Jake let him stay, stroking his back. Calms the nerves.

"I miss him—give him an ear scratch for me."

"Done. He said thanks—I think you can hear his purr."

"Definitely." Her voice sounded hesitant, and Jake realized his heart was still beating distractingly hard. "Things have been going so fast here in New York with the show and all. I'm ... uh, sorry I haven't been in touch ... before now."

"No problem." He tried to sound nonchalant, pretending to himself for a moment that he was a man who had not had her face burned on his brain—or who had scanned the pic on his phone like it was a friggin' masterpiece. "I know your life there is really busy. But hey, guess what? Good news."

He heard an intake of breath. "Did you hear from Taggarts?"

"Yep."

"And??"

"5-star."

Her voice exploded with warmth. "Congratulations! That's wonderful! I'm so happy for you. You really deserve it, Jake— you, and Iris, the team, and the inn."

"Thanks. It does feel pretty good." That, and hearing her voice.

"Is the review up yet? I'll have to go online and look."

"Yeah, it went live Wednesday. Short, very general, but already good PR for the inn. Or at least, for the barn as a venue."

"That's so great. I'm sorry I haven't been in touch," she said again, sounding hesitant.

"No problem. Like I said, I can't imagine your life there in New York." Though he had tried, way too often. And since he usually ended up imagining something that made him jealous, it was better not to go there. "And besides, I'm the one who owed you a call. Getting the review was great, and you were a big reason it happened. I—the whole team—can't thank you enough," he said, hoping this was a way to ease into all he knew he needed to say.

"Oh, you're welcome. You know I needed to do it for myself too." Her voice was warm, if a bit distant. "I hope it's spreading the word about the inn."

"Definitely. Things are kicking into gear here. Just since yesterday we've gotten two more bookings for this summer, several inquiries, and people coming to see it tomorrow." Was she really interested in this? Is that why had she called? Just to ask about the review?

"That's wonderful." She still sounded muted. "So it sounds like you've got your hands full?"

"It's getting that way. But that's what we want. I'm going to start looking for an assistant manager." Though it must sound lame compared to the fast lane, he mentally added.

"Good—you need one. You're going to keep your hands on the controls, though, right?"

Of course, he had control over his own inn. Why did it sound like she was trying to get at something?

"Are you kidding?" He forced ease into his voice. "Of course. I'll keep doing the hands-on with all the property stuff and the vendors and subcontractors we use. But I need somebody to handle calls, questions, do a lot of running interference and handling the details of getting everything coordinated for the actual events. And social media." Justifying all the control he had was starting to sound out of control. Damn, what was it about Anna? He could almost fall in love with her if she didn't keep getting under his skin.

"You're really making this happen, Jake."

"Yes, I am—we are." Jake realized they'd only been talking about the inn, and he couldn't yet figure out how to bring up the comments to Samuels. Needed to stall for a few more minutes, see how the conversation went. Or maybe even suss out why she had called, which wasn't quite clear to him.

Much as he didn't want to hear about her fabulous life in New York, he knew the next step was to ask, if only to be polite. "Speaking of making things happen—how's the pilot coming?"

A pause. "Not so great, actually."

His jealousy temporarily subsided. He might not like the idea of her with ... whatever men were around. But he loved her work, her ideas, her vision. "I'm sorry. What's happening with it?"

"Some important pieces don't seem to be coming through."

"Like?"

"Well, like all the things you've done right at the inn, we've done wrong. You really do know what you're doing, and I'm afraid we don't. We're not much more than a week away, and the permits for the café space aren't coming through yet. The certificates of inspection and ... I'm not sure what else. Sierra and Rubin are handling it. But it's looking risky."

Permits, certificates ... Jake let out a low whistle. He knew that territory well. "That stuff can really mess you up if it's not done right. Is there any way it can come together? Any Hail Mary pass?"

There was another silence, long enough that for a second, Jake thought he'd lost her. "Anna?"

"I'm here." Another pause. "Jake, there is one last Hail Mary pass that might be possible."

"Good, then you should throw that football. I know—we threw enough of those passes around here getting this place put together."

"Thanks, Jake. That's encouraging. OK, so I'll throw the Hail Mary."

"Good for you. What is it?"

"It's you."

Iris squinted into the bright morning sunlight from where she knelt, trimming a few zinnias. They'd sprung up early that year, bright pops of color in the raised beds around the back patio. And they were gorgeous.

"You know, Jake, this is the next piece we need here at the inn." She waved her clipper in his direction. "We can start to develop the inn as a café, not just the barn as an event spot. If you think about it, that way the inn and the barn could be perfect companion pieces. Maybe Anna's pilot is just a way for us to get started in the café business. Maybe it's our pilot too."

Gloves on, hammer in hand, Jake was reinforcing the wooden border of a nearby bed. Haven and Tom walked up, carrying more bedding plants from the back of his pickup and setting them out along the edges of the trees.

"How?" Jake said, trying to keep his voice proportionate to the casual conversation instead of to the confused emotions he'd been cycling through since Anna's call the night before. The one where her suggestion of doing the pilot at the inn had totally derailed his complete intention to tell her about his comments to Samuels—at the event and then on the call. He'd barely gotten through the wedding reception, keeping everything under control, and now this. Though of course, he'd agreed to it. Taken off guard by her call in the first place, then further thrown by the request—and even more thrown by how good it felt just to hear her voice again. So he'd said yes, just like he'd said yes, sort of, to the wedding cake. "Anna's the one with the vision and the know-how. And the team. Not us." Which could only mean more loss of control on his end.

Iris shrugged, unperturbed. "Well, first, we're all the team, and I'd bet dollars to doughnuts Anna would be the first one to tell you that. And second—I don't know yet how it could work for us after they all go back to New York, but it's possible. Just see what you learn from it. Talk to Anna about the fact that you'd like to do this for real with the inn. She'll have good ideas."

"Iris is right," Tom said as he set down the last of the plants. "This could give us a lot more options. We'd have one-off events down at the barn. And up here could be a regular stream of people. Plus, if we got a good baker up here," he winked at Haven, "then that could also be another option we can offer for events at the barn. More value."

"Sounds good, though I'd have to balance it with the Filling Station." Haven brushed off her hands as she stood up. "Like now, Jan is filling in for me—I'm going to get her to do it more regularly, bring her along. Like I did there when I was a teen too. Especially if I can start to get some jobs making wedding cakes! When are you going to find out what else we need to do to get ready for the TV show, Jake? I talked to Tina about refreshing the plants front and back, but also about doing stuff *inside* the inn. And on the back patio."

"We can finally get a flow of people inside this old place, not just around it," Iris agreed, snipping off another hot-pink bloom.

Jake tapped the other end of the board with the hammer, lightly securing it to its neighbor. "I'm not sure. I'm supposed to talk to Anna again soon. Probably tomorrow. She had to check some specs out and get back to me."

"Good," Iris said emphatically, though whether about Anna or the flowers, Jake wasn't sure. "Let me know what she says. And now—anybody want iced tea?"

Tom waved his hand. "Count me in."

She pointed inside the back door. "It's in the fridge. Made it this morning. Can you bring it out for us?"

"Definitely. Haven, help me?"

"You bet."

As they disappeared into the front door, Iris glanced back over at Jake with a sly expression.

Oh no, more emotional directives. This was getting old.

"OK, Jake, you do know this is fate, right?"

"We're fated to have a reality show at the inn?" He could yank her chain a little.

She narrowed her eyes and snipped another bloom, this one yellow. "The chance to talk to Anna."

"I did talk to her."

"Yes, because she called to ask you about doing the show here. But not because you called *her* to talk about the two of *you*."

Jake sighed wearily and tested the strength of the raised wooden border, avoiding Iris's eyes. "She's got a great life, Grandma, a real life. I'm sure she charms everybody that comes her way. I'll look like this lame guy from her hometown who fell for her like every other guy." His voice had an edge. "Besides, I'm just getting everything up and running with the barn as an event venue. I don't know if we can manage adding on a whole new café thing after Anna … leaves again."

"You know what sounds lame? That does." Iris snipped serenely.

He rested his forearm on his knee and waved the hammer pointedly at her. "Look, I'm a guy who hauls mulch. And checks the plumbing and sets up tables. And worries about getting bookings. She's a … star in New York. A successful, smart, talented … sweet, funny …" His voice trailed off as he went back to hammering. He didn't need 'successful, smart, talented, sweet, funny' so close to his own precarious business that he wanted to both holder her closer and push her away.

"Still not adding up, my dear. Is this about Margaret getting remarried?" When Jake shot her a glance, she added, "Haven told me."

Jake shrugged. "Nah, I'm fine. I want Margaret to be happy. She deserves it."

"You both do. You know, Jake, it was right after the divorce that you did a swan dive into your work here. And I don't think you've ever resurfaced."

"The inn needed the work. We couldn't put it off anymore. You know that, Grandma." Jake banged the wood harder than was necessary.

"That's true. But isn't it also true that you could have let it be the justification for not opening that space back up in your own life?"

"Geez, Grandma, should I have a therapist's couch delivered out here? It'll fit right there beside the peonies."

Iris laughed, her profound love for her grandson shining through. "OK, 'nuf said, as Haven always says. But I do think there's something to that. And now that you know she's happy and on her way, it'll free you up to do the same thing. And the timing's good, don't you think?"

"What do you mean?"

"The barn is really starting to work. You've got that done. And Anna shows up with …"

"With what?" With meddling interest in his business right as it was finally feeling like it was going somewhere? Or with ease, companionship, and loveliness that filled an empty spot he'd desperately ignored? Maybe Iris had a point.

She sidestepped him. "I'm not sure. That's what you'll need to find out. The café sounds like a good chance to do that."

Jake felt oddly heartened. To tell the truth, that's how it felt to him too. But mixing business and pleasure had backfired before. He couldn't bear it if it backfired with Anna. "Then why did she bolt?"

"I don't know. You have to ask her. And you have to tell her."

"Tell her what?"

"That you don't want this to be the end."

Jake's defenses sprang back up. "What are you talking about? Her life is in New York. And mine's … here." He paused, looking at the gardens, seeing the years and layers of work he'd put into every square foot. "What are we supposed to do? Date long-distance?" Weird how even just saying it brought him both pleasure and pain.

"I don't know. Sometimes you can't see anything but the step that's right in front of you. And only once you take it do you start to see the next, and then the next. So take a step. What have you got to lose?"

The success he was barely managing to put together in his own life, Jake thought dryly. "I could end up looking really … lame."

"You won't know till you try. The only way out is through."

CHAPTER 9

"I've never been on a movie set. This is so exciting!"

Haven sounded like a kid in a candy store, Anna thought, grinning.

The two of them stood at the front gardens of Cedarwood Spring Inn as smart, white Mercedes vans with the name of the production company stenciled on the sides maneuvered into parking spots along the driveway. Crew members bustled around, carrying sound and lighting equipment, cords dangling.

"Well, remember it's not a *movie* set, it's a *TV* set—sort of. It's really only the same inn that you know so well. We're just borrowing the first floor to set up the café in."

"So all the baking and prep in the kitchen, but also the customers?"

"Yep—customers too. We're opening it up to anyone, but the cool thing is, it's mostly people from the area who've signed up."

"Well, it's all the same crazy-exciting to me. How long will all this take?"

'Forever,' Anna thought, then pursed her lips; where had that come from? "Four or five days or so. I'll just show up when and where Sierra tells me to." Anna knew that she was as excited as Haven. But for a range of reasons—not the least being her mixed feelings about the sweet, seasoned owner of the inn—she was committed to keeping her cool.

It did feel good to be back, she had to admit—really good. As she'd pulled off the interstate at Exit 13 that morning—this time under a sunny blue sky—she'd reflexively sent up a little prayer for where this second trip into Cedarwood Spring would take her. When she'd driven up the inn's driveway and remembered driving up it in the storm in Jake's truck, joy had outpaced trepidation. Since this time, it was no detour. It was completely intentional and had taken rerouting a lot of things in her life. Even if only for a few days.

It had been a week since Anna had proposed Sierra's brainstorm to Jake on the phone—a mind-spinning week. He'd agreed to the idea of the shoot at the inn, but was a little stiff about it. He sounded nervous about the logistics and how to protect his team amid the specialists the producers were sending in. Jake had called her a couple more times, asking questions—which had actually been pretty nice. Even though all they talked about was the inn, at least it made chatting a little more natural. It felt like it was a way to ease back into ... what? She wasn't sure.

Anna half-smiled to herself—Jake was ever the manager, ever the worrier, ever the overachiever.

Then again, look who was talking.

The pilot was a first for her and had certainly given her a few angsty midnight self-confessions. But she'd mentally crossed her fingers, confident in Sierra, Rubin, and the producers. So instead, her angst had detoured away from the pilot and toward Jake Petersen.

Or rather, toward the idea of talking to him about what had happened the night of the wedding. That kind of vulnerable honesty would be a first too, and for that one, she didn't have a director handling all her questions.

Not that Sierra hadn't been a director of sorts for this process too, she thought wryly. *I lucked out and got a director and a life coach at the same time.*

Speaking of which, where was Jake?

"Um ... so where's your big bro?" Anna asked casually.

"He's in the barn, or at least he was. Come on, we need to let him know you're here. He'll be so glad to see you." Haven headed toward the back gardens, pulling Anna with her. As they rounded the corner to the back of the inn, Anna stopped in her tracks, her eyes wide. "Haven! It's amazing—and in a totally different way than at the wedding!" she exclaimed, surveying the patio.

Small café tables were set with two and three chairs apiece among Iris's raised gardens, the plants she'd put in especially to look colorful and smell even more beautiful.

Haven giggled. "Ha! I surprised you," she bubbled. "Tina and I worked on this last night—we set up seating out here and also inside in the dining room and part of the living room. I can't wait to show you that too. The other half of the living room is for people to gather, sit, and wait for a table. Doesn't it look great out here?"

"It's just perfect." Anna stood, gazing at the chairs. "It's like a mix between a Paris park and ... Pennsylvania countryside."

"You really like it? You see so many amazing places in New York." Haven seemed to continually seek her approval, Anna noticed—an interesting experience to have back in Cedarwood Spring.

"I do like it," she said emphatically, hugging Haven from the side, then leaning over to trace one of the table tops with a finger. "Each one looks like a mosaic. Who did that?"

"Tina and Pete started making these awhile back. They had them ready to go. They use local recycled blue and green glass that people bring by the shop. And wait'll you see how Iris's painted mason jars look out here, each one with fresh herbs in it so that you have that fresh smell in the seating area, not just the kitchen."

"I love it. We can even coordinate that with the time of day, like the pastries and the drinks."

"Brilliant!" Haven clapped her hands. "And we can use the cut herbs for cooking the next day. Can you work them into pastries?"

"You bet. Herbs are great for savory breads, and savory scones too. I especially like rosemary. And we can use lavender in shortbread, and mint in all kinds of things. I have great recipes for cocktails and mocktails that use herbs and ginger."

"I can't wait." Haven looked around, sighing. "Do you think this is where you'd like to be serving customers for the show? Like, the right vibe?"

"The vibe is perfect," Anna said, running her finger along the scrolled top of a chair. "Just the right mix of sophistication and relaxed charm. Using small tables like this keeps people close. It means they're there for conversation—for company, to stop for a moment and see the world around them. That's exactly what I like." In fact, it *was* exactly what she liked—and felt like a contrast with the staged rush of the crew from New York.

She breathed deep, taking in the gentle fresh smells. It felt so good to be back. Could she really have bonded so much with this place in a week? Or was it that the bonds went all the way back … ?

"We'll put out all the table settings and sideboard tomorrow," Haven was saying. "But see the plants? Tina's sister Dorey did that—Dorey had her whole From Seed team out here, working like crazy." She pointed to the containers of summer flowers that sat here and there along the perimeter of the garden at the edge of the trees. "Come on now, let's head down."

As they went across the patio to the pathway, Anna felt a twinge at the memory of the path that night, the lanterns showing the way. She watched the barn as they headed down. The wedding garlands were no longer there, of course, and the barn was back to its simple self. And it was no less lovely for that simplicity.

The doors stood open, and in the bright day, the interior beyond simply looked dark. She squinted a bit, as Haven called, "Jake! You in there?"

Anna's heart gave a double-bump as she saw his form emerge, coming toward her from the shadows. Relaxed, he seemed to be in his usual easy work clothes of worn chinos and a soft, somewhat frayed oxford-cloth shirt, its sleeves rolled back. His pale hair was combed back in waves, and slightly sunburnt skin crinkled around the edges of his eyes. The everyday familiarity of it was nice. And ... breathtaking. How could something be both everyday and special?

"He-ey! Welcome back!" His heartiness sounded a little bit forced. "I think we've got everything in shape for you."

Anna stepped forward, and reached toward Jake for a quick, awkward hug—at the same time flashing on the last time they'd been this close, and ....

Stepping back, Jake ducked his head and crossed his arms. "It's good to see you."

"Well, here we all are again," Haven piped up. "And so soon! Who knew?!"

Jake raised his eyebrows and looked up toward the New York crew moving around in the inn. "Yeah, who knew?"

Anna swallowed, regaining her professional buoyancy. "Well, let's hope the success is as sweet as last time. You set a pretty high bar there, mister."

"I'm sure it'll be fine," Jake said, again looking beyond them in a way that seemed distracted, or maybe distant?

She spread her arms out, determined to stay on track. "Well, everything looks great. Thank you so much."

Jake looked from Anna to Haven. "Yep, we had the same

team come back in. They really crunched it these past few days to make sure the place is wearing a bow tie."

"It's been so much fun," Haven said, glowing. "Peter and Tina and Dorey. And Albert with Purveyor, and Tom and his crew. Everybody's really leaned in."

Jake gave her a sideways hug. "You too, kiddo. You've all been great."

"We love it," she said. "This is our place too, bro, and don't you forget it. You're not getting rid of us, come hell or high water!" She paused, turning toward Anna. "Do you need the barn for anything? We set up everything up at the inn—inside and also out in the gardens."

Anna nodded. "I think that's right. The barn has its own life —so to speak. We'll just borrow the inn for a few days for the shoot." She felt a twinge and avoided Jake's eyes. "But still, I hope it'll be good PR for you."

"We had never been sure how to use the inn itself—not enough room for big events, but potential for … for something," Jake shaded his eyes. "And the pastry-and-drink café is a good concept."

"It might be just the ticket," Haven said. "Nobody else is doing exactly that. I mean, I've got the muffins and cookies beat covered. Albert does desserts that he caters. There's a couple of restaurants. But nothing as unique as your café, Anna. Hey, maybe you could become a chain!"

Anna avoided Jake's eyes, busying herself scanning the back of the inn. The thought of an ongoing café here—after she left—got stuck in her mind for a second, and Anna felt a strange mix of hope and sadness. The thing was, she couldn't figure out which feeling went with which idea. "That would be great," was all she said.

"So you like what we did with the place?" Jake asked, a bit sheepishly. It was sort of like his phone calls, like he needed to reassure himself of something. "You think it'll work for your, uh ... idea?"

"It's exactly what I'd want—so charming and cozy. But it's also got a unique edge that uses local materials—and people." Anna nodded, briefly averting her eyes.

Jake gave a small smile. "Great." He seemed more grounded than a moment ago.

"Hey, remind me of the timetable again? All these people getting here—it's so exciting. Some cute guys!" Haven said, giggling.

Anna glanced at Jake. "Well, as we'd talked about ..." he nodded as she continued, "we'll be here a few days, with Sierra and Rubin and the crew staying at the hotel in town—they were lucky to get rooms because it's midweek. We'll spend a couple of days setting everything up on the first floor of the inn. Which is sort of the set, only we don't call it that. I've been learning all this stuff. And then we'll spend a couple of days shooting."

"Ending on the solstice." Jake's voice was soft.

"The romantic solstice," Haven chimed. "I looked this up and found out about the young women dreaming about who their fiancé will be." She looked from Jake to Anna and back. "Maybe I should try it?"

"Sure," Anna said with forced gaiety. "Let me know if it works."

Jake's eyes caught hers.

"Maybe you should try it too, Anna," Haven said impishly.

Anna gave her a small smile, struggling to keep her professional polish. "Let me know how your research goes first."

Jake cleared his throat and changed course—thank goodness, Anna thought.

"So, Anna ... did you get settled back into your room? Iris said she had it all ready for you."

"I did. It looks great, of course. It's really nice to be back in there, Jake. Already said hello to Putz."

Anna felt her phone vibrate in her pocket. She looked down quickly. "Oh, geez, I'm sorry—it's Rubin." She quickly scanned the text. "He's out front looking for me, which means he'll bug everyone till he finds me."

She slid the phone back into her pocket, looking up at Jake, unsure of what to say.

But he took care of it for her. Stepping toward her, he cleared his throat. "What are you doing for dinner? Probably have to be with Rubin?"

"Whatever I'm doing, it won't be with Rubin," Anna said, laughing. "Have you ever tried to make dinner conversation with him? It's like an Olympic sport." She hesitated, glancing at him. "I … I don't have plans, actually. Why? Is Iris cooking?"

"Iris has the night off—getting some rest. I thought I'd have something simple. If you're up to take a chance, why don't you join me?" Jake's expression was courteous, casual. She wondered if that was the way he felt.

In spite of her nervousness, she felt a nice shiver. Hmm, this could fun, if she could figure out how to talk about the wedding night.

The wedding night. She wished there were something else she could call it. "Alright, you're on."

"Meet you in the kitchen—around seven?"

"OK, then, seven."

As she headed back up the hill, Anna took a deep breath. Would being with Jake hold more of what the kiss had shown her? Or would it only hold more pain?

Jake stood with hands on hips, surveying the kitchen. One of the things he loved about the back end of the house was how the windows he and his dad had installed captured the feeling of the sun's light—different for morning, afternoon, and early evening.

Good call, he thought, seeing how the pinkish light from the setting sun suffused with the paler light of Iris's cozy kitchen lamps.

He glanced at his watch—almost seven—and nervously checked the front of his white oxford-cloth shirt for lint or spots, which somehow always seemed inevitable. He peered through the back room to the garden patio.

Among the café tables sat one at the center with a chair on either side. A lit candle stood on its top beside a whitewashed mason jar with sprigs of rosemary springing from it. The basket of food sat on the next table. The clear ferry lights they'd used for the Abbott event were strung back and forth over the patio and even a bit over the raised garden beds.

It had been jarring to have the New York crew descend on him—on the inn, that is. He'd agreed to it; but then how could he have said no to Anna, when she needed help, and giving her help would mean it brought her back here. Not that she could stay, of course. But maybe it would give them the resolution he'd so unsuccessfully copped out on in phone conversations with her. At least he didn't have to be in the show himself; he was a behind-the-scenes kind of guy anyway. And soon enough, they'd be gone, and maybe he and Iris and the team would get some PR out of it.

Some PR, and another painful departure by Anna. But somehow the chance to resolve things felt more pressing. Not that he had any idea exactly how it should look. But at least having this little dinner out back, before all the filming started, was a way to claim this time for both of them. And maybe just get past the weird jumble of events that had happened and get on with things.

He hoped she'd like the table setup—these touches were usually the domain of Iris or Pete and Tina. Hopefully he'd learned something from hanging out with them. At least she'd never find out about his cookie fiasco.

Jake took a deep breath, digging his hands into the pockets of his chinos.

Iris had been right. It was time to try to talk to Anna, to ask her why she'd left. What was the worst that could happen?

Well, total rejection. But at least it would only be in front of the cat. And, as he repeated so often to himself as if to train his thoughts to stay in line: *She'd be gone soon enough.*

He heard a step at the kitchen door and turned. Anna stood, framed by the doorway to the living room. Her face was fresh and open, and her eyes squinted into smiles beneath her graceful arched brows. Man, he loved that, fleetingly remembering the teenage Annie. Which only made the real Anna who stood before him even more endearing and amazing.

"Hi," he said. Brilliant opener. "Uh … what do you think?" He gestured through the open door out to the patio.

Anna stepped forward past him, toward the door, and as she passed by, Jake could smell a faint musky fragrance. Inconveniently, he found himself wanting to bury his face in it. *She'll be gone soon enough.*

She pulled in a breath. "Jake, it's beautiful. This is for dinner? For us?" She turned toward him.

"Yeah. I, uh, made a sort of picnic. I didn't want to muck up the kitchen, now that you and Iris and everybody are getting things ready. And I thought we could give a café table a test drive—see how it feels?"

"Good idea. Research!" She laughed, holding up a slim finger in a habit he was finding irresistibly endearing.

"Right, of course, research." He indicated one of the chairs.

Anna sat down, smoothing her silky white blouse printed with tiny flowers—which, Jake noted, looked fabulous—and shaking her thin shimmer of silver bangles down her tan arm. Jake felt her watching him as he lifted an open bottle of wine from a nearby table along with two glasses.

"Why don't you pour, while I sort all this out," Jake said,

pulling sandwiches and plates from the basket, followed by strawberries and two small lemon tarts.

"It's perfect," she said, smiling as she poured. "What is that, chicken salad? You made it?" Annoyingly, her voice was a bit incredulous.

He shot her a glance. "Well, I could pretend I did, but with your finely tuned palate, you'd recognize Iris's trademark herbs pretty quickly. She made it this morning—I think she knew it would find somewhere to land tonight."

"And the strawberries?"

"From the farm stand right outside town—the one Albert uses."

"Excellent. And the tarts?"

"Haven. When she gets nervous, she bakes. And then delivers. Her anxiety goes down, and the edibles in the kitchen go up. It's a win-win."

Anna laughed. "And the wine?"

"Local winery. Of course. A pinot grigio. Let me know what you think."

He looked over at her, sleek and friendly in the blouse that made him think of the gardens. Her thick dark waves were in a loose chignon, and small silver loops hung from her ears.

Time to stop staring. He cleared his throat and held up his glass. She welcomed him with a smile as they touched their glasses with a light ping.

Might as well be bold, he thought. "To storms?"

"To storms," Anna agreed.

They took a moment to sip. The quiet felt palpable.

Setting down his glass, Jake motioned to the food. "Well, help yourself." He picked up his own sandwich, wondering if this was the right moment.

"Rubin and Sierra really love the place," Anna began.

OK, not the moment yet. Might as well follow her lead. "Good, good. I'm sure there's some changes to make, but I hope we got it into good enough shape to get everything rolling. So ... tell me more about reality TV. I mean, I've seen some of it, I guess. But I've never really thought about how it works." That seemed a safe enough topic for now. Nothing too close to home.

"Ah." She held up a slender ringed finger—charming, again, he thought. "A good question. Without a clear answer."

As Anna launched into descriptions, Jake nodded, listening but also noticing. Her eyes were animated—smiling eyes, as he'd come to think of them—and her glance danced as she spoke. The Annie he'd known before had really blossomed. Man, it was good to have her sitting back here, no matter how messed up he felt about trying to talk to her about ... what had happened.

"We wanted to get back to a better vibe than where a lot of reality shows have gone," she was saying. "Too many of them are about embarrassing people. You know, making someone feel bad, or like they have to win or lose. And then they have to do those interviews where they spill their guts and talk about each other."

Though he had no idea what she was talking about, Jake nodded.

"And we wanted to get back to something more like one of the first shows of this whole ... trend."

"Which was?"

"*The Real World*. On MTV back in the '90s. Don't you remember? I think we were starting high school. Or somewhere around there."

Jake couldn't remember much more from those days than playing football and worrying about the inn. And chatting with Annie at the store. Habits start early. "Sort of," he lied.

"Well, we want it to get back to being ... sweeter. Not too edited. Mainly how people come together in a workplace. Because we all have workplaces in our lives. But ..." She held up her finger again, which he found as cute as the first time. "...

for this, we needed a workplace that has something people *like* in it."

"Like your amazing pastries and cakes and breads?"

She giggled girlishly, which he also found he liked. He was liking a lot tonight.

"Exactly. But also the drinks. We're making sure they're really carefully sourced—we know the places they're made, the people who roast the coffees or make the liqueurs, that kind of thing. And then the drinks are matched up with the time of day and the pastries, or bread or homemade crackers or whatever, being served. Just … simple. And kinder."

"And they're filming you doing all this? Seems like a lot for one person to carry off. You know—lots of focus just on them." Though why not? He was having no trouble focusing only on her.

Even in the dim light, he could see her blush. "No, it's supposed to be about all of us—staff and customers. I've got a great colleague back in the city, Colleen, she's my backup, in case I get sick or something."

"Like, detoured?"

She smiled deeply. "Like detoured. Colleen would have been here with me, but she couldn't get out here from the city just now—she's got a beautiful new baby boy! I love seeing them together."

To hear Anna mention a baby … why did that have an effect on him too? "Can't leave that. You going to be OK on your own?"

"Oh definitely. That's what Haven's covering—what Colleen would have done on set."

"Glad to hear it." Was good to hear one of his 'own' was getting something out of this.

"We've also got some interviews with makers out here for some of the drinks," Anna continued. "Of course, now we can get more ingredients right here. One of Sierra's assistants is working on it, but I told them you'd know all the best farm stands." She glanced shyly down; was she, like him, remembering all their old haunts?

Just watching how animated her face had become made it clear to Jake how much the café meant to her. But by now it was all about the café itself; the reality-show part of picture now seemed almost absent. "I like it. I'll have to start getting into reality TV," he said, with a touch of curiosity. "Did you always have a thing for it?"

Anna paused. "No, not really. I hadn't really watched much of it since those early days."

"What did you like about the idea for this one? If you didn't like a lot of reality TV, what made you say 'yes'?"

Anna stopped for a second, fork poised before spiking a strawberry. "You know? No one's ever asked me that."

"Well, someone just did."

She thought a moment. "I guess that when Rubin had this idea and pitched it to the producer, it felt like it might help show real life in a real workplace—sort of like what *The Real World* did for a living space. Not hyped-up drama, just real people showing what they can do, I guess."

Jake nodded, listening. It was nice to hear her follow her own thoughts. He flashed back on recent conversations with the Anna he was coming to know, or at least, know better. "You mean, showing their talents?"

She nodded slowly. "Yes. Showing what they can do."

"And having it be on TV would mean …"

She finished his thought and his sentence. "… that it was really seen. No one would be hidden." She reached her fork to thoughtfully spike a strawberry.

A small piece of pain cut through the softness Jake had been feeling, and internally, he wheeled around to face the guilty memory that had been shadowing him.

OK, this might be the moment, he realized, feeling Iris and

Haven prodding him over his shoulder like little devils. At least time to try. The kiss, her departure ... and his comment to Samuels. But wasn't his guilt his problem? He'd fixed it, after all. Why drag her down? Except that it felt like it was coming between them, if only in his own head, and he didn't like that feeling.

Jake picked up a strawberry nonchalantly. "So you'll do this one show, then everybody goes back to the city?"

Her eyes clouded. "I think that's what the producer is thinking. That this bought us time to finish up the place in Soho."

Why wasn't she meeting his gaze? "You too?"

This brought her glance back to his. "That's the idea," she repeated slowly.

Jake cleared his throat and sat up straighter, setting down the berry. "Anna, I ... I'm sorry if this sounds kind of awkward, but ..." He fought to keep his gaze steady as her eyes widened slightly. "When you left before, after the Abbott event. You went ... so fast. We didn't have a chance to talk. And I feel like there's something I need to say."

She set down her fork. Her voice was low and calm. "I know I left quickly, Jake. I'm sorry. I want to apologize for that. It was impolite."

He shook his head. "We knew you had to get back to work, to the city. I just ..."

"What?" She was listening intently.

OK. Showtime. He took a breath. "Look, I know I ... I took a chance and kissed you, and it probably wasn't the right thing to do. But I'll take one more chance and say this ..."

Anna was leaning forward cautiously, her hand forgotten on her wine glass.

"I'm sure you get guys interested in you all the time. Hell, I don't even know if you have a boyfriend." He glanced away from her. It was easier to talk that way, now that he'd started. "And I shouldn't have just done it like that. I owe you an apology. But Anna, I … I felt something between us, and I didn't think. I can't tell if it is something old or something new. But it was there. It .. it *is* there. And …" he finished quickly, shrugging, "it's just that I'll be sad to see you go again."

There. He'd probably sounded like an idiot, but at least he could tell Iris and Haven that he hadn't backed down.

He looked up at Anna, steeling himself for her to give a kind but clear rejection. But she didn't.

Instead she lifted her hand and slowly, tentatively, touched his right fingers where they rested on the table by his glass. Reflexively, at her touch, he jumped slightly, then shifted his palm upward so that hers lay in it.

"Me too, Jake." Her voice was almost a whisper. "I did too. And I don't know if it's old or new or … or both." She gave a quick smile, looking at him intently. Jake had no idea where the conversation was going, but it sure felt good to be in her gaze—and touching her hand. "By the way—I'm not seeing anyone. And for the record … I was glad you kissed me."

Jake didn't realize how clenched he'd felt until relief swelled in him like a wave at the beach. The chances had felt so slim that she would meet him on what seemed like this tiny strand of a high-wire act—and yet somehow she had. He nodded slightly, resisting the urge to grasp her hand fully in his. "And still … you have to go back."

She pursed her slips slightly and squinted thoughtfully at the lights overhead. "This feeling … that we're talking about. It's … so new that I don't know what to do with it." She looked back at him and gave a small shrug. "Do you?"

There was a strange clash of fear and longing in his gut. "New York's not very far away," he said weakly, not sure of what he meant by it.

Anna nodded, looking down. "But it feels far away." She pulled her hand back—Jake mirrored it with his own—and furrowed her brow. "You know, you asked about my leaving so quickly before."

Apprehension began to rear its head again, and Jake leaned back, crossing his arms defensively.

"I wanted to—" She stopped and gave a rueful smile. "Tonight suddenly seems to be about saying things that aren't easy to say. Were you finished?"

Jake shifted uncomfortably. Not yet—talking about that night wasn't complete without talking about what he'd then said down at the barn. But somehow, it felt like too much weight for this moment.

"Finished enough for now. Your turn," he said evenly.

"OK, here goes." She took a visible breath. "This is kind of embarrassing, but … I don't know if you remember that Albert had a videocam set up at the barn? So he could know what was going on when he was up in the kitchen?"

"Of course. I thought it was smart. Especially since the kitchen and the event were in separate buildings." Jake tried to sound conversational, but he was totally baffled about what could possibly be coming next. What the heck did Albert's cam have to do with anything?

"Well, after the event, after the … the kiss … I was up in the kitchen with Albert cleaning up. You were down in the barn, talking to Mr. Samuels." She paused. "From Taggarts? And with … Mr. Abbott."

A dark realization began to creep into Jake's awareness. Oh, crap, he thought. No, surely, she didn't hear …

But she had.

"I heard you," Anna continued hurriedly. "I didn't mean to, it was just on. But when he asked you about the cake, you didn't even say my name. You didn't even act like I … like I was there."

As he saw the pain that finally fully showed itself in Anna's beautiful face, Jake felt punched in the gut—by his own stupid actions. Unwittingly, he put his palm to his forehead, grimacing, as he pictured the moment she must have heard it.

"Anna, I apologize. I … I remember that moment, and I feel awful about it. I've thought about it over and over since then, and I know it was the wrong thing to do. And … and I've fixed it. Please, let me try to explain."

Her eyes still flickered with pain and wariness, her hands withdrawn into her lap. How he wished he could rewind time, give the right answer to Samuels, and have her hand back up on the table touching his. Talking about the kiss.

The kiss. This was right after the kiss. Oh, geez, that made it even worse.

"That was right after I … kissed you." He pushed out the words, as she gave a slight nod. "Damn, that must have felt like whiplash."

"Yep."

Jake plunged ahead, knowing there was no way to stop now. "One of the things Samuels liked so much about what we were doing with the inn was how it used local people. Artisans and farmers and all that. He had talked about it with me several times before. And when he asked about the cake, I just panicked. Like, if he knew you'd done it, he would think we didn't really stick with the program, like it was just a gimmick. Like I had brought in a pro from the city or something." Jake glanced down at the table, then back up. "It was lame. I knew at the time it felt wrong. And now I realize, Anna, it's like what happened to your dad."

Anna was just sitting there, her brown eyes wide. He wanted to know what was going on inside her—and he wanted more than anything to pull her up into an embrace. Nothing made sense.

As if making one last-ditch effort for a woman he had no reason to feel he had any kind of dibs on, he caught her eyes firmly with his own.

"Anna. I'm. Sorry."

He looked so vulnerable that it made her heart hurt.

Anna wanted to believe him. What she would do with that belief, she had no idea. But for better or worse, she wanted to.

Relief began to thread its way through her, but before she could speak, Jake swung his face back forward again. "I was dishonest about giving you credit for the cake. But there's another way I was dishonest."

"Which was?"

"I was dishonest about you being part of 'us.' About you belonging ... here." His arm swept down toward the darkened barn. "I know your life is in New York now, I'm not saying that's not true. But it felt like you really were part of the team, like you belonged here."

Anna blinked, trying to take it in. She wanted to pause and land on each thing he'd said, but he was galloping forward, and all she could do was try to keep up.

"And Anna, I fixed it. I hope. When Samuels called to tell me about the review, I told him. I didn't care if it changed how he thought about me or the inn or anything. I told him about your growing up here, you and your dad, and how you made the cake to help us out. But that you were local. Not just in the past, but in the present. Because ..." He looked agonized for a moment. "It feels to me like you *do* belong here. I know it can't work that way. But it's just ... how I feel."

He sat back, looking spent and vulnerable, his hands resting on the small table.

Anna peered at him, trying to process what he'd said. Shocked relief and tender gratitude began to flow inside her. Somehow he'd taken what had been something that dug painfully into her past and transform the whole thing into a present where she belonged.

When she finally found words, her voice was hoarse and soft. "So what did Samuels say?"

Jake's voice was quieter now. "He said it was great. He knew about you, knew your work. He thought it was … cool that you were from here. He said …"

She leaned toward him unconsciously. "What?"

"That this was some 'unfolding story.' Like there was more to come, more to the story, I guess."

"So you told him it was me?" Anna fought the distant sensation of tears. "That I was part of the story?"

Jake just nodded mutely.

Instinctively, Anna reached forward and rested her hands over his once more. She knew she didn't know what could possibly come of it all, and she didn't care. This moment felt complete.

"Jake, thank you. It feels like that to me too. Like I reconnected with … this place. And to be totally honest, maybe I've been reconnecting with parts of me from the past. Parts I didn't want anymore. But I didn't realize …" She raised her eyebrows as she looked into middle distance. "I can't leave parts out. It just doesn't work that way."

Jake watched her intently, his hands motionless under hers. "Is that why you wanted to come back to do the pilot?"

"Of course." Then again, it wasn't the only reason. It wasn't only about the past and who she had been then. It was about who she was now—and who Jake was now. They had both been daringly honest. Why stop now? "But there were other reasons too. It hurt when you said that to Samuels. But it wasn't something I could just … walk away from."

"I'm glad you didn't." Again, Jake slowly turned his hands upward so that they were palm-to-palm with hers. "So … was Samuels right? Does the story go on?"

Panic rose in her as Anna once again felt she was straddling irreconcilable worlds. The inner world she felt now, with Jake. And the outer world, of all the work and goof-ups and successes that had brought her to this point. That had made Anna out of Annie.

She tried to smile, but knew it was weak. "Of course. This place will be a success, and hopefully the show will too. And we'll …"

She felt Jake's hands stiffen under hers.

"We'll stay in touch. Of course."

In the silence that followed, Jake's open face seemed to change gears. He nodded, giving her hands a quick squeeze, then pulling back to himself.

His small smile seemed forced. "Well, at least we got that night sorted out. Glad we got it resolved. And I'm sure the show will be great."

"They weren't married long," Iris offered as she and Anna sipped tea.

Baby-fresh sunlight blessed the kitchen, and the old-fashioned hands of the farmhouse-style clock on the wall said 6:10. Anna had woken early and padded downstairs to find Iris up and humming. And somehow, amid serving tea and slicing the bread for her traditional toast, the older woman had toggled gracefully from talking about how big this week was for Jake, to the news that Margaret was remarried, as if she and Anna had been in the middle of some ongoing cozy chat about it all. But then Iris made everything feel cozy.

"I'll let him tell you details—those are his to tell," she was saying. "But I will say that none of us thought it was a match from the start. I think he thought they'd be able to be partners in taking care of the inn, the way his mom and dad had been. He thought he was doing what was expected of him. I don't think he stopped to think of what he wanted for himself."

Anna frowned. "Jake just did what was expected? It never looked that way to me. He always looked so … assured. And I was so opposite."

"Don't let looks fool you," Iris said. "You know the old adage—don't compare your insides with someone else's outsides. He was always trying to measure up to some legacy about this old place. Having no roots in your hometown can be tough, I imagine." Iris's glance was purposeful, as she continued, "But so can having roots that go too far back. I'm not sure his dad was always very helpful in that regard. He praised Jake a lot, but I think it ended up making Jake think he had a lot to live up to."

Anna narrowed her eyes as a little more insight into Jake began to dawn. "I never thought about it that way before. I always assumed that being part of this family, this place, couldn't be anything but perfect."

Iris gave a small sigh. "That's exactly what Jake felt like he had to live up to. Maybe partnering up with Margaret seemed like an answer. Then they saw that he wanted one thing for the inn and she wanted something else—and Jake got stubborn, like he will, and held onto his vision for it. She's a smart business-woman with her own ideas. And, well, the short version is, they broke up. But since they were both from these longtime Cedarwood Spring families, I'm afraid the whole thing was public. Margaret moved to New York and got involved in real estate there, but Jake was left to sort it out here."

Anna felt her heart squeeze. "How awful for him."

"Yes, it really kicked him in the gut. He felt like the whole town saw him fail. I don't think he ever understood that nobody blamed him or Margaret. They were both so young."

"I remember her from high school. I never knew her though. I don't think she noticed me." Warmed by the honesty of the conversations, she added without thinking, "I didn't think most of the kids did."

Putz wove back and forth between their feet.

"So you felt left out?" Iris regarded her.

Anna nodded. "Yeah," she said with a sigh.

"You know, I thought I could see something like that back then. You were sort of shy but also always so observant," the older woman said softly. Anna thought back to the girl she'd been and how sweet it was to think that Iris had seen her with such compassion. What a difference it would have made to her to know it back then.

Iris brought her back to the present. "And do you feel that way now?"

For a second, Anna wondered if it was OK to be talking to Jake's grandmother about … her deepest feelings, most of which she was still figuring out. But it felt good to lean on the older woman's wisdom. And in some way, it felt like it helped make sense of the strangeness of finding herself back at the inn, again.

"I don't know," she ventured. "I thought I had gotten past it. I worked so hard in New York, and in lots of ways, I feel *very* seen —probably way too much. But back here … and back at the Abbott wedding … there was a moment when … well, when I felt invisible again." No need to bend Iris's ear with the details.

Iris looked at her. "Did that have anything to do with why you left without saying goodbye?"

Anna nodded, keeping mum on the specs.

Iris reached out and lightly patted Anna's hand. "But you're back now. And I'm glad. And I know my grandson—and I know that he's glad too."

A couple of hours later, Anna stood among the front flower beds in her sleek New York casual—so different from her vacation casual from a couple of weeks before—watching the crew quickly and efficiently begin to build a new reality here at the inn. Everyone was crowding around the breakfast van that had pulled up to the front for them, well stocked with fruit from the local stands and goodies from the Filling Station.

As she bit into an almond croissant, gripping a fresh cup of coffee in the other hand, Anna glanced up to see Rubin rounding the corner of the inn. With Jake.

Rubin was talking fast and gesturing vividly, while Jake looked at a loss for words.

Wow, Rubin and Jake—that was cognitive dissonance. New York and Cedarwood Spring, past and present, colliding into some new Picasso-like jumble.

Quickly wiping crumbs from her mouth with a napkin, Anna swore once again to maintain professional demeanor. After all, though the success of the inn had been on Jake and team a few weeks before, it now oddly felt like some part of that success was on her. And her talk with Jake the night before had left her feeling close, raw, and excited—and suddenly vulnerable to a broken heart. Her growing desire to never walk away from Jake again was utterly at odds with logistical reality.

Even as she felt a kick of anxiety, she raised her cup toward them and called out, "Good morning, guys. Over here."

"Oh, there you are," Rubin answered. "I just got word that the production company wants to bring in an outside designer, some catering backup, a florist, layout design. You know, all the usual. They want the inn to have more international appeal—for a broader audience. Better chance at getting picked up by affiliates. It needs to lose the name Cedarwood Spring Inn—too cute, too local. At least for the show, they want a name that hinges on the solstice. Of course, I'm still voting for Love Bite—it look me a lot of margaritas to come up with that one. But out here, they want to change it to Lunar View, or Solstice View, or something—"

"What?!" Anna broke in incredulously, blinking. Now she understood the flashes of pain on Jake's face. It was one thing when Rubin muscled things his way through stuff in New York. But this? It clearly trampled over everything Jake had invested here—the inn, the concept, good heavens, even the name of the place.

Even as her feelings about Jake played tag inside her, they were quickly outpaced by righteous anger on his behalf. Time to reroute this before it went any further. Just then, Sierra emerged from one of the vans. Good, she needed reinforcements.

"Look, Rubin," Jake began, trying to respond, "I had agreed to work with this, but ..." He broke off, looking angry and miserable.

"Morning," Sierra said, joining them.

"We have to act fast," Rubin pressed on, undeterred. "The graphics designers have to crunch this tonight. And the company has to get their own people here to make sure everything's right."

"But what about Pete and Tina?" Jake said, and Anna had the impression he was repeating something he'd already said to Rubin before. "And Albert, and Tom, and Haven? I promise, they're the best. Pete and Tina moved down from Brooklyn a couple of years ago—"

"I'm sure they're darling," Rubin said, glancing at his phone as he talked, "but we need a team of pros to take this to the next level." There was a sudden rustle as Putz darted among their feet and into a raised flower bed. Rubin let out a yelp. "And somebody get rid of that damn one-eyed cat. He keeps freaking me out."

Anna thought quickly. Sometimes a crisis puts things into perspective real quick—and though she wouldn't have been aware of it last night over dinner, it was suddenly crystal-clear to her exactly what she felt dedicated to—and if forced to choose, which this definitely felt like, she didn't choose the show. She chose the inn.

The inn—as in Cedarwood Spring Inn. Not Solstice blah-blah-blah.

And right now, that meant choosing Jake. Funny, how easy that suddenly was.

Anna stepped firmly toward Rubin, as Jake looked on agonizingly.

"Rubin," she said, "a team of pros has already taken this place to the next level. They've done it before, they can do it again. If you haven't looked around, please do. And be sure you've got those glasses on. This place looks perfect. It's why Sierra and I chose it, and it's going to be hard to top." She gestured to the gardens, to the bowery that Pete and Tina had created over the iron archway, and to the boxes of fresh food Albert had unloaded at the front door. And to the sign: Cedarwood Spring Inn.

"I know these people and they know me." She glanced uncertainly at Jake, who was watching her. His eyes seemed to give her permission, and she turned back to Rubin. "And you couldn't find anybody better. It's what Cedarwood Spring Inn is. If you want to base the show here—if you want me in it—you have to do it on Jake's terms. And no one else's."

Holding her croissant with all the authority she could muster, she posed her hand on her hip defiantly. Wow, she hoped it was working. "And that includes the *cat*." She emphatically punched the air with the croissant.

Rubin looked up from his phone, raised his eyebrows over his glasses, and whistled. "OK, OK, Anna, you go, girl! This is why I love ya. You know I've been wanting you to lean into the show. And here you are. Careful what you ask for!" He laughed at himself. "Anything to get this damn pilot off the ground! You know I'll do anything for you, so I'll do this too. Even if it costs me." He gave a faux-baleful look.

"Remember what we said?" she retorted, trying to let banter return them to normalcy. "I'm a pâtissière, babe. I know chemistry and timing. Jake already has the right chemistry here, and now we have the right timing. Don't mess with a good thing."

"Got it. I'll call them now. Pray for me." Rubin reached out to shake Jake's hand.

Jake took it, not looking directly at Anna. "Good deal," he said, watching as Rubin turned, waving, to head back to one of the vans.

Anna glanced sideways at Sierra who, out of Jake's sight-lines, gave Anna a two-thumbs-up, then moved in front of the couple.

"Well, glad that's settled," Sierra said efficiently, giving Anna a quick hug. "You got game, girl."

"You too, girl," Anna said, remembering their convo back in New York and watching as Sierra headed over to talk to crewmembers.

Looking absently toward the crew, her own words still echoing in her mind, Anna felt a finger brush her hand, summoning her attention.

She fleetingly froze, as Jake's finger hesitantly linked into her palm and her hand lightly closed around his. As she thundered into the moment, Anna had a flash of uncertainty. She hoped he didn't mind her taking charge that way. She'd thought she was saving him, but there was every chance he didn't see it that way.

Struggling to retain her professional poise in light of the feel of Jake's hand, she looked up at him cautiously. "Jake, I hope that was OK. I hope it didn't come across like I was trying to … to speak *for* you. You've done great work with all of this, and you don't need help from New York. I'm just trying to make sure the inn stays … well, that it stays yours. Yours and Iris's," she added hastily. "And besides, I'm used to dealing with Rubin. He's great, but he takes some getting used to."

Jake's eyes softened.

"What are you thinking?" Anna pressed.

"I'm thinking we're quite a pair," he said slowly. "I didn't know how to make it work both for you and for me. It felt too much like it had to be one or the other. He took me by surprise. I just … couldn't see a solution. But you did. One that worked for both of us."

Anna breathed a sigh of relief. "It works *fine* for both of us. Look, these New York guys will love hanging out with our team here at the inn. I mean—" she broke off, realizing with a blush that it had felt like all the people she'd been ticking off to Rubin were her team. "I mean, *your* team."

"Anna," Jake spoke slowly. "I'd love it if they were *our* team, together. Yours and mine. Can we agree to do that—just for the shoot?"

Anna nodded, avoiding Jake's eyes. Trying to stay in the moment and step carefully around last night, and around the feel of his hand and the warmth that rose in her chest. "That's perfect, Jake, thanks."

His eyes searched hers again. "And … after the shoot?"

She met his gaze, her heart fluttering. "After?" she asked weakly. This was not helping her professional demeanor.

"There's something here, Anna. I don't know what to do with it. But I … I want to talk."

She took a deep breath and squeezed his hand before releasing it. "You're right."

"About what?"

She took a deep breath, briefly closing her eyes. "What's here, with us." What's here. But—where was *here*?

"So we can talk?"

She nodded emphatically, looking purposefully up at him and wrestling her heart for self-control. "Definitely. But right now, I've got to go get ready for some interviews Rubin set up. And then all afternoon, I have to work with Sierra on the kitchen layout." She smiled at him, feeling more on track.

"Of course," Jake said. "Um, I've got a full schedule too.

How about tomorrow morning? I have to drive into town on some errands before everyone starts pouring in."

"Lights, action, camera," Anna said. "Sounds right—I'm sure I'll be up for a break to get my head straight."

"Anna!" Rubin was leaning out the door of his van. "Need you now!"

"I'm being summoned," she said and, heading over to Rubin, turned to give a thumbs-up to Jake. "Tomorrow morning it is. We're almost there."

As she stepped into the van, her last glimpse of Jake was his open smile, intent on her even from yards away, his thumbs crooked through his belt loops as he stood back on his hip, framed by the beautiful stone home behind him. There was no denying it after last night … her heart was here.

But hearts didn't always know what was good for them. Her heart would have to learn to negotiate.

CHAPTER 10

T he truck was already purring as Jake leaned across the seat to push open the door. "Hop in."

"Thanks," Anna said breathlessly, hoisting herself up to the seat and pulling the door shut behind her. "Sorry I was running a little late."

She quickly perused his silhouette. Jake looked a bit more spiffed up than his usual workday clothes around the inn: the same chinos and shirt, of course—only newer-looking and missing the usual smudge marks. His hair, still damp from a morning shower, was smoothed back in pale waves.

"You look ... nice," she said, at the same time thinking, God, I hope I sound like I'm just being polite—instead of crazy-happy to see how really, *really* dashing he is.

In a way, it made the teenage Jake, as cute as he was, look like a guy who hadn't really grown into himself yet. But this Jake—he was all grown-up.

"Thanks. You too." Jake tossed a smile as he slipped the motor into gear.

Anna gave a quick laugh and smoothed her hands down what she had come to think of as her inn clothes, versus "in-clothes"

—comfy jeans and a soft, lightweight blouse with rolled-up sleeves. Sort of like Jake … come to think of it. "Yeah, right. I'm not supposed to look good yet—they'll take care of that later. Though if they tell me to 'love the camera' one more time, I'll throw eggs at them. And not the boiled kind."

He smiled, his eyes crinkling at the edges as he glanced back at the driveway. "You don't need to love any damn camera. You look great, just like that."

Anna felt a flutter in her stomach that wasn't about the show.

"So how are you feeling?"

She let out a puff of breath and looked at him nervously. "I'm feeling everything."

"Like?"

"Well, scared. Of course. This is something new and big. And I've never done anything like it before. Lots of interviews, sure, but nothing like this. And there's so much riding on it. For Sierra and Rubin—and for the inn." She looked at him with eyebrows raised cautiously, not quite sure if that was the right thing to say.

It seemed to be OK, since Jake nodded. "I know the feeling. So, what else?"

Anna watched the trees blur as they headed toward the end of the driveway, flashing back for a second on that stormy night a few weeks ago when Jake had first driven her up this driveway. But no need to add that ingredient into the conversation.

"Oh, just hoping it'll be fun for everyone. That even if it's work, that everybody has a good time. It's the whole idea behind it, after all."

"And the name of the café?" His gaze was straight ahead.

Anna smiled over at him. "You'll be glad to know we left Love Bite back in the city, and I nixed all Rubin's other equally dubious suggestions. I wanted to keep it simple. It's just the Cedarwood Inn Café." She paused to let it sink in. "Has a nice ring to it, don't you think?"

Jake drove steadily. "I do. So it'll air in a week or so? I still don't get how they do it that quickly."

"Me neither, actually. But that's the magic the editing and production crew do in those white vans. All their equipment is in there. Jake, it was super of you and Iris to let everybody set up shop on your property. You've had people crawling all over the place for days."

"No problem. So ... do they like the inn?"

"They love it. I've heard from so many crew members about how this is the vacay they needed this time of year—and that they're coming back." She hoped her voice sounded encouraging —and not as empty as her gut felt when she thought about leaving here ... again.

"Great. And ..." He took a deep breath. "Do you think *you* will be coming back?"

Anna felt her stomach say hello. But wasn't this why they were driving in together? To talk?

"I hope so," she said quietly. "I ... I want to."

Jake steered down what were once again becoming familiar roads to Anna. That weird old/new thing. It tugged at something deeper inside of her, some place she'd forgotten about. It was like closing a loop that she hadn't realized was still dangling loose.

"Anna, I know I said I wanted to talk to you. But there are so many people we know in town. Do you mind if we take a quick detour?"

"Not at all. I'm getting pretty good at those lately." Her voice was quiet.

"Thank goodness." He steered up a nearby hill that she knew led to a spot that overlooked the entire valley. She hadn't been here in years, but she remembered coming up here to watch the setting sun with Papi, often at the end of the afternoon's deliveries. It would be nice to see it again.

They reached the overlook, where an outcropping of rock sat

poised over a sweep of valley below. Jake pulled over, and they climbed out of the truck.

Anna walked over where she could see the expansive span of the green fields that lay before them, each one plowed and planted slightly differently so that the whole picture looked like a beautiful soft green crosshatch quilt. "Jake, this is so beautiful. I'd forgotten," she murmured, slowly drinking the view in with her eyes. She realized she was thirsty for it.

Suddenly, she felt him arrive beside her. His hands rested on his hips as he squinted into the morning sun, shifting his weight to one hip. Nestled in the valley, Anna could see the cluster of buildings that was the borough of Cedarwood Spring, and in the midst of it, the small steeple of Old Trinity Church where they'd been to the Abbott wedding.

"Coming up here was a good idea before all the craziness today. Keeps things in perspective," she said, pivoting slightly toward him.

Jake nodded and gestured behind them to a wood-and-iron bench that looked like it had been added recently. "There's a bench over here. Want to sit?"

As they settled onto the bench, Anna was aware of a gentle creak from their weight and the clean smell of Jake's shirt. She held the silence that was between them like it was a delicate baby kitten and she was waiting to see what sounds it made. Though her eyes were still on the valley, she closely tracked Jake in her left periphery.

He leaned forward, elbows resting on his legs and hands clasped together. Like Anna, he kept his gaze on the vista. The breeze ruffled his hair loose.

"I know we talked last night. But there's something else to say. And it's about Margaret."

Anna's eyebrows raised.

Glancing at her, Jake hastily continued, "It's not like I've seen her, or need to. It was more the news she had remarried."

Anna asked the question that had been resting on the edge of her mind. "How was it to hear that?"

"It was OK. It really was. In fact, I think it kind of helped me." A dry chuckle. "Iris said it would. It helps me feel like maybe it's not that I just screwed up. Maybe for a while, it was that Margaret and I needed each other to learn."

"Learn what?"

Jake gave a small shrug. "The way forward. What was most important to each of us. And then ... finding out that the way forward was apart."

Anna took a slow breath, steadying her mind. They were saying newer, deeper things to each other. Maybe there was space for one more question. "Jake, can I ask you ..."

"Sure. You're already getting TMI."

She turned toward him. "Didn't you date after your divorce?"

He switched his gaze back to the valley. "I tried, a couple of times. But it always felt like it made my life into ... into less. Not more." He paused. "You?"

Oops, wrong direction. She wanted to talk about him, not her. But no way to dodge it. "Yeah, Carson. We were involved for six years." That always sounded ridiculously long when she had nothing left to show for it.

"And?"

Anna sighed. He'd ponied up, she might as well do the same. "He always seemed to like the glamour of ... whatever life I was making there in New York. He always pushed in that direction—the parties, the media. The show, even. He kept saying the show would help me break out. Whatever that means." Anna tucked a loose wave behind one ear. "But he never seemed OK with just ... me. With me just liking to create and make up recipes and dishes, and talk about my mom and papi back here. I think it made me feel like I had to hide that part of me. Or like I had to keep trying to run away from it."

Jake was silent for a moment. "You broke up with him?"

"Well, yes, but only after … after I figured out he was starting to see someone else." She glanced quickly at him, then just as quickly looked away.

He grimaced. "Sorry about that."

"Thanks. It was all through Facebook and a tag that led to a comment that … Look, no need for the details. But I ended it, and he didn't seem too unhappy about it. And I put the pedal to the metal with my work. And then the pilot came through." She gave a sardonic half-smile. "He'd be so pleased."

Jake looked back at her, his voice level. "And are *you* pleased? With the show?"

She paused. "It's what I thought I wanted. Or what I should want. It seemed like the next logical step. But now, after … these past few weeks, I'm not sure. I mean, don't get me wrong. Having the show is great. And it's not a done deal. We have to see if the producers buy it, if they want it to be more than the one-off deal."

"But you're not sure you want it. Sounds like a lot of work for something you don't know you want."

Wow, he was really nailing everything that was going on inside her, only he was doing it better than she could. She shook her head, trying to keep up, let alone get ahead. "It is a lot of work, and I love work. But what I'm wondering is … is the show the work I *want*? These past few months, I've spent more time with directors and producers and crew and designers than I have in the kitchen. Though I think Sierra is great—"

"Me too, for the record."

"And time with Rubin and 'soft scripts' and how to make a kitchen be easy to get good camera shots in—"

"But not easy to actually bake in?"

She nodded emphatically. "Exactly. And now I'm feeling like somewhere along the way, the priorities got turned upside down. I thought I was getting what I wanted, and then it seemed … like I lost what I wanted."

Jake looked down at his hands. "What is it you *do* want, Anna?" Though his voice was light, the words felt heavy to her.

"That's just it. I thought I knew. I thought that getting this show—I mean, getting that top slot if it went to a series—was perfect. I thought it would be the answer to everything. But the reality ..."

Jake gave a teasing half-smile. "The reality of reality TV?"

Without thinking, she laughed and reached over to give his hand a small fist bump. "The reality of reality TV is that ... I mainly want to bake. Without compromising my own space, my own vision, my own customers. And the past few months, getting ready for the show, I realize ... I've lost so much direction in my own baking, my own craft, whole new things I want to explore with it. And it's left me feeling kind of empty. I got too far from ... well, too far from home."

"A detour?" Jake's voice was almost playful.

She gave a quick dry laugh. "Yeah, ironic. And what helped me see that I was too far from home was how good it felt to be back here. With you and Iris, in the kitchen." As she heard her own words, she frowned and pulled herself straight as if she'd just realized something. "You know, I haven't said that out loud before—or even in my head."

Jake was looking down at where her hand had briefly touched his, and then slowly lifted his hand, held it open for a second, and reached over to circle his fingers around hers. Anna watched it, any more words stuck in her mouth. It was warm, and it felt like it cradled her entire soul.

This made no sense, no sense at all. But ... sitting here, looking at the valley and holding Jake's hand, was *exactly* what she wanted.

"Jake." Her voice was almost a whisper. "Can I ask you one *more* question?"

"Of course." His grasp tightened slightly.

She was still looking her hand resting in his. "Why did you kiss me?"

He gave an almost inaudible laugh. "Well, I can give you several reasons."

"Like …" She couldn't resist a note of affectionate teasing.

"Like, you're …" he glanced at her, then quickly looked away, his hand tightening impulsively. "Isn't it obvious? You're smart. And talented and fun. Beautiful, of course. And you have great ideas that actually end up coming true. Not just … dreams." He squinted. "And you make everyone around you feel good. You make me feel good. You always did." He looked intently at her. "Those are reasons. But really, in the moment, it just … felt right. And I should have asked first," he ended hastily.

She tilted her head toward him, and her voice was soft and slow. "I would have said yes."

He met her eyes. "Really?"

Anna nodded silently, her heart beginning to brim.

"Well." His eyes slightly narrowed. "What about now? I'm asking."

She held her breath. Could this really be happening? Not by chance, not in the dark, but full-on with the valley sweeping before them. Maybe it was the morning light, but she felt fearless. "The answer is still yes."

Suddenly and with a quiet power, he pulled her up by her hand so that they rose, his left hand somehow already making its way along her face. He scanned its edges, lightly tucking a curly wisp of hair behind her ear. Anna drew herself up toward him, and the space between them closed as they angled their mouths against each other. Anna felt herself breathe against his face, as his own breath brushed her cheek. Heat rose in her chest.

He pulled back, glancing down at her, then held her against his chest. "Anna?" His chest rumbled lightly against her ear as she buried her head against his shoulder, even while looking down at the valley. A breeze danced around them.

"Hmm?" Actually forming words felt too hard to do at the moment.

"Your life feels like it's so far away. I know New York's not really so far, but I don't mean the miles. I mean, some other way. It seems so … fast."

She nodded against the cloth of his shirt, smelling his fresh, clean musk. "I think I'm scared to take my foot off the gas. I'm afraid of what will happen."

"If you slow down?"

"I don't want the past to catch up with me." Though even as she said it, Anna realized that the past was already here on the high ridge, swirling around them as Jake held her.

It was part of the present. And maybe the future.

And right at that moment, it wasn't clear to her why the difference between present and future was a problem at all.

"I wish …" he began, hesitating.

"What, what do you wish?" Anna drew back to look up into his face.

"I know it's crazy impossible, but I have to say this anyway. You're going to be gone soon, and who knows when I'll see you again." He ran his thumb along her jaw. "You may not know what you want. But I know what I want. It might not be possible, but at least I know what it is. And what I want is that somehow … somehow … it could work for you here, Anna. Here, in Cedarwood Spring. It's crazy, but that's what I want. God help me, but I do."

Anna rested her hands on his arms, feeling a little space wedge between them. "I want it to work for me too, but—"

Jake grasped her shoulders, and she felt the strength of his arms. It felt gently fierce. Involuntarily, she took a half-step back.

His voice was clear. "How? How could it work for you? Tell me."

Anna felt like she was poised high on a seesaw, that precarious moment when it hits the top and starts to head back down, but your stomach is still flying upward. She tried to give a weak laugh. "I don't know. I'm doing pretty good just to know that I want it to."

"What about your contract with the producers? Are you locked in?"

Geez, he was talking real specifics. It was both thrilling and utterly overwhelming.

"The contract gave both parties—them and me—the option to decide after the pilot."

"And if you don't take it?"

She shook her head slowly. "They could still take the idea and run with it. That's why Colleen was on the job. She can carry it off. Now that I've set up the concept."

"How would that feel?"

As she looked at his face—familiar but new, handsome but careworn—a brief flash of fear overtook her. She loved this man. And there was so much at stake—so much that could be lost. All that she had built, all that she had dreamed about, and pushed for, and sweated for, and dreamed about again.

Could she really hold onto that … back in Cedarwood Spring, or would she become Annie again? And an even more frightening thought: If she lost Anna, would she lose Jake as well?

She squeezed his shoulders and let go, turning back toward the truck. "I know what I wish, Jake, it's what you wish too. But 'how' is a whole other question." She stopped with her hands in her back pockets and turned toward him, the breeze blowing out her full mane of hair almost wildly. "I'm really glad we came up here. It was the right place, the right moment. But we should probably finish the errands. We have to get back."

As she silently pulled open the door to the truck, Anna knew, maybe for the first time, where her heart truly rested. But she had no idea how her life could follow it there.

~

"That's a wrap!" Sierra circled her forefinger high in the air. The cast and crew broke out into cheers and applause, clapping high-fives and sharing hugs.

From where he stood learning against the kitchen door, Jake couldn't help but feel proud. But that pride made for a pretty lousy cocktail with the bitter ambivalence in his gut from hearing Anna say she didn't know if she even wanted this show—and yet she didn't know if she wanted Cedarwood Spring either. At least, that sure was how it had sounded to him. And he'd been sitting there on the bench with her, saying this sensitive stuff about Margaret. Not your best moment, Petersen.

Sierra stepped from behind the cameras and into the pool of brighter, bustling light that had been the kitchen all day. "Wonderful, everyone, wonderful. And you, lady …" She pointed to Anna. "You were a rock star. Everything went off even better than I'd hoped."

All the customers had left a couple of hours ago, raving about the experience. It had been hot on social media, Jake had noticed, and throughout the day, people had come who hadn't RSVP'd in advance, with a cheery, bustling queue right out the front door. Exactly what he would have hoped for the inn … and for Anna.

Since then, the crew had been clearing everything away, cleaning up, and getting the last of the footage, "tucking the kitchen in for the night," as Anna always said. Jake watched as she and Sierra hugged, wishing he could do the same. Haven came up to join them. "Group hug!" she called out.

"You did great, Haven," he heard Anna saying from the

tangle of arms. "You really shone. My colleague back in New York, Colleen? You did just as well. You're an excellent boulanger."

Haven clapped her hands together and held them up to her chin. "You think so? The fact that Colleen had a baby was my winning ticket. I'm a boulanger and I never even knew it. Who knew making bread and muffins and scones came with a title."

"Oh, but being a boulanger has a long, great history. Name it and claim it, girl."

"I'm so sad this has to end," Haven said as she turned to another cast member. "Anna, I wish you didn't have to go back." Her voice faded into a hug as Jake, watching, felt an inner kick and kept his eyes on Anna. She was smiling but looked tired. Was it his imagination, or did she seem a little detached?

She was ensconced in a chattering group of cast and crew, but Jake saw her look his way, scanning quickly for him. She was basking in praise, but still, she looked vulnerable and tentative … and looked for him. *Him.*

When she saw Jake, her eyes smiled, like they were asking him something, but he didn't know exactly what.

What was she thinking? He wanted to yell, "Come talk to me," but instead gave her a smile and a thumbs-up.

She shot him a frazzled, relieved-looking smile before being swept up into yet another group hug. As he watched, Jake felt an unexplained sadness swirl through his gut. Or was it really just the fear of sadness to come?

He turned and stepped through the back room and out the back door, where the café tables sat still and silent beneath the pattern of fairy lights. Watching the shoot from the sidelines these past two days, he hadn't been crazy about seeing people make decisions about his property, his home. But Anna had been fierce, making sure they consulted with him and negotiated anything he didn't like. And his own team shone just fine. The New York crew would be gone soon enough—about which he was pretty mixed. Having them here wasn't the most comfortable thing in the world. But as long as they were here, so was Anna.

She had sparkled, she'd been elegant and poised, all while managing things like the total pro she was. She didn't hesitate to speak her mind but always seemed to be low-key about it. An art he wasn't sure he'd ever really mastered.

And he had to admit, she'd brought the inn alive. Not the barn—he'd done a good job there already, he knew that. It was the vision his parents had had, and he'd carried it forward.

But the inn—before this, it had been unknown, like Sleeping Beauty waiting to be wakened. And Anna had wakened it.

And him.

He started, feeling a light touch on his back. Turning, he saw the finger belonged to Anna.

"So? What did you think?" she asked.

To hell with this hands-off thing. Still bold from their kiss the day before, he slipped his forefinger against her palm and felt her hand close around his. "It was great. The customers ..." he gestured toward the empty tables, "were knocked out. All I heard was raving about what a great idea the whole concept is. They want more. We had to turn people away."

Anna looked up at him, eyes tired but gleaming. "Thanks. I'm so glad they liked it. Everybody was great during the filming." She lightly squeezed his hand. "But Jake, I meant you. What did you think about it all? At your inn."

How honest could he be? This was her night, her celebration. He kept his voice casual. "I felt ... proud. But I wasn't sure if I had the right to be proud."

"Of course you do," she exclaimed. "Are you nuts? The inn is what made the whole thing work, and you're the motor that drove it here."

"No, I mean, it wasn't simply being proud of the inn. Don't

get me wrong, the team did great. I mean I was proud of … of you. And that's what I wasn't sure I had the right to do."

Her smile widened. "I love that you felt proud of me. I'm not sure anybody's said that to me—other than my mom! I was proud too—of you. I love showing off what you've done here at the inn."

"This was good for us—for Iris and me, for the inn." He glanced around at the quiet tables. "You showed us some real possibility for it. I was always good at imagining how to use the barn, how to turn it around. But the inn—that was harder to know. I could never get my head around it. And you did it so easily."

Her smiled faded a bit. "You know, the guys on the crew were asking about a B&B here."

"Yeah, definitely. That's a good idea. I'll talk to Iris about it." He looked away, down toward the barn. Funny how he always seemed to return to that view. It oriented him, like a compass. "So—what about your next steps? When do you hear from the producer?"

Anna's hand felt limp in his. "Soon, I hope. They'll call Sierra, and she'll let me know as soon as they do. You know, it's funny."

"What?"

"We stood right here, in this same spot, a few weeks ago at the wedding. We were wondering about the Taggarts review for you. Now here we are again, wondering about the show for me."

This conversation wasn't helping that sense of dread along the edges of his gut. "Yeah. What a coincidence."

More laughter and noise poured from the house out into the gardens. It was clear the New York crew segued naturally into party mode.

He still stung a little from the unresolved talk on the bench. But he knew she could slip away at any moment, and the questions inside of him rose to the point of imperative. Everything had a now-or-never quality.

Glancing toward the door and reassuring himself that no one was about to interrupt them, he turned back to her. He reached up to rest his hands on her upper arms, feeling the gentle rise of her muscles—kitchen muscles, she always called them.

"Have you thought any more about our talk yesterday?"

"Of course I have. It's been there nonstop. Even with all of this."

He nodded slightly. "Me too. So let me say this, and then I'll … I'll get out of your way. Anna, you deserve this show, and all this success. You're amazing, and I hope that really good things come. I would never want to get in the way of that."

"You're not in the way—"

"Let me finish," he interrupted her, placing his finger lightly on her lips, then hurried on. "If I could pick up and move to New York to be with you—if that's what you wanted—then I would. But I've thought about it, and I don't see how I can leave the inn, and Iris, and all the stuff that's finally starting to happen for us. And I know you have to stay in New York, that it's where you belong. I also understand that Cedarwood Spring is too far from the life you want—"

Anna was the one to put her slender finger up to his lips—and the feel of it drove him crazy. He stopped talking, lightly kissing it before she lowered it.

"Jake, that's just it." Her voice was a whisper. "Maybe it *is* the life I want. Right here. But I don't know how it's supposed to look."

His hands tightened on her. "I don't know how it's supposed to look either. But I do know how it's *not* supposed to look."

"How?"

"Like you in New York, and me in Cedarwood Spring, and a few texts or calls and visits that end up being cancelled because something else came up. I don't want that for us." It felt good to say "us."

"Neither do I," she said wanly. "I don't know. Maybe ... maybe we should wait and see what the word is from the producers? What might or might not be there for me in New York. Then I'll take it from there."

A little flare of anger went up inside him. Jake knew that was probably the best he could hope for, but after the past few days, it didn't sit right. They had finally come close to something so good that it should matter more than a boardroom decision.

"You mean that whether or not we get to be together depends on a New York production company? And TV network execs sitting in a boardroom somewhere?" He spoke brusquely, and he knew his pain was translating into irritation, but he didn't care.

Anna's eyes revealed a clash of emotions. "I'm sorry ... I didn't mean ..."

Damn, he had come on too strong. A Jacob Petersen trait. "No, *I'm* sorry, Anna." He slid his hands down her arms, squeezed her hands, then released them.

"This isn't fair to you. I guess I didn't want to be Plan B."

She smiled down, then glanced back up at him softly. "You're not. I promise."

"Maybe it's because I'm new to show biz, but it always amazes me how fast a professional crew can take down a set—or strike it, as they call it," Anna said. She and Iris stood at the front of the inn, bathed in summer-morning sunlight and breezes, as the final crew members maneuvered the last boxes and pieces of equipment onto the vans and trucks.

After having to worry constantly about how she looked during the shoot—cultivating casual /sexy/perfect while trying to make sure the cinnamon buns rose the right way was no easy feat

—it was great being back in a loose skirt, a delicate blouse tied at her waist and hair blowing loose. It felt like breathing again.

Which, she realized, meant she'd been holding her breath. For how long, she wasn't sure.

"I know. It's like magic," Iris was saying. "And also a little bit sad. I'm sorry to see it end. Sort of like the day after Christmas."

Couldn't have said it better myself, Anna thought. "Me too. I hope it's good for the inn, and we didn't throw everything off too much."

"Oh, of course not. This was great for us. We already had the 5-star for the barn, for the event business there. And now people are buzzing about the café. They want more of it." Iris linked an arm through Anna's. "You need to leave us with some of your know-how. I know how to do a lot of good basic cooking, and Haven is a fine baker. But this whole idea of the pastries and drinks and how perfectly they went together—that's your vision, and no one else's."

Iris had no idea how precisely she was echoing the feelings in Anna's gut—or maybe she did, Anna thought ruefully, knowing the older woman's knack for insight. "Thanks," she said weakly.

Iris crossed her arms loosely, still watching the crew. "Anna, can I ask you a question?"

"Of course."

"Did you enjoy the filming?"

Ouch. Anna glanced at her. "Enjoy?"

"Yes. Was it just work—or was it really satisfying for you? You know—do you feel like you really used your talents, what makes you happy?" She eyed Anna. "What you dreamed of all those years ago as a kid in Cedarwood Spring? What you left your dad's store for?"

Anna looked at Iris with frowning playfulness. "You might have been watching from the side, but you sure saw a lot. But then, you usually do." She looked back toward the vans. "If you must know—no … no, it didn't feel as great as I'd thought. As great as everybody said it would. I was happy for them. But not really happy for me."

"Ah, I thought so. Tell me more."

"Well, I'm trying to figure all this out. But …" Anna's gaze drifted up into the bright blue where birds flitted and whistled in the treetops. "I didn't feel excited as much as … anxious. And worried. All the time. There was so much pressure on every little thing. And every time I got close to doing something that would have felt more natural, more like … like me, somebody told me to pay more attention to the set. Or to a camera. Or to the next thing the staff was doing."

"So then, what would have felt more like you? Just getting lost in the hands-on baking?"

Anna nodded. "Exactly. This is hard to say, but …" Sadness welled up, a contrast to the sunlight spilling over her. "I worked so hard for this. Months and months. I'd left my job at La Chaise to help get this off the ground. What would happen if it turns out that I was working for … something I didn't really want? Where would I go from there?" She looked appealingly at Iris, her eyes becoming damp.

"What would happen is … you would be free for whatever you *do* want to do. And that might not be as hard to figure out as you think."

"Iris?"

"Hmm?"

"About that. This week—these past several weeks, really—something's happened. Part of me feels like that even when I went back to New York, the special feeling of coming home … well, it stayed here. In Cedarwood Spring. And not just the town. But here at the inn." She shook her head and sighed. "I don't know what to do with that."

"I see. How big a part is it?"

Anna gave a wry smile. "Pretty big. It's like … like my heart and my life are playing tag. And I can't tell which one is winning."

Iris's and Anna's shared chuckle was suddenly stopped by a shout from one of the vans.

Sierra and Rubin emerged, spotted Anna and Iris, and waved.

"Anna! Anna! There you are. Great news!" Rubin scurried across the driveway toward them, clutching his ubiquitous zippered folder.

Anna shielded her eyes. "What's up?" It was always funny to her to see Rubin scurry—it ended up looking more like a waddle, she thought, as he reached her, a bit breathless, Sierra a few steps behind.

"We got a call from the producer. The network liked the rushes." He glanced at Iris. "That's the film footage that we send to the producers right away so we can see if they like how it's going." He pivoted back toward Anna. "And they think it's going great. Loved it, *loved* it! Plus they've finally gotten the restaurant permits in Soho sorted out. So—it's a go!" He threw his hands up high, dropping the folder in the process. "'Love Bite' is a series! Congratulations!" Rubin gave his awkward version of a "mwah, mwah" hug, then scrambled for his folder.

"Congratulations, Anna," Sierra said more soberly, giving her a quick squeeze. "You deserve this."

Anna stood, looking from Rubin to Sierra and back again. This moment was such a strange collision. In the few minutes with Iris, she'd dared to name something inside her that had finally come clear. And Rubin's news felt like cold water suddenly thrown on her—which was exactly the way she knew it *wasn't* supposed to feel. It was supposed to feel like birds released from a bird cage … right?

"I … I don't know what to say."

"What *is* there to say?" Rubin threw his hand up. "You'll be an instant celebrity. This is everything you wanted. Now, I need to get more media lined up, and meetings with the network and the producers, and we need time with Sierra at the restaurant." He pointed a teasing finger at her. "The point is, I need you back in New York, lady, like, yesterday. And your time is all mine. No more running off to country inns. Now, when are you getting back home?"

His words were fast, but Anna heard them in slow motion, taking each one in as if it were a complete realization in itself. And at his last words—"When are you getting back home"— something clicked into place inside, the last puzzle piece completing a sweeping scene. Why it clicked at this moment and no other, she had no idea. But click it had.

She glanced at Sierra, who watched her intently. Anna knew her next words would be important—like she was navigating in the wilderness and she could as easily end up on the wrong path as on the right one.

"I'm not sure, Rubin," she said slowly. "I know timing is everything here. I don't want to mess you up, but ..." She looked up at Iris, who simply smiled and gave a small nod. Anna turned back to Rubin. "I'm not sure when I'll be back in New York. But I'll let you know real quick, I promise."

"What's the problem? We need to get to it—we have to make sure you're on solid ground here."

Anna watched her manager with fondness and understanding. "That's just it, Ru. I do need to make sure I'm on solid ground. Which is what I have to do now. I'll get back to you in a few." She turned to Iris and lightly touched the woman's arm. "Iris?"

Iris smiled. "He's down at the waterwheel."

As Anna turned and headed toward the back of the house, her feet felt light as the early-summer day.

～

She headed down the path—the path of the lanterns, the path where Jake had first kissed her, the path she'd come to know like her own already—and her skirt moved softly against her knees, the breeze from the valley rising to tickle her. She began walking faster, and she knew that she wasn't walking away from something, but toward something better.

And then the joy of that something pulled her feet into a jog off the path and through the thick grass. Rounding the barn, she could hear the stream before she saw it. As it came fully into view, she saw Jake standing at its opposite edge, his hands jammed in the front pockets of his chinos. He looked down into the water, lost in his thoughts as the wheel rhythmically churned above the old white bridge.

She suddenly wanted to be closer to those thoughts than to anything else.

He looked up, startled, the bright sun glinting off his gray-threaded blond waves. Anna knew her own face had to be showing what she felt, but finally, she didn't care.

"Jake!?"

"Anna." His voice was flat, and his eyes held a mix of emotion that she couldn't quite read across the stream. He didn't make any move toward her. "Are they finished packing up?"

She nodded, wishing she could touch him. But there seemed to be this stream in between them. And maybe something else. But she could take care of both things. "Yes. They're almost done."

"They did a great job. Really." His voice had a quiet resignation. "And Rubin and Sierra?"

"They're getting ready to go. Jake—I have news."

He stood still, watching her carefully across the moving water.

"The producer called Rubin." She saw him stiffen.

"And?"

"And it's a go. The network loved it, people responded well, and believe it or not, the restaurant space in Soho actually came through." She met his stillness with a stillness of her own, her hands dropped by her sides. "They're gonna do the series."

Jake ducked his head, looking back down into the water, his face impassive. "That's great. Congratulations, Anna. You'll … you'll be terrific." He looked back up with a polite smile.

Anna's heart couldn't hold back. "No, Jake, that's just it. I've figured something out. Finally. Something really … big. Something I need to tell you." Her hands were loose at her sides in the folds of her skirt. She took a deep breath. "I don't want it."

Jake straightened. "You don't want what?"

"The series, the whole thing. Jake, I know what I want now, and it's not that. I mean, yes, I do want to bake and run a café, and I kind of love doing interviews and talking to people about it. Letting them see what I can do. And teaching—it was so great showing Haven the ropes. But in *my* own way. I want to create and bake and have my own place. I want …"

Jake's eyes were widening. He pulled his hands from his pockets and began moving toward the bridge, and Anna's feet moved automatically to meet him, picking up speed as she went.

"What? What do you want, Anna?"

At the same moment, their feet thudded from opposite ends against the gray wood of the bridge, and they reached each other just as Anna thought she couldn't bear not holding him any longer. Her arms went around his waist as his went firmly around her shoulders, his face in her hair. She felt him draw back for a second, holding her billowing hair out of her face, and then he ducked forward once more, their mouths meeting.

Finally, heart and life were landing in the same place, Anna managed to realize. *When are you getting back home?* Rubin had asked.

I'm there.

Jake loosely caught his fingers in her hair, pulling back to look at her. "You know, when you went back to New York? I missed you. I missed you so much."

"I missed you too."

"I don't want to miss you again."

"I don't want that either," she said, her eyes locking into his. "It's so strange. The stuff we feel when we're kids, teenagers … so much of it doesn't end up being the truth. But this … this feels like the truth. It just hasn't been time … until now."

"This? Meaning?"

"Meaning, here. Cedarwood Spring. The inn."

"But the celebrity that Rubin was talking about, the success. You've worked so hard for all of it."

"Yeah, I did work hard," Anna said slowly, pulling back slightly from him. "But I think I'm figuring out that that's not what I worked hard for. It's just where I ended up. Those are two different things." She tugged gently on his waist. "Time for a course correction."

"Like what?" Jake's smile dispelled the shadow that had seemed to lay across it, the edges of his mouth and eyes crinkling in the way she so loved.

"What I worked hard for was baking and creating and making people happy with it. Coming up with great new food for people to love, and doing the classic stuff too. Looking at sourcing and collaborating with great people like … oh, I don't know, like Pete and Tina and the crew. And mainly seeing regular people every day. People who know me, and know my team, and what we make and the space we're in, like the café. And they come back for more. I just think … it turns out I can do more of that here."

"In Cedarwood Spring?"

She nodded, as he moved his hands to frame her face. Her heat and hope rose. "In Cedarwood Spring."

"Hmm, I see." There was levity back in his voice. His left

eyebrow rose. "Well, I'm not sure where you can do that. I mean, if you did it in town, it would upstage Haven ..."

She narrowed her eyes thoughtfully. "Right. I definitely wouldn't want to do that."

"And if you made it, say, catering, it wouldn't do Albert any good." He gave a mock-frown.

"True. So ..." she said, giving a sideways glance. "Do you know of any place that might be up for a café? Like, I don't know ..."

"Like an inn where they just filmed a reality TV show about a café? Maybe?"

She held up her finger. "That's it! Brilliant!"

He held her finger and gave it a light kiss, folding it back into his grasp. His voice became low and serious again. "Anna, really, would you? Would you ... work here with Iris and me?"

She sighed and looked up toward the gardens and the back of the inn. "Well ... how do you feel about a partner?"

"I think I'm finally ready for it." He took a deep breath.

"I'm not sure yet exactly how a dessert-and-drink café will work with what you're already making this ... this wonderful place to be," she added hurriedly, "I don't want to get in the way of what you've thought about in the past."

The past didn't seem anywhere near him. "We'll figure it out."

"We have to figure out the business plan. Talk to Iris, and—"

"Anna, Anna," he said, smiling and running his hands down her arms to grasp her hands. "Of course, we'll do all those things. It'll take time. But it'll take time ... together. That's what's important. As long as we know we want that, we'll figure the rest out. But first, we have to say yes."

Anna felt his hands curling around hers more tightly, and her words were working better than her thoughts. She peered at him. "Say yes to what?"

"To being together, Annie Diaz. You and me. Isn't that what we're talking about?"

She nodded slowly, feeling the answer clear and real. "Yeah, I think it is."

Jake suddenly spoke with urgency, as if her 'yes' had unleashed something that had been pent-up for a long time—too long.

"If you're game, Anna, we can do this. We'll figure out how to do it so that we make something together that ... that ... I don't know, that lets us both do what we thought we were dreaming of. Only better. Like when I thought all I wanted was to fix up the inn, I didn't realize what was missing. And now I do. You were missing. And now it feels ... whole. I was scared that that would take something away from me. But it gave something to me."

Her eyes gleamed as she looked up to him, daring to believe what she saw and heard. "Me too. I had a lot of the right pieces, just ... in the wrong order."

Jake ducked his head, still speaking fast. "We'll keep your place in Brooklyn, if you want. So you can still keep your media work going and everything for your ... your career there—"

She put her finger up to his lips, and he stopped talking. "Shhh. Like you said—we'll figure it out. It'll just take time. And we have time."

"You've already brought so much to this place. I thought I could imagine all it could be. But you imagine more."

A light fear once again crossed Anna's face. "I hope you don't feel like I did too much—"

"You don't get it, do you? How can I make this clear?" He pushed her hair back with his hand. "I don't want to do this without you. How's that?"

She hugged him, smiling into his chest. "OK, we'll do it together," she whispered. The breeze swirled around them, as the waterwheel chugged steadily on.

"What about Rubin?" Jake asked. "What'll he say?"

"Oh, he can manage me here as well as he can manage me in New York. He's pretty portable. And Colleen will get the break she was hoping for, the break she deserves. It may take a little time, but she's got a good team. Remember—I know chemistry and I know timing."

Jake smiled, cupping her jaw lightly with his hand. "Yes, you do. So how's our chemistry and how's our timing?"

"It's good. So …" She cocked her head and gave him a side-long glance. "Quoting myself to Rubin … don't mess with a good thing."

Jake laughed, his strong arms pulling her close to his warm body and into the heart of the laughter. He spoke softly into her hair as it billowed in the breeze. "Yeah. It's funny about chemistry …" Jake turned her face up to his.

"And timing …" Her voice was a whisper, just before his lips found hers once more. There was a lot they didn't know yet. But Anna did know this: She had arrived.

As he pulled back, his face became serious again.

"I lost you once—well, twice. I don't want to lose you again. I don't know how everything is supposed to look, but I know I have to say this." He paused, scanning her wide-open face. "Anna, I … I think there has to be another wedding here. Don't you?"

Her heart sprang into her throat, and she couldn't quite believe what she was hearing. "What do you mean?"

"I know that this is what I want." He took her hands and enclosed them with his own, learning down to brush a kiss against her fingers. "Anna … marry me?"

"Really?" she whispered, as joy and tears welled up.

He nodded, pulling her close again, whispering into her hair. "Yes."

Her face was against his chest, enveloped in everything that Jake was. "Then yes. Yes, I will."

"Hey, you two, it's about time!" Startled, Jake released her as Haven bounced into view, utterly unfazed by any sense of supposed decorum about what you're supposed to do when two people you love finally … *finally* … get together.

Jake laughed and turned toward her, still holding his arm tight around Anna's shoulders. "Where did you come from, kiddo?"

"The last van just drove off, and I wanted to come tell you people were calling the inn and all over social media asking about when the café will be open here. I came down to ask—and here you are. This took you long enough, by the way!" She gestured toward the two of them.

"Yeah, it is about time. How many years?" he asked with mock-seriousness, turning to Anna.

"Hmm." She met his frown and raised a finger to her chin. "A ridiculous number of years. Like twenty? Way too long, and … just the right amount."

"So what are you going to do? Can we keep you here or not?" Haven asked.

"We-e-ell," Anna said, looking inquiringly at Jake. "Is it solid?"

"Is what solid?" Haven demanded.

"It's solid," Jake said quietly to Anna, then turned to Haven. "OK kiddo, get ready—Anna's staying here to manage the Cedarwood Inn Café. And we're doing it … together."

"*Together*? You mean, not just business partners, I hope." Haven pulled her hands emphatically onto her hips.

Anna shook her head. "Life partners." She looked up to Jake and took a deep breath. "We're getting married."

Haven's squeal made Anna's eyes widen. "Anna, you did it! It was the solstice. You looked into the water and saw Jake!"

Anna laughed. "I'd forgotten about that! But it's one of the most lovely things I've ever heard. Yes, I guess I did see my future husband. Maybe it really works. The longest day." She glanced up.

Jake hugged her to him. "And the shortest night," he whispered into her hair.

Haven peered mischievously at them. "I think I'll hang out here at the pond awhile, throw some flowers in. Maybe I'll see the man *I'm* going to marry. Hey, speaking of which, when are you guys doing it? You've got to give the whole team time to really do it right."

Jake looked back at Anna. "What d'ya think? You know I'd do it tomorrow, but … we gotta let the team do their thing. And," he said, pressing his mouth into her hair, "I want you to have the wedding you want."

"The wedding I want is whatever we do," Anna assured him. She thought a moment, her eyes drifting down to where her hand rested in his. When she spoke, it sounded almost shy. "You know what? I'm so thankful. Just really grateful. This might sound silly but—how about … Thanksgiving? It's so beautiful here deep in autumn."

Jake gave an emphatic nod. "Thanksgiving it is."

Haven reached out to grab their arms in another three way hug. "Oh my gosh, can I … can I make the cake?"

Anna's laugh was silvery as she felt Jake's arm holding her close. "I wouldn't have it any other way. Let's start planning."

SNEAK PREVIEW

Cedarwood Spring is a magical place of connection, community, and love longed for, wrestled with, and fulfilled, all amid cozy small-town charm nestled in the beautiful Pennsylvania Dutch countryside. Be sure to follow Anna, Jake, Haven, and the mysterious, frustrating man she's about to meet and find out what happens to them over the whole Cedarwood Spring series —and life. Visit ericasams.com to stay on top of the latest.

Here's a taste of Book 2, *Flipping His Heart*, where Haven faces high stakes as she struggles to fight for her beloved Filling Station ... even as she finds out that her opponent is also the man who makes her heart shimmer every time she sees him.

Flipping His Heart
Book 2 of the *Cedarwood Spring Clean Romance Series*
By Erica Sams

Come on. Men giving presentations at stuffy business conferences aren't supposed to be *that* good-looking. This guy belongs at a bachelorette party. She stopped just short of imagining how he'd be dressed.

Haven Martin swatted the thought away at the same time she pushed a stray wisp of straight brown hair back behind her ear where it belonged but never quite seemed to stay. She shifted in her front-row chair, trying to get comfortable. Her navy-blue suit had looked a lot crisper that morning.

The day had been long—though, she had to admit, the speakers had been great. One after another, entrepreneurs, investors, and influencers in the Philadelphia real-estate development scene clustered in the grand Philly hotel ballroom to support, inspire, and teach. Each one gave a story about their life's ups and downs, with each "up" or "down" bringing them to a new stage of growing their approach to business and even growing just as human beings. They'd been inspiring and full of know-how.

And Haven knew she desperately needed know-how. Her little piece of life—her little bakery back in her hometown—was on the line.

Feeling more settled in her seat, she took a minute to check in with herself. Her gaze rested on the empty podium, but her mind's eye was scanning her town of Cedarwood Spring, about an hour outside Philly in Pennsylvania Dutch country, where she'd head back to in, oh, no more than an hour. And boy, would it feel good to get home. The small town was the perfect setting to hold the gem of her own little bakery, the Filling Station, right there on Main Street.

The Filling Station—a historic old service station she'd worked at as a teenager when it was a coffee shop. Then after college, she'd put everything she had into taking it up a notch and converting it into a bakery. Everything she had, everything she loved, and probably everything she lacked, including all the skills she was trying to up her game with, went into that tired old place, and despite her masterful ability at doubting herself, even she had to admit it had become one of the best spots in town.

Unaware she was beginning to smile, she flashed on all the different moments it took to get here: working double-time through college to learn baking and business, then, when the manager of the coffee shop retired, convincing the landlord—Charlie—to take a chance on her opening her own bakery with a goofy-cool name like the Filling Station. Specializing in muffins. Of course. At least to start with.

And he had. With the help of all her close friends there, together they'd gotten every display case, café table, bucket of paint, and farmhouse-style light fixture in place. She smiled even bigger—sometimes it felt like it was all held together with Band-Aids and chewing gum. But it was home—right down to her little apartment in the back of the building.

She noticed people moving to their seats, and her smile began to fade. Charlie had passed away not long ago, and some distant Philly firm had snapped it up. Some place called "PDP." The memory of it made the erasure of her small smile complete. They had said they were looking at whether to keep it or flip it. And the ground she'd barely begun to feel under her feet had shifted. She was due to go into their office sometime soon—they hadn't yet said when—and make her pitch for why it was the best possible thing for Cedarwood Spring for them to renovate it —and keep it. With her as manager.

So how to fight for the life of her Filling Station? By fighting fire with fire. She'd get better at business. If their question was a business question, she'd give them a business answer.

And months of after-hours study and courses out at the Cedarwood Spring Community College had brought her here. Three days of top-notch speakers, breakout sessions, and group chat. She'd hung onto every word.

And it felt like it. Her eyes felt strained, and she was actually getting tired of hanging onto words or anything, thank-you-very-much. But she figured she'd give it one more go. After all, the schedule said the speaker was a pro at assessing properties for further development. Exactly the skills she needed. Maybe she could even get him to coach her.

She rubbed her eyes and squinted back down at the conference program. Brook Sutherland, it said. Developmental architect. What the heck was that?

Looking back up, she saw the almost off-puttingly handsome man she'd just spied talking to the facilitator walk toward the podium, nervously adjusting his earpiece mic. His thick dark-blond hair kicked in waves off his face, and this close, she could even glimpse the paleness of his gray eyes. His neatly groomed, closely trimmed beard was even lighter than his hair, highlighting a squared jaw. For a split second, it felt like he was walking toward her, and her heart gave a pleasurable beat.

Yikes, definitely time to wrap up the day.

"Testing, testing …"

Oooh, nice voice. Sort of dark and warm—like chocolate. Or maybe she was just so tired she was hallucinating about her favorite baking ingredients.

She looked at the program once more. "Brook Sutherland, Development Consulting Services." The topic of his talk? "Evaluating Your Assets: When to Let Go."

Let go? Her eyebrows furrowed. She'd only just begun.

"Good afternoon." The stiff handsome guy cut into her thoughts. "I know we're all tired at the end of a long day. And I haven't been outside for hours, but I hear it's a pretty gorgeous October day here in Philly. So let's get right to it so you can get home."

Haven narrowed her eyes attentively as he flipped through a very polished series of PowerPoint slides with charts and graphs that always seemed to fade into the next one before she could nail down exactly what it said. But then again, that's why she was here: to get better at what she didn't know about business.

Yet still, as slide by slide went by, Mr. Sutherland occasionally scanning the front row while he talked, she could follow his comments. And maybe it was the fatigue, but it wasn't sitting well with her.

Things like, "Be brutal in your evaluation."

"Lean into the competition."

"Emotions cloud your judgment."

And "Don't get sentimental—be detached, especially if you're dealing with social contacts."

Social *contacts*?

Did he mean *friends*? She unconsciously gripped the small notebook in her hand, given to her by the conference organizers who invited everyone to jot down their fears, hopes, and learning. She'd taken it very seriously, writing thoughtfully during each presentation, so she felt painfully and physically aware of her "fears, hopes, and learning." As she gripped the journal, it was as if she were gripping those very things.

And she knew that the only way she'd ever established the bakery, let alone gotten it off the ground, was by *attaching with* her friends. Her amazing, talented friends, right down to dear old Charlie, who wasn't even here anymore. Don't get sentimental? There wasn't a day that passed that she didn't feel sentimental about the whole thing—like when, for instance, friends had helped her pump all the water out of the basement when a bad storm had hit last summer. She could get pretty darn sentimental over that, for starters.

She knew she shouldn't get upset. This was just a presentation; she'd never see this guy again, thank goodness. And she was probably misunderstanding. After all, she was the newbie here. Surely, he'd clarify that he meant something totally different.

But no. As Mr. Sutherland wrapped up his presentation, he seemed to pause over his conclusion, relishing each word: "Always remember to assess the facts objectively. Your feelings will mislead you. But the figures never lie. That's the key to the difficult decision of whether you take that older property and retrofit and upgrade it—or whether you just flip it."

And that was it. There was a drizzle of applause as, tired and ready for the cocktail hour, people began gathering their materials.

Yet Haven wasn't on that page. In spite of her fatigue or

maybe because of it, she felt a spike of anger as she flashed on all that was at stake for her in that very question. How could he be saying this? Had he never been helped by people who believed in him—and had he never dared to take their belief to heart? Maybe he'd just never needed to, this stiff gorgeous guy with dark-blond waves along his face and the suggestion of muscular shoulders framing the suit.

Anger pulled at the edges of her mouth. It was her friends' belief in her that had gotten her where she was—and dang, she wanted to stay there. If she'd had to believe in herself to carry it all off, the Filling Station would have stayed a flimsy idea, for sure.

And what if this approach was the kind that developers always took? The fear that had been on the edges of the day pushed its way into her gut. Would this be the kind of attitude she'd have to fight against with the development firm that owned the bakery … her bakery? Haven's head became a jumble of images, exhaustion, memories, and faces, and before she knew it, her hand shot high into the air. "Excuse me. Question! Can I ask a question?"

The smattering of hand-claps stopped, and Mr. Sutherland nervously adjusted his tie and picked up a glass of water. He shot a startled expression over at the woman in the front row, his thick blond hair still perfectly in place.

"Uh … sure," he said, with a little less bravado. He glanced at the facilitator who nodded, looking at his watch.

Automatically slipping into the drill from high school— "Stand when you address the room"—Haven quickly stood up. She was vaguely aware that her notebook slipped to the floor, but that was inconsequential. The suited blond man had seemed far away during the talk, but now he seemed disconcertingly close. She smoothed her skirt and cleared her throat.

"Mr. … uh … Sutherland."

He only nodded, still looking uncomfortable.

"Don't you think there are times when your feelings can lead you in the *right* direction? And not the wrong one, as you say?"

Sutherland visibly relaxed a bit, taking on a more authoritative air. "Sometimes. But in business, it's hard to tell when those times are. You might not find it out till much later. Till it's ... too late."

"But I disagree." Anger still pricked inside, and Haven was talking before she could realize that she was probably only consoling her younger self who had so relied on her friends. "There are times when your feelings help you understand how to interpret the facts. You have to understand a place, you have to understand its whole context to know whether to ... to *flip* it." The word suddenly felt personal and bitter in her mouth.

But the more she dug in, the more Sutherland did too. Only in the opposite direction. She pushed, he pulled, glancing nervously around the restless room.

"There's no interpretation. Facts are facts. You don't interpret them. You just accept them. If you let sentimentality or attachment to a neighborhood fog your thinking, you can't make a sound decision about the fate of a property."

Fate? That did it. Anger shoved the fear aside, as once again she flashed on the image of friends helping her haul defunct kitchen equipment out to a pickup truck after last summer's flood.

"What if the facts include how people have helped you? And what you want a place to be? Not just what it is but what it can become?"

"Those aren't facts. They're just ..." He shrugged. "... circumstances." He glanced questioningly at the facilitator who nervously smiled at the crowd.

"But what about belief in yourself, Mr. Sutherland? What if you need people to believe in that with you? Is that a fact or a circumstance?"

Sutherland gave a cautious scan of the room. "Belief in yourself? That's, um, about belief in your skills to execute a job. The better you know your skills, the better the execution."

"Execution? Are you building something or killing it?" Haven shot back in spite of her usual caution.

The facilitator clapped his hands. "O-k-a-a-a-ay," he said loudly with a pasted-on grin, walking over to shake Sutherland's hand. "Thank you so much for your question, ma'am, and I think we're all pretty tired here. Thank you all for your attentiveness at this last session of the day. And as you know from your agendas, the last thing—I'm sure you're happy to hear—is the reception in Ballroom B. With open bar! See you there!"

A much heartier round of applause greeted that announcement, as the facilitator turned to Brook Sutherland and shook his hand.

Haven stood, still mouthing the next words she'd wanted to say. "But … but …" As the din of the room rose up around her ears and her own words echoed in her mind, her heart sank in embarrassment, and pink flared in her cheeks.

Maybe it was the exhaustion, but tears suddenly sprang up behind her eyes, as a mass of feelings clutched in her stomach.

Oh no, not crying. She hated this about herself—anger so easily went to tears. But not here, not in front of all these professionals.

And for heaven's sake, not in front of this guy Sutherland.

Haven pressed her lips into a firm line, seeing nothing but the jumble of people shaking hands around her and chatting collegially. Trying to focus in the midst of the blur of people and sound, she automatically grasped her jacket and the strap of her handbag from the back of the chair and, ducking her head quickly and miserably, made a beeline for the door.

As she reached it, she glanced down at her watch: 5:15.

If she hurried, and with a little traffic luck, she could just make it to the 30th Street Station in time to be on the 5:40 back home.

To Cedarwood Spring, to her own little bakery ... and to her friends.

It was all she had, and it felt like this stiff conference guy had just taken it away. At least it was the last she'd ever see of him.

Little did she know the fate of the Filling Station rested in the hands of this infuriating and infuriatingly compelling man.